The Child Within

Mind's Eye Investigations, Volume 2

Margaret Lashley

Published by Zazzy Ideas, Inc., 2020.

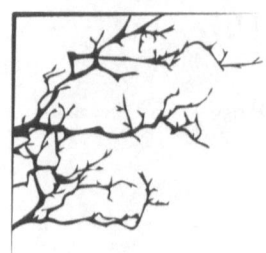

Prologue:

GOD RODE IN ON SWIRLING thunderclouds,
    His voice echoing in the rain.
    Watery whispers to quench his thirst.
    His life was not in vain.
    Crackling buzz, like an angry bee.
    He leaned closer despite the pain,
    Of pins and needles in tiny boats,
    Racing sharply toward his brain.
    Sparks and stars danced inside his skull,
    Whispering their secret, sad refrain.
    He knew he must obey their words,
    No matter how insane.

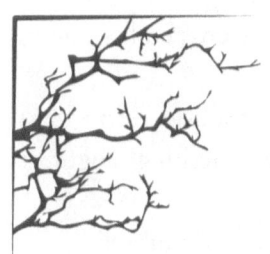

Chapter One

"NURTURE THE CHILD WITHIN. Neglect it at your own peril. For one day that child could flame up with rage and burn your life to cinders."

HE CRACKED OPEN THE door and peeked through the narrow slit. His eye darted left, then right, peering through the curtain of rain.

The monstrous thunderstorm roiling above had done its work, aging the afternoon sky prematurely gray and clearing the streets of prying eyes.

No one was watching.

He stepped out into the deluge. The rush of cold rain soaked through his clothes, slapping his mind awake.

Life surged within him. He was—*as light as a feather!*

Lightning crackled in the sky above. He looked up and felt a strange kinship with the clouds being shot through with electric veins.

He spread his arms wide and imagined himself riding the wind like a leaf, surfing the frenetic gusts that swirled around him, clawing at his face and kicking up debris.

He laughed with delight.

God's washing me clean!

A sudden pinch of doubt pursed his lips. He crossed his fingers, just to be safe.

As if on command, the torrential downpour subsided to a light, gray drizzle. He turned to go back inside—but something caught his eye.

Looming at him from the damp gloom was a red umbrella.

A sign!

Robert, he thought. *Robert's here!*

Frozen with awe, he stood and watched in silence as the figure carrying the umbrella passed by on the sidewalk and disappeared from view.

"Wait for me!" he almost yelled. Instead, he dashed through the yard toward the figure. As he reached the sidewalk, a sudden thought jerked his body to a standstill.

Things don't always turn out so well when Robert's around.

He slowed his pace, trailing a safe distance behind Robert as he made his way along the sidewalk's uneven hexagonal pavers. Mesmerized by the red umbrella bobbing and twirling in the light rain, he forgot about the damp and the cold.

Giddy elation turned his skin to goosebumps.

I'm on a mission—with Robert!

In the dim gray of dusk, he furtively followed Robert down another block and around a corner. He stopped and swiped damp hair from his eyes as he peered from his hiding spot behind a palm.

Robert scurried up the front walk toward a faded, two-story frame house and climbed its sagging front steps. Under the sanctuary of the covered porch, Robert lowered the umbrella to shake off the rain.

But as the umbrella collapsed, so did the silent watcher's face.

That's not Robert! That's—a woman!

He glared at her as she leaned the umbrella against the wall by the front door.

She tricked me!

The woman reached inside the pocket of her beige trench coat and retrieved a pack of cigarettes. She tugged one loose with her lips, then stuck the pack back into her pocket.

She struck a match.

Oh, no!

Bad girl. Bad, bad Harriet!

Harriet must die.

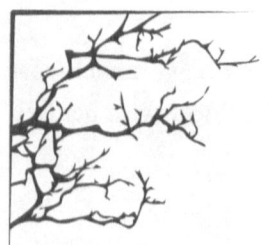

Chapter Two

MARCUS BLATCH WAS WASHING meatloaf grease from the dinner dishes when he heard the first siren. He dropped the sponge and sprinted into the living room. Through the foggy front windows of the Craftsman bungalow, he watched a red firetruck jostle quickly past on the street.

A hand landed gently on his shoulder. "What's going on?" Deloris asked.

"Not sure, Mom," Marcus replied, his eyes scanning the street. He turned to face his elderly mother. "You wait here. I'll go check it out."

Deloris Blatch's delicate features pinched with concern. "Be careful."

Marcus nodded. "I will. And don't worry. I'll be home before your cherry cobbler's done baking."

Deloris doled out a resolute smile. She knew nothing she could say would stop her son from helping someone in need. That was his most endearing quality. She handed him an umbrella. "I hope everybody's going to be all right."

"Me, too." Marcus pressed the umbrella back into her hands. "I think the worst of the rain is over. I'll see you soon."

He hugged his mother, then slipped out the front door of the house, hoping his neighbor wouldn't notice.

He only made it ten steps.

"You going down to check out the firetruck?" Art Melman asked from his rocker on the front porch.

According to neighborhood gossip, "Old Man Melman" had been living in the house next door since the giant oaks lining the streets were nothing but acorns. A perpetually angry-faced, stick-figure of a man, Melman had already been well-entrenched in his plain, white-brick bunker of a house thirty years ago, when Marcus himself had arrived after being adopted by Deloris and Dave Blatch at the age of thirteen.

While Marcus had stumbled through puberty and learned to drive a stick shift on a rebuilt Ford Mustang, Melman had supervised his every move from the jury box of his front porch. A cynical sentinel, he'd eyed Marcus with a skeptic's certainty that any day now the sprouting young misfit would screw up and prove he'd come from bad seed.

Instead of giving Melman the satisfaction, Marcus had followed his new father's advice. He'd tried not to let Melman's comments anger him. Instead, Marcus had made it his mission to treat his nosy neighbor with unwavering respect.

Eventually, Marcus had realized it was the best way to piss the old man off.

But after three decades, even Marcus was ready to admit the game—along with his patience—was wearing thin. Marcus' attempt to kill his crotchety neighbor with kindness had failed. In the meantime, Dave, the only father Marcus had ever known, had passed away five years ago, proving the old adage that only the good die young.

"Yes, sir," Marcus said, addressing Melman as if he were his military commander. "I thought I'd see if the firemen need any help."

The old man's face soured. "What could *you* possibly do to help?"

Typical Melman, Marcus thought, ignoring the man's sarcastic tone. "Well, I *was* a police lieutenant, in case you forgot."

"I didn't *forget*," Melman said bitterly. But his eyes conveyed traces of worry—fear there might be some truth to his memory beginning to falter.

Marcus recognized Melman's self-doubt. He had plenty of it himself. Lately, more and more, Marcus had the niggling fear that perhaps the old geezer in front of him had been right all along.

Maybe he was no good, after all.

At forty-two, Marcus was painfully aware he was on the bullet train to becoming "that guy." Divorced. Unemployed. Living with his mother. The beginnings of a middle-age paunch setting up shop around his waistline. All he lacked was a basement apartment and evenings spent playing videogames in his boxer shorts with his "internet friends."

He grimaced and glanced back at his mother's bungalow. *Thank god she doesn't have a basement ....*

"Got yourself another job yet?" Melman barked, looking Marcus up and down.

Marcus rankled. "Yes, sir. I started my own business." *So why don't you mind yours?*

"Uh huh," Melman said skeptically. "Well, back in my day—"

"Sorry. Gotta run, Mr. Melman," Marcus said, cutting him off. "You take care, now," he added, and took off jogging down the sidewalk in the direction of the firetruck.

MARCUS SMELLED THE smoke before he saw it.

Jogging west on 12th Avenue, he sprinted past seven or eight beautifully restored wooden bungalows similar to his. He crossed the street and ran down the sidewalk bordering another block of turn-of-the-century homes.

"New England with palm trees," was an apt description of the ritzy, Florida neighborhood. Abutting gorgeous Tampa Bay and a bourgeoning downtown district, the quaint homes in the Old

Northeast section had become the most sought-after in the city of St. Petersburg.

Most of the homes had stood for well over a century. But as Marcus stumbled onto Oak Street, he gasped and wondered if they would make it through the night.

Flames were shooting up above the rooftops. Neighbors were pouring out of their houses, gathering in the streets and wringing their hands.

Shit! he thought. *These old homes are tinderboxes. The whole neighborhood could burn to the ground within hours!*

Marcus caught his breath, then hooked a left on Oak Street and ran in the direction of the flames.

Halfway down 10th Avenue, he saw two firetrucks unrolling their hoses and hooking up to hydrants. Short of breath from the acrid smoke, Marcus pushed on until he reached the scene of the fire.

It was horrific.

Against a backdrop of dull, gray sky, a two-story, wood-frame boarding house was being roasted alive by a whirling inferno—a forty-foot tall tornado of fire.

Marcus caught a glimpse of the familiar roofline before it was engulfed in flames. He recognized it as Mercer Arms—one of the many once-stately homes that absentee landlords had cobbled into too many apartments back in the 1970s, when the economy had collapsed and property codes had gone creatively lax.

Back then, the Old Northeast neighborhood, along with most of St. Petersburg itself, had languished in neglect for decades, earning the unenviable reputation as a has-been city—a place for Social Security pensioners to retire to Florida on the cheap. By 1980, the town had become known mainly for its green benches crammed with derelict seniors idling by-and-by until their name was called up yonder.

As a result, St. Pete had been dubbed, "God's waiting room."

But in the mid-1990s, a new generation began to rediscover the forgotten beauty of the city's quaint old homes and tropical locale. A resurgence spectacular enough to be called a rebirth got underway.

By 2007, when another economic collapse had sent other cities stumbling, sassy, shiny, hip St. Petersburg had simply yawned and applied a little more sunscreen.

Despite the city's glamorous rise, a few holdouts like Mercer Arms had remained stubbornly unkempt and unrepentant. Eyesores of the community, the old tenement buildings were deprived of renovation by their cash-cow investors. Protected from code violations by grandfather clauses, they continued to slip through the cracks like crafty cockroaches.

Mercer Arms had been one such frustrating neighborhood holdout.

But no outdated law could protect it now.

It was toast.

Marcus watched as firefighters aimed their hoses at the mango trees and artsy bungalows surrounding Mercer Arms. He knew what that meant. The firemen had given up on saving the building and were focusing on containing the fire's spread.

Marcus glanced around at the sea of people crammed together behind a line of yellow police tape. He spied a familiar face among them—a young, sandy-haired police officer named Jerry Davidson. He'd come on as a new recruit six months ago, shortly before Marcus had quit the force.

Marcus gave him a nod. Davidson nodded back.

Marcus worked his way through the pink-faced gawkers to Davidson. "Got you working crowd control?"

Davidson smirked. "Wow. Great powers of deduction, Blatch. I can see now why you decided to become a private investigator."

Blatch fought not to wince. To survive on the SPPD required political savvy and a wolf-pack mentality. Successful cops learned quickly to eat their young. Marcus, however, had never acquired a taste for it.

"Good one," Blatch said jokingly. He slapped on a grin and noticed Davidson's face relax a notch. "You know, I never understood how a house could burn down in the middle of a rainstorm."

Davidson glanced around at the crowd, then leaned in toward Blatch. "I heard it had a little help."

Blatch leaned in closer. "Help?"

Davidson straightened his shoulders and chewed the inside of his cheek. He was still contemplating whether to say more when a young boy around five years old snuck past him. The tot had wormed his way through the crowd's forest of legs for a better look at the fire.

Suddenly, the child darted out beyond the yellow tape toward the flaming tenement building.

Before Davidson could react, Blatch reached out and nabbed the red-haired boy by the collar of his Smokey the Bear t-shirt.

"Not so fast, little man," Blatch said, pulling him back to safety.

"There you are!" a woman screeched, her face a mother's mask of worry and weariness. She grabbed the boy up in her arms. "Young man, you're in a heap of trouble!"

The child patted his mother's cheek, then leaned into her shoulder and sucked his thumb.

His mother nearly broke down with gratitude. "Thank you, sir," she said to Blatch.

He smiled and tousled the kid's auburn hair. "Don't be too hard on him. Boys will be boys, after all."

As the mother and child disappeared back into the throng, Davidson nudged Blatch on the arm. "Thanks." He leaned closer and whispered, "Could be arson. Found a gas can in the bushes."

Blatch whistled. "Not Smokey the Bear's, I hope."

Davidson snorted. "It's down at headquarters being run for prints as we speak."

Blatch nodded, then grimaced at the smoldering hull of the boarding house. "Anybody inside when it happened?"

"Won't know until they sift through the debris."

An awful groan reverberated through the damp twilight. The two men turned to see the Mercer Arms curl in on itself and collapse. Sparks flew up like the remnants of demons, only to be quickly struck down by jets of water from the firemen's hoses.

Davidson turned to face Blatch. "You miss the force?"

"I miss some things about it, yeah," he admitted.

"Bet Captain Castleberry isn't one of them things."

Blatch locked eyes with Davidson. Castleberry had been his boss for two long, painful years. The man was a political shark. A master manipulator. And a complete dick.

Castleberry had hand-picked Blatch to mentor, but both men had quickly realized that neither had anything the other wanted—especially respect. Someone had to go. And, as was the custom of the world in general, the shit had rolled downward.

Blatch hesitated, wondering which way he should he play it with Davidson. *Screw it*, he thought, and slapped on a wry grin. "I'll say this much."

"What?" Davidson asked, his eyes keen.

Blatch smirked. "I'm happy to report I no longer need a hemorrhoid cushion."

Davidson snorted, his stoic blue eyes suddenly alive with mischief. He opened his mouth to reply but was interrupted by a crackle from the walkie-talkie clipped to his belt. He unhooked it and held a finger up at Blatch, a silent *wait a minute* request. Blatch nodded and turned to watch the final flames flicker out on Mercer Arms.

Davidson grunted into the walkie-talkie a few times, then clicked off. "Got a match on the prints," he said.

Blatch raised an eyebrow. "That was fast."

"The miracle of AFIS." Davidson glanced around. "Wanna know who it is?"

"Sure."

"Asshole named Gary Lee Preston."

Blatch's brow furrowed. "You're kidding."

Davidson studied him for a moment. "You know him?"

"Yeah. Sort of."

"Think he could've done this?"

Blatch shook his head. "Not a chance."

Davidson's head cocked sideways. His eyes bored into Blatch. "You seem pretty confident."

Blatch nodded. "I am."

"Why?"

"Because six months ago, I watched Gary Lee Preston die."

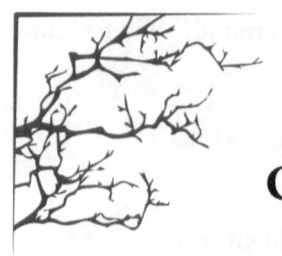

Chapter Three

MONDAY MORNING, BLATCH made his way down the hall of the office building and cautiously turned the knob on the frosted glass door labeled *Blatch & Smalls Discrete Investigations.*

It was unlocked.

"Dammit," he cursed under his breath. He'd thought for once he'd finally beaten his partner, Barney Smalls, to work.

Not today.

Blatch pushed open the door and winced when the bell above it clanged out its rude alarm. Smalls had insisted on hanging the bell. It was an idea as old-fashioned as Smalls himself. As Blatch hung his jacket on the coatrack, he pictured Smalls sitting at his desk, snickering victoriously.

Blatch checked his wristwatch. It was quarter to eight.

Smalls needs to get a life, he thought, then rolled his eyes. *Who am I kidding? I need to get a life.*

But right now, both men would've settled for getting a client.

The two private investigators had solved three related cold cases barely a week ago. News coverage had sent the calls and queries pouring into their office. But so far, little had materialized from the deluge. The business coffers were running dry. If it weren't for the influx of cash from their new partner, the check for December's rent would've bounced higher than a bungee-jumping pothead.

Bracing for his partner's sarcasm, Blatch dragged himself into the office area he shared with Smalls and peeked around the doorframe.

A short, bald man—as tan and leathery as dried tobacco—was tapping a pencil on his desk. The handset of the office landline phone was pressed against his weathered ear. Smalls looked up and gave Blatch an *I got you, sucker* sneer, then turned up the dial on the snark he was dishing the poor person on the other end of the line.

"Now let me get this straight. You wanna prove a dead guy isn't dead?" Smalls used the pencil to draw circles in the air beside his left ear and mouthed the words, *Looney on the line*. "Listen, I appreciate the call, but—"

Blatch lunged forward and snatched the phone from Smalls' hand. He blurted into the mouthpiece, "Hello. You need to be speaking with me, Marcus Blatch."

Smalls rankled. "What the?" He tried to grab the handset back, but Blatch was younger, taller, and faster.

Blatch put his hand over the mouthpiece and elbowed Smalls away. "Cut the crap!" he whispered. "I'll explain in a minute."

"I see you two are hard at work," a woman's voice rang out.

The two men stopped scrabbling with each other and turned to stare at the beautiful blonde standing in the doorway. Their new partner, Deanna Young, had arrived early, too.

"Morning," Smalls said, and gave up trying to steal the phone back from Blatch.

Blatch gave Deanna a nod, put a finger to his lips to shush them both, and spoke overly loud into the phone to compensate for the surrounding chaos. "Yes. I'm the one named in the case. What can I help you with?"

Deanna's eyebrow arched with surprise. New business would be a welcome shot in the arm. She would've given Blatch a thumbs-up if her hands hadn't been occupied with the large cardboard box she was carrying.

Smalls walked over and hazarded a peek inside the box. He eyed Deanna suspiciously and crinkled his nose at the strange-looking appliance within. "What's that?"

"Shh!" Deanna scolded. She gave Blatch a quick nod, then turned and headed down the hall toward the breakroom kitchenette. Smalls followed, hot on her heels, mumbling behind her.

"Geez. You're not gonna junk up the place with a bunch of lady stuff, are you?"

Deanna smirked. "I've got a thirty-three percent stake in the place. I'm entitled to a few necessities." She plunked the box on the counter and wrestled out a rectangular assemblage of stainless steel and black plastic.

Smalls frowned. "What is that? Some kind of manicure machine?"

Deanna shot him a *really?* look. If he and Blatch hadn't just saved her life, she'd have given the old-school detective a piece of her new-school mind.

"I'm a psychologist, Smalls. Not a nail technician. If I'm going to work here, I need access to a decent cup of coffee."

Smalls groaned. As a private eye, he was used to working alone. But after watching fifty-nine fly by his rearview mirror, he'd decided to find a partner to help him with the investigative footwork. He hadn't counted on *two*.

As first partner, Marcus Blatch fit the bill pretty well. The younger man possessed the physical stamina Smalls found fading in himself. And Blatch's police training meant he knew how to handle himself. But what cinched the deal for Smalls was Blatch's ambition. His dark-brown eyes had the hungry look of a guy who still had something to prove. To Smalls, that trait seemed to be getting rarer and rarer.

Over the past few months of working together, Smalls had also figured out Blatch's weaknesses.

Like himself, Blatch was no salesman. He also suffered fools badly, though not as badly as Smalls himself. And Blatch appeared to have a soft spot for stray damsels in distress—he'd hired Deanna to be their secretary after meeting her by chance at a café.

Blatch had thought he'd hired a pretty face. But both he and Smalls had been in for a surprise. Deanna was smart, insightful, and had come packing a secret weapon—eight years' experience as a practicing psychologist in New York City.

She'd also come packing sex appeal.

Except for a noticeable bump on the bridge of her nose, Deanna had a model's face and figure.

She'd sparked a fire within Blatch. And although Deanna fought to hide her reciprocal feelings, to Smalls, the chemistry between the two was as obvious as the hairy mole on his ex-mother-in-law's chin.

Blatch was smitten by Deanna's looks. But for Smalls, it was the woman's pluck he found fascinating. Two days after nearly being murdered, Deanna had dusted herself off, quit her practice in New York, and made the men a business proposal that would help keep their faltering agency afloat—for now.

They'd needed the cash. Deanna had needed a new life. Politics had no monopoly on the making of strange bedfellows.

"Humph," Smalls grunted and folded his arms over his chest. He eyed Deanna skeptically as she leaned across the kitchenette counter and plugged in the cappuccino machine. She scooped dark roast coffee into a stainless steel receptacle, twisted it into place, and turned a knob.

"Look at that thing," Smalls groused. "Looks like something out of Willy Wonka's chocolate factory."

Deanna laughed and flipped another button. Steam began to hiss through the machine's inner workings.

Smalls studied the contraption and scowled. "I'm telling you now, that gizmo's a workers' comp hazard."

Deanna kept her eyes fixed on two thin streams of expresso filling the white ceramic cup. "It's perfectly safe, Smalls. Tell you what. You don't like it, you can go back to your K-cups."

She turned and handed Smalls the cup of espresso. He shot her a look. "What am I? Your Guinea pig or something?"

She gave him a *just do it* stare. Smalls conceded and took a sip. "Humph."

Blatch poked his head into the breakroom. "What's going on in here?"

Smalls shoved the cup back into Deanna's hands and shook his head at her. "If that thing's staying, you need to hang up a *Use at Your Own Risk* sign." He turned and glared at Blatch. "Partner meeting. *Now*. You two—follow me."

Smalls marched out of the room.

Blatch turned and smirked at Deanna. "Nice work. I've never seen him give anything such a glowing endorsement."

Deanna grinned. "That's Smalls. Bite first, ask questions later."

Blatch touched Deanna's arm. "Do me a favor? Make us all a cup before you join us in the conference room?"

Deanna's nose crinkled. "You forget. I'm a partner now. Not your secretary."

"So?" He shot Deanna that charming smile of his—the one that reminded her of every underdog hero in every romantic comedy ever made.

Deanna softened, but only slightly. "*So?* Since when do I have to make the coffee?"

Blatch's face sobered, but his tone remained flirtatious. "Partners share the load. Each of us does what they do best."

Deanna rankled. "Are you saying—?"

Blatch grinned. "What I'm saying is, at present, you're the only one who knows how to use that fancy thingamabob of yours. So this morning, coffee falls to you."

Deanna shot him a sideways look and conceded. "Fair enough. See you in there."

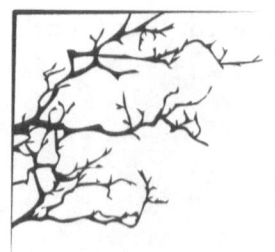

Chapter Four

THE SKY REFRACTED SHADOWY, rainbow hues on the iridescent wings of the black bird. It soared like a drone above the patchwork of gray and brown rooftops, spying on the yards and houses that delineated its territory.

A member of the raven species, the bird was curious of mind and omnivorous of appetite.

And smart.

Smart enough to use tools.

Smart enough to plan.

Smart enough to feel paranoid.

Of these three attributes, it outpaced its arch-nemesis by one ....

The flashing glint of a shiny object below caught the attention of the raven's round, black eyes. With a subtle shift of its wings, it circled back and down.

Its new trajectory landed the bird on the lawn of a suburban house. It hopped over to inspect the gleaming object.

It was a clear, glass bottle.

Inside it was a chunk of raw flesh.

The raven tapped its pointy, black bill along the bottle's shiny surface, trying to break the unseen barrier between it and the tasty-looking morsel. When its beak reached the tapered mouth of the bottle, it pierced through the flimsy paper lid.

Cautious, the bird withdrew its beak.

Its head pivoted right, left, up, and down as its eyes scanned both the sky and the nearby perimeter of grass and hedges.

Satisfied, it stuck its beak deeper into the bottle.

The flesh inside remained tantalizingly out of reach.

The raven plunged its beak deeper, then deeper still, until its head was completely inside the bottle.

It seized the half-rancid meat in its beak.

Blood oozed from the flesh, forming a thick, dark pool inside the bottle as the raven tugged and strained to free it from its glass coffin.

Engrossed in its task, the raven was caught unaware by a sharp sting in its neck.

It heard a cracking pop.

Its body went limp.

Paralyzed, the bird's shiny black eyes reflected the image of its captor, who stared back with keen interest as the bird's eyes grew dull and its life ebbed away in yet another dark pool of blood.

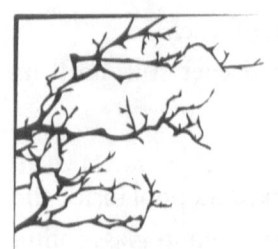

Chapter Five

DEANNA PLACED THREE cups and saucers on a silver serving tray, along with a trio of cloth napkins and tiny silver spoons. She added a silver sugar jar, then carried the tray into the conference room to join Blatch and Smalls.

Smalls looked up from his seat at the head of the conference table. Although his stake in the private investigation firm was only one percentage point more than his partners', he'd founded the company, and thus felt entitled to the director's chair. He used his commanding view of the door to scowl at Deanna as she arrived with her fancy coffee service.

"More girl stuff," he groused.

Deanna shot him an amused look. "I thought our clients might appreciate something more upscale than Styrofoam cups and that plastic tray you lifted from McDonald's."

"We haven't got the budget for haute cuisine," Smalls said.

Deanna set the tray down on the table in front of Smalls. "Consider it an early Christmas present."

Smalls groaned. "Aww cripes! What next? Secret Santa?"

Deanna grinned. "Speaking of Christmas, would it kill you to hang a wreath on the door?"

Blatch eyed Smalls, then grinned at Deanna. "Quite possibly, yes."

Deanna laughed. During her years as a psychologist, she'd seen plenty of tough cases. Barney Smalls was what she'd come to term a "burnt marshmallow"—crusty on the outside, but with an inner core of pure goo.

22

Marcus Blatch, on the other hand, was a bit more complicated. Sometimes he seemed downright cocky with confidence and charm. At other times, when he thought no one was looking, she'd caught glimpses of him looking as lost as a puppy in the rain.

Deanna handed Blatch a cappuccino, then turned to Smalls. "Offering a decent cup of coffee to clients is good for business. Besides, I did the math. Per cup, this espresso costs less than K-cups. And I'm sorry, but those artificial excuses for coffee don't exactly impress anyone."

"We're not here to impress," Smalls grumbled. "We're here to solve cases." He took a sip of cappuccino and tried to hide his delight behind a twitching scowl. He rolled his eyes and sighed. "Fine. You can keep your crappuccino thingy. Can we get down to business now?"

Deanna smirked. "Sure."

"So? What've we got going on this morning?"

Blatch shifted uncomfortably in his chair. "Not much."

Smalls unfolded *The Tampa Times* newspaper in his hand. "Not much in the papers worth following up on, either."

Deanna shook her head. "Honestly, Smalls. You must be the only person on the planet who still gets an actual newspaper delivered."

Smalls wagged his graying eyebrows and clicked the top of the red felt-tip pen clenched in his fist. "What can I say? I like to circle things. You got a problem with that?"

Deanna frowned. "I don't think the paper's the best way to drum up new business. We're not ambulance chasers, are we?"

Blatch winced. "Not *yet.*"

Smalls' eyes narrowed in on Blatch. "What about that call you were just on? Anything come from that lady trying to find a dead guy?"

"Oh. Right." Blatch nearly blushed. Being close to Deanna had temporarily scrambled his thoughts. Again. He needed to nip that bad habit in the bud.

Blatch sat up straight and cleared his throat. "The woman's a claims adjuster for Mutual Peninsular. She wants to take another look into the death benefit claim for a client named Gary Lee Preston."

Deanna set down her cup. "Why?"

"The company's about to hand over a hundred-thousand-dollar life insurance payout to his widow."

"So what's the issue?" Deanna asked.

"The claims adjuster said she got some suspicious news this morning." Blatch turned to Smalls. "Preston's name came up in connection with that fire you've got circled there in red, chief."

Smalls glanced down at the paper, then back at Blatch. "A dead guy? Suspected of what? Arson?"

"Yeah."

Deanna's brow furrowed. "On the phone, didn't I hear you say something about being involved in some sort of case?"

Blatch nodded. "Yeah. I was a witness to the traffic accident that killed Preston around six months ago. I didn't work the case officially, but I gave a statement to the traffic officer as to who was at fault."

"I don't understand," Deanna said. "If this Preston fellow is dead, how could he be a suspect in the fire?"

Blatch shrugged. "I wondered that myself. I was going to tell you guys that last night, I watched Mercer Arms burn to the ground."

Deanna's eyes widened. "Really?"

"Yeah. It could've been a disaster for the whole neighborhood. Thankfully, the firehouse is right off 25th Avenue. They had it contained within minutes. And Mercer Arms was no great loss. Not the building, anyway. That place was a fire trap."

"So how does Preston play into this?" Smalls asked.

"A cop at the scene told me Preston's prints were found at the scene. Knowing he was dead, I figured it had to be a mistake. The insurance adjuster, Aanya Gill, confirmed it this morning. She's already checked with the police. They told her the officer involved gave inaccurate information to the reporter who wrote the article in *The Tampa Times*."

Deanna frowned. "Sounds like it's all been settled. Why call you?"

"It's Gill's job to perform due diligence. She needs to cross every T to be certain Preston didn't somehow fake his own death for a payout."

Deanna looked incredulous. "Is that possible?"

Blatch shot her a mischievous grin. "I've seen people do a lot worse for a lot less."

Smalls snorted. "For a hundred grand, I'd consider it myself. Just think. If that Preston guy actually did pull off this fraud, he'd be one *lucky stiff.*"

Blatch and Deanna groaned.

Blatch turned to Smalls. "The coffee quality might've gone up, but your jokes sure haven't." He cleared his throat and continued. "Anyway, Gill is emailing over a contract today with specific things she wants me to double-check and recertify. It's piecemeal stuff, but at least it's work."

Smalls grunted. "I guess."

"Well, *I* have some news," Deanna said. "I'm actually seeing a new client this morning."

Smalls' left eyebrow perked up. "Really? You planning on filling us in on it?"

Deanna shrugged. "Not really. It's a case for my private therapy practice."

Smalls scowled. "I thought you were giving that up."

"I plan to. But as much as I'm looking forward to being your full-time psychological profiler, I enjoy the thought of keeping a roof over my head even more."

Smalls flinched. "Business will pick up. We're still getting calls from the Snyder case. Hopefully, some of 'em will turn into real work."

"Right," Blatch said. "In the meantime, you keep scrounging through *The Tampa Times*, chief."

Blatch smirked and pushed his chair out to stand. "If that's it, I'm going to get started—"

"Wait," Deanna said.

Blatch froze mid-stand. "What is it?"

Deanna cleared her throat. "I think we should change the name of the agency."

Smalls nearly choked on his espresso.

Blatch sat down again. "To what? Blatch, Smalls & Young?"

"No." Deanna chewed her lip. "It just doesn't have that ring to it, you know?"

"Yeah," Smalls deadpanned. "Sounds like something you'd hear from a dermatologist. Hey buddy. Let me cut off that 'blatch' while it's small and young."

Deanna shot Smalls a grin. "Precisely."

Blatch frowned. "Okay. How about Smalls, Young & Blatch?"

"Sure," Smalls said, mimicking a carnival barker. "Step right up, folks. We got a special on small, young 'blatches.' Buy one, get one free."

Deanna stifled a smirk and glanced over at Blatch. "He's got a point."

"Okay," Blatch conceded. "Our names suck together."

Deanna chewed her lip. "What about something without them?"

"Like what?" Smalls asked. "Private Investigators, Inc.?"

"Not that generic, but yes." She drummed her nails on the conference table. "Something that sets us apart from other detective agencies."

"You got any ideas?" Blatch asked.

"Well, let's talk this out." She looked at Smalls. "You bring what—thirty years' experience in detective work?"

"Thirty-*two*," Smalls corrected.

She turned to Blatch. "And we've got your connections with the local police, and your way with people. And as far as what I have to offer, well—"

"Hold up," Smalls said. "What about *my* way with people?"

Blatch shot Smalls a sideways grin. "Right now, we're talking about *assets*."

Smalls sneered. "Har har. Okay, okay. Carry on."

Deanna's face grew serious. "I think adding my profiling skills to your investigative ones is something that could really set us apart. We need a name that conveys that."

"How about Seeing Eye Private Eyes?" Blatch suggested.

Smalls scowled. "Sounds like a strip club for blind people."

Deanna laughed. "Well, keep working on it, guys. I've got to go." She stood, picked up her coffee cup, and left the conference room.

Blatch followed her. "So, who are you going to see?" he asked as they walked down the hall.

Deanna shrugged. "It's confidential."

"Oh, right," Blatch said too casually.

Deanna smiled to herself. "She's an acquaintance of Jodie Havenall's. One of those art-patron types who visits her gallery. Jodie said the woman was in 'a situation' and was looking for some emergency life counseling. Jodie recommended me. I figure it'll just be the one session. Maybe two. I'll be done before you guys even need me."

"Well—"

Deanna turned and pressed her dirty cup into Blatch's hand. "Look, I've got to go. I won't be long. Do you mind cleaning up the dishes?"

Blatch balked. "What?"

Deanna grinned coyly. "Your mother says you wash dishes better than any man she's ever known. And *you* happen to be the partner with spare time on his hands."

Blatch gave her half a smile. "Touché."

Deanna laughed, patted Blatch on the shoulder, and headed for the front door.

As Blatch filled the sink with hot water and dish soap, Smalls sauntered into the breakroom. He poked Blatch with his empty cup and nodded at the cappuccino machine. "You know how to use that thing?"

Blatch eyed the contraption warily and shrugged. "How hard can it be?"

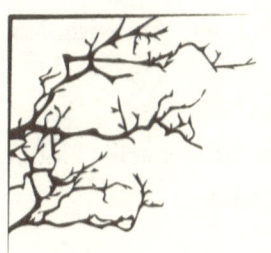

Chapter Six

CALCULATING.

That was the first word that popped into Deanna's mind when she laid eyes on Cecilia Count.

Everything about the woman screamed tactical, from her spikey, black haircut to the sharp tailoring of her stone-gray business suit to the pointed ends of her fingernails lacquered the color of fresh blood. Tall, slim, and in her late thirties, the woman had the perfect face for poker—narrow and angular, with not a single soft edge that might betray an emotion.

Either the woman's a stone wall or she's hiding behind one, Deanna thought as she shook the woman's hard, boney hand.

"A pleasure to meet you," Deanna said with a smile. "Jodie Havenall told me—"

"Look, I don't have a lot of time for small talk," Cecilia said curtly. She squeezed Deanna's hand hard enough to break bone, then terminated the handshake just as abruptly as she had Deanna's attempt at a polite greeting.

"Certainly," Deanna said. "You're pressed for time. Shall we go inside?" Deanna opened the glass door to the small coffee shop around the corner from her office.

Cecilia hesitated a moment.

She eyed Deanna up and down. Apparently satisfied, she pivoted on her stilettos and marched inside. Cecilia chose a corner table for two and arranged herself in the chair that offered a view of the door and the pedestrians bustling along on the busy sidewalk.

Deanna sat across from her. "So, what can I help you with, Ms. Count?"

Cecilia stiffened. "Not *me*. My son. Conrad."

Deanna's eyes widened slightly at the thought of Cecilia Count being mother to anything beyond a stock portfolio.

"Your son?"

The corners of Cecilia's mouth turned down infinitesimally. "Yes. Are you hard of hearing?"

Deanna willed her expression to remain pleasant. "No. I'm just surprised. Jodie didn't mention the nature of your request."

The right side of Cecilia's mouth puckered slightly. "As flakey as that woman is, Jodie Havenall knows how to keep her mouth shut. I'm hoping I can count on you for the same courtesy?"

"Absolutely."

"Good. I'd like you to sign a non-disclosure agreement. I prefer paper to promises."

"I don't have a problem with that," Deanna said, somewhat surprised. "But I retain the right to terminate should I deem your case of a nature to which I prefer to remain unaffiliated."

Deanna's mouthful of business-speak seemed to impress Cecilia. The woman's shoulders relaxed an inch. "Agreed."

Deanna offered a hint of a smile. "So, shall we—"

"You two ready to order?" asked a slim young man sporting a millennial-style man-bun, relaxed posture, and "whatever" attitude.

"Cappuccino?" Deanna asked Cecilia. The woman gave a quick nod. Deanna looked up at the waiter. "Two cappuccinos, please."

"Cool. So, you want like soy milk, almond milk, or—"

Deanna nearly groaned. She shot the young man a tight smile. "Two old-schools, please. Real milk. Real espresso. Real cups."

"You got it," he said, and shuffled off to the coffee bar.

Deanna turned to face Cecilia and thought she detected a fissure of pleasure in the woman's stony face. She figured she might as well try to crack it open a bit further while the woman might possibly be in a good mood.

"So, Ms. Count, you said you're concerned about your son, Conrad?"

Cecilia sighed. "Correct. I really don't know what to do with him anymore. He won't listen to reason. It's like he's in his own little world."

"Have you had him tested for autism?"

Cecilia looked offended. "Of course. He's on the very lowest end of the spectrum. I don't think this has anything to do with that."

"What do you mean by *this?* Has he done something unusual?"

The woman's ice-blue eyes glanced around the café to make sure no one was watching. She leaned over the table and whispered, "I caught him playing with a ... a dead bird!"

"I see," Deanna said, somewhat taken aback. Cecilia's voice had displayed concern, but not of the motherly type. It was more a tone of inconvenience, as if her son were an employee on the verge of being dismissed for unethical behavior.

"Did he kill the bird, or find it dead?" Deanna asked.

Cecilia stared into Deanna's eyes. "I don't know."

"How old is Conrad?"

"Six."

Deanna pulled a small notebook from her red leather satchel. "Has he done this before?"

"Not that I know of." Cecilia's eyes followed every line as Deanna wrote in the notebook. "What are you writing?"

Deanna looked up. "I'd like to meet with your son for a private assessment."

Cecilia's face registered relief. "Good. Of course. Should we meet at your office?"

"Your cappuccinos, ladies," the waiter said, oblivious to interrupting their conversation. He fumbled the cups onto the table and

stood there staring and smiling, as if he were waiting for one of them
to hand him a gold star for his spectacularly average performance.

Deanna tapped a silver pen on her notebook, actually grateful
for the waiter's intrusion. She needed a moment to think. When
she'd woken up this morning, she'd had no clients—and no idea
she'd be getting any so soon. She had yet to procure an office. She
didn't even have business cards.

Still, the hard-faced woman sitting across from her didn't appear
to be the kind who liked to wait—or to be told "no."

According to Jodie, Cecilia Count was a lawyer with deep connections to St. Petersburg's business elite. Screwing this meeting up
was out of the question. It could quash Deanna's chances of getting
new clients in a far-reaching way from which she might never recov-
er.

I need an office, and now, she thought. *But where? I can't exactly
take them to Blatch & Smalls. Smalls is about as discrete as an election-
day politician ....*

Deanna looked up at the expectant waiter. He beamed at her.
She smiled awkwardly and said, "Thank you ... uh?"

"Skyler."

"Of course. Thank you, Skyler. I think we're all set here."

As the waiter shuffled away, Deanna racked her brain trying to
think of how to answer Cecilia's question about meeting at her office. Stalling for more time, she leaned in toward Cecilia, reached for
a sugar packet, and asked, "How dead was the bird?"

One of Cecilia's neat, angular eyebrows raised slightly. "Why?"

"I'm trying to determine if Conrad found the animal dead, or
killed it himself."

"Does it make any difference?"

Deanna nodded. "Yes. I'm afraid it does."

Cecilia's lips pressed into a thin line. "I think I know why. Isn't killing small animals one of the first signs that your offspring may be a psychopath?"

Deanna blanched, mainly from Cecilia's description of her son as "offspring."

"I won't sugar coat it," Deanna answered. "Harming animals is a sign of psychological disturbance, Ms. Count. But I don't think we should jump to any conclusions just yet."

Cecilia stared at some point to her left. "I should have known. Charles Count was a sadistic bastard. Why should I have expected his son to be any different?"

Deanna cleared her throat. "What do you mean by 'sadistic bastard'?"

Cecilia glanced around. "Listen, Dr. Young. I appreciate you meeting me on such short notice, but this just isn't the place to be discussing these things. You *do* have an office, don't you?"

"Yes, of course," Deanna lied.

"Good. Shall we meet there tomorrow? I can fit you in between my morning depositions and afternoon business lunch. Say, eleven?"

Deanna flipped through the blank pages in her notebook and made the pretense of checking her empty calendar. "I would love to accommodate you, Ms. Count. It's just that, at the moment I'm having my office—*redecorated*. It's supposed to be ready by—"

"I know!" Cecilia interrupted. "You can come to my house. Would that work?"

Deanna's gut went slack with relief. "Yes. Actually, it would be preferable. Meeting Conrad on his own turf would allow you to introduce me as a friend, not as a scary doctor. It could help build trust and rapport. And if he could show me his room and where he found the bird, it would aid me in assessing his social and environmental influences."

"Impressive." Cecilia said, and offered Deanna a brief glimpse of her upper teeth. "Jodie said you were from New York. I'm glad to finally find a therapist with some sophistication."

"Thank you," Deanna replied, wondering how many other therapists the woman had already tried.

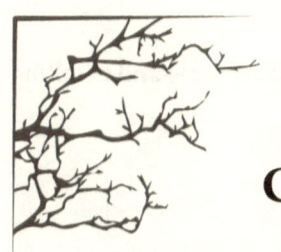

Chapter Seven

BLATCH PRINTED OUT the email from Mutual Peninsular and studied the claims adjuster's request. In all, it looked like two or three billable hours, tops. If something didn't break soon, he might have to start chasing ambulances after all.

"What you got?" Smalls asked, eyeing the printout.

"Not much. Looks like they want me to review and recertify the points I made in my accident report statement—and to interview the neighbors of Preston's widow to see if she's been 'acting suspicious.'"

Smalls snorted. "Living the high life on her ill-gotten gains?"

Blatch smirked. "She hasn't gotten the gains yet. According to this, she's still living in a trailer in Pinellas Park. I just need to make sure she's not smuggling Gary Preston under the floorboards."

"Dead or alive?"

"Either one."

Smalls nodded. "Right. Well, have fun and pet some Pit-Bulls for me."

Blatch shot Smalls a look. "Okay. It's not sexy stuff, I'll give you that. But it's solid work."

Smalls snorted. "Yeah. Of the *grunt* variety."

Blatch scowled. "So, what have *you* got going on?"

Smalls' chin lifted an inch. "I've been reviewing some cold case files."

Blatch nearly rolled his eyes. "Not *those* again. Don't you have them all memorized by now? We need to be looking toward the *future*."

Smalls balked. "I have been!"

"How?"

"I've been working the calls from the Snyder case—and thinking up new names for the business, all right?"

"Fine. Got any?"

Smalls' eyes narrowed. "Any what?"

"Names."

"Sure. Better than your lame ideas."

"Yeah? Let's hear 'em."

Smalls puffed out his chest. "BS&Y."

Blatch snorted. "Sounds like a dime store. Hey Smalls, pick me up some dog food at BS&Y. No, wait. That's a lot of BS and let me tell you *why!*"

Smalls scowled. "Har har."

Blatch blew out a breath. "I thought we all agreed our names suck."

Smalls nodded a concession. "Okay. How about this, Discrete Investigation & Profiling Services."

Blatch chewed on the idea for a second, then burst into a grin. "Talk about your sucky acronyms. D-I-P-S. DIPS! I can see the advertising slogan now—Hey everybody, why not let a bunch of dips work for you?"

Smalls grunted and wadded up the paper in his hand. "Maybe we should hire somebody to handle this."

"Sure," Blatch said. "We'll take it out of petty cash since we're rolling in dough."

Smalls sighed, his face etched with worry. Blatch put his hand on his partner's shoulder. "Don't sweat it. It'll all work out, chief."

"I hope you're right."

Blatch grabbed his coat and handed Smalls a stack of papers. "Here. In the meantime, make yourself useful."

Smalls' face came alive with interest. "What's this?"

Blatch grinned. "A manual on how to operate Deanna's fancy coffee machine. I hear baristas are in high demand."

Blatch reached for the doorknob, then turned back and shot Smalls a wink. "Never hurts for an old dog to learn a new trick."

Smalls sneered. "I hope you catch fleas."

AT THE OFFICE, BLATCH had joked with Smalls about the old man's career being played out. But when he pulled up to the dilapidated trailer next door to Tandy Preston's equally squalid one, Blatch worried he might be staring at a vision of his own dismal future.

If this private eye business doesn't pick up, I don't know what I'm gonna do.

Shoving the thought away, he opened the door of his innocuous, dark-blue sedan. It was a forgettable model manufactured in a forgettable year. Not good for picking up chicks, but perfect for blending into the scenery—especially *this* kind of scenery. From what Blatch had seen of Palm Court Mobile Home Park, "down and out" would've been a step up in the world.

He climbed out of the car and onto the crumbling asphalt road, then picked his way along a dirt path through the knee-high Bahia grass and weeds that made up the front lawn. Garbage and plastic toys littered the yard, lying forgotten and bleaching in the sun like skeletal remains.

Blatch put a foot on the rickety steps of the makeshift wooden deck scabbed onto the single-wide trailer. Fairly certain the boards would hold his weight, he made his way across the deck and pressed the doorbell. The brittle plastic button fell off the wall, leaving a round opening in the trailer's aluminum skin reminiscent of a .38 bullet hole.

"Great," Blatch said under his breath. He rapped his knuckles on the worn beige paint on the dented door. The wood beneath his feet began to vibrate.

Someone was moving around inside the trailer.

Blatch felt for the Glock tucked inside his waistband. In this kind of neighborhood, neither the residents nor their visitors knew what to expect from each other. Still, even if Blatch had known the name of the trailer's inhabitants, he wouldn't have called ahead. People with police records usually weren't too keen on making appointments with ex-cops or private eyes.

The trailer door cracked open enough for a voice to escape. "What you want?"

"Just wanted to ask about your neighbor, Tandy Preston."

The door opened halfway, revealing a cloud of cigarette smoke and a woman nearly as wide as she was tall. Dressed in a dirty t-shirt and bulging polyester leggings, the woman's bottle-blonde hair sported a skunk stripe of brown roots. "What you want with Tandy? Poor woman's been through enough."

Blatch tried to look both charming and concerned. "Oh. What's she been through?"

"Lost her husband a while back. And last week her damned trailer nearly burned down."

"Wow. That's a shame."

The woman's smile conveyed that, to her, it really wasn't *that* big a shame.

Going with it, Blatch leaned closer and whispered conspiratorially, "From what I hear, Tandy would've been better off without both Gary *and* that trailer." He shot her his best flirty smile.

The corners of the woman's mouth curled slightly. "You knew Gary?"

"Yeah. We had business together."

"Business, huh? What's your name?"

"Marcus Blatch."

She eyed him suspiciously. "I never heard him talk about you."

"Well, to be honest, it's been a while." Blatch smiled again. "I'm looking for something."

The woman laughed. "Well, if it's the keys to Tandy's chastity belt, honey, you're a bit late to the party."

Blatch let his eyebrows collide. "She's got herself a new guy already?"

She grinned coyly. "Well, there's new, and then there's *new*, if you know what I mean."

"Not exactly."

"She's back with her old beau."

"Gary?"

The woman's eyes flew open wide. Her chin met her neck. "*Gary?* Naw!" She shook her head at Blatch. "What are you? Some kind of ghost hunter?"

"No. I just ... well." Blatch made a show of hanging his head. "Gary owes me money." He shot her an upturned glance. "Are you sure he's dead?"

The woman's lips pursed into a sour line. "I'm sure. Get in line. Gary owed everybody money. I tell you what, if he wasn't already dead, I know a shitload of folks who'd be happy to help his ass get to his just reward."

"I heard that," Blatch said, and nearly blushed at his attempt to sound cool. The woman didn't seem to take offense, so he carried on. "So, who's Tandy seeing now?"

The woman's brow furrowed like a Shar-Pei's. "Do I look like I would know? I mind my own business around here."

Her head jerked to the left. The sight of an approaching car made her face crumple. "Oh, shit!" she said, and slammed the door in Blatch's face.

Blatch turned to see a rusty, red Camaro pull up in the overgrown lawn in front of Tandy Preston's trailer.

A woman climbed out of the driver's seat. The man in the passenger seat pulled a ball cap down nearly over his eyes, and then piled out of the car, slinking behind Tandy like a kicked dog.

Even with the ball cap and black wig disguise, Blatch felt certain he'd seen the man before.

He looked a lot like Gary Lee Preston.

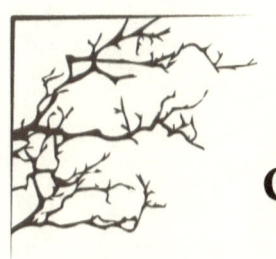

Chapter Eight

SHINY, BLUE-BLACK FLIES buzzed in a frenzied cloud around the dead raven.

A figure inched its way closer and crouched among the feeding insects. He closed his eyes and smiled with delight at the tickling feeling the flies' legs made as they crawled all over his arms and face.

He opened his eyes and leaned forward to study the dead bird for a moment.

It was time.

He maneuvered himself into position.

His eyes danced with anticipation.

He waited patiently for the buzzing insects to settle once more onto the pungent carcass.

Whoosh!

In one quick motion, he pounced down on the dull, lifeless raven, trapping it and the swarm of flies within the thin parachute of a plastic grocery bag.

Carefully, he scooped the bag along the damp ground underneath the raven, then hurriedly tied the bag's handles together in a pair of tight, choking knots.

He raised his prize to the fading light and smiled.

Hello, my new friends. You'll teach me to fly ... or else.

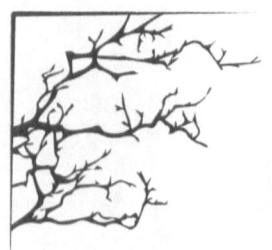

Chapter Nine

DEANNA PAUSED AT THE door of the coffee shop, her mind churning with thoughts about her new client, Conrad Count. She'd never worked with a child so young before. Usually, it took patients quite a few more years to wander far enough off track to require her kind of psychological counseling services.

Conrad was only six. How sick could the poor little guy be? Still, his mother had left in a hurry after securing their appointment for tomorrow. Deanna wondered yet again where Cecilia Count's priorities lay.

I guess we'll find out, she thought as she stepped out of the café. Preoccupied, she ran headlong into an elderly woman laden down with fancy shopping bags.

She nearly knocked her over.

"Oh! Excuse me!" Deanna exclaimed as she grabbed the woman's elbow to keep her from toppling to the ground.

The woman laughed. "My fault, honey. I get so distracted this time of year. Can you believe Christmas is almost here?"

Deanna shook her head. No, she really *couldn't* believe it. She helped the woman pick up her bags. "Looks like *you're* ready, which is more than I can say for myself."

The woman winked. "What's not to like about shopping? Happy holidays, hon!"

Deanna watched the elderly woman disappear among the crowd of people bustling along the sidewalk, then turned to admire a small shopfront laden with Christmas cheer. The holiday décor of St. Petersburg's merchants didn't compare to those of downtown New York's, of course. But then again, neither did the weather.

If Deanna had been in the Big Apple, the wind chill would've bitten right through her thin trench coat. And she most certainly wouldn't have chosen to walk the mile to downtown from her house on Coffee Pot Boulevard.

Deanna thought about the crumbling old mansion and groaned inside. She'd inherited the house when her mother passed away last month. Once a true beauty, the pink, 1930's Mediterranean Revival boasted soaring ceilings, arched entryways, and wrought-iron balconies overlooking the inlet of dark water known as Coffee Pot Bayou.

As a child, Deanna had loved the house. But after thirty years under her mother's neglectful watch, the place was falling apart at the joists. The faded stucco was coming off in scabby chunks. The rusting wrought iron railings were spilling coffee-brown tear stains down its sides. The wooden windows were shot, half eaten away by termites.

The only saving grace was the derelict landscaping. From the street, the overgrown Ligustrum hedges hid a multitude of deferred maintenance from the curiosity of strangers passing by.

Deanna strolled along the sidewalk toward the waterfront, barely noticing the quaint shops, busy cafés and restaurants, and funky, refurbished hotels as she passed.

Ever since her return to Florida, her mind had been preoccupied—caught up in a debate on what to do with the moldering mansion that had suddenly become her sole responsibility.

Should I decorate the house, or detonate it? she wondered.

Her mother's life insurance policy was enough to cover a great deal of the repairs the house needed, but there would be nothing left over for living expenses. Deanna could sell the house, but she felt certain the ghastly revelations recently discovered there had surely caused its market value to plummet.

Deanna chewed her lip. As a pragmatist, she knew the logical thing to do would be to make a list of pros and cons to determine the best course of action. But as a psychologist, she was well aware that logic was of no consequence in affairs of the heart.

The cool breeze picked up as Deanna turned the corner of Central Avenue and Beach Drive. The clanking of sailboat riggings caught her attention. She paused to admire the skiffs and catamarans bobbing in their harborages on Tampa Bay. Many of their masts and bows were strung with holiday garlands and lights.

She took a deep breath and smiled at the unexpected holiday cheer.

A few blocks further down Beach Drive, Vinoy Park came into view. The shady strip of green was usually quiet during mid-day. But with the holidays approaching, it was alive with visitors enjoying the city's homespun Santa village and forty-foot tall artificial Christmas tree.

Deanna smiled wistfully. It seemed as if the holiday spirit had invaded every nook and cranny of St. Pete—except her place.

Not yet ready to face the reality of her rundown house, Deanna stopped at 400 Beach Tavern for a quick lunch. She chose one of the high-top tables overlooking the park and soon found herself entertained by a steady flow of families strolling by.

Children carrying letters for Santa were especially intriguing. Their eager little eyes shone with anticipation as they tugged their moms and dads toward Santa's big red mailbox across the street, where every wish was sure to be granted.

She smiled through the pain. *If only that were true.*

"Merry Christmas, lady," a joyful voice squealed.

Deanna looked down to see a little blonde girl holding a handful of candy canes. She offered one to Deanna.

"Thank you," she said, taking the candy. "Merry Christmas to you, too."

The little girl beamed, her cherub face a picture of innocence and joy. Deanna watched her make her way toward the mailbox, her mom in tow.

Suddenly, Deanna felt herself unexpectedly caught up by the holiday spirit as well. She smiled, took a last sip of chardonnay, and thought, *Maybe there's such a thing as a happy childhood, after all.*

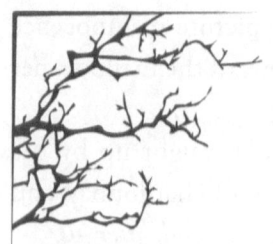

Chapter Ten

BLATCH DROVE HIS SEDAN around the corner from Tandy Preston's rundown trailer. Once he was out of sight, he pulled over to weigh his options. If the guy in the wig and ball cap disguise really *was* Gary Lee Preston, his job for Mutual Peninsular was over.

And maybe his life, as well.

From what Blatch could recall of his police record, Gary Lee Preston had a history of taking pot-shots at stray dogs with a sawed-off shotgun. With a hundred grand at stake, the guy would probably be willing to up the ante.

Blatch pulled out his cellphone and tapped Smalls' number. "Hey. I think I might have found something."

"What?"

"Gary Lee. Alive and kicking. I don't want to face this guy alone."

"Be there in fifteen."

Blatch clicked off the phone. As he reached to put it back into his jacket pocket, it rang in his hand. He didn't recognize the number, but answered anyway, hoping it wasn't a robo-call.

"Hello?"

"Hey, Blatch. You sure this Preston guy's dead?"

It was Jerry Davidson, the young cop he'd met at the fire last night. *I was just going to call you and ask you the same thing,* Blatch thought. "Uh ... pretty sure. Why?"

"This whole thing stinks," Davidson said angrily. "The *official* story is the thumbprint comparison wasn't conclusive. But I saw what I saw, Blatch. The print was a match."

"Okay. So, why are you calling *me*?"

"You told me last night you saw Preston die. I thought you were pulling my leg. Then I saw your name in Preston's accident report. Captain Castleberry saw it too, and went ballistic."

"Shit. Did you tell him we talked last night?"

"No. But when I insisted the thumbprint was legit, he threw me out of his office and put me on Scooby patrol."

Blatch glanced over at Tandy Preston's trailer. No activity. He turned his attention back to Davidson. "Uh ... Scooby patrol?"

"Yeah. Castleberry said if I wanted to chase ghosts like a cartoon mutt, that was my prerogative. Then he slapped the file in my hand and told me to have at it. I thought that was the end of it, but when I came in this morning, there was a jar of dog biscuits on my desk labeled Scooby Snacks. Shit, Blatch. I'm nothing but a joke to him." Davidson hesitated, then added, "I really shouldn't be talking to you."

No shit, Blatch thought. "Then why are you?"

"Because I want to kick that asshole Castleberry in the balls. I want to figure out how Preston's thumbprint got on that fuel can and shove the evidence up his—"

"I get the picture."

Davidson coughed. "Right. Given your history with the guy, I thought you might want a piece of the action. I guess I was wrong."

Blatch mulled it over for half a second. "Actually, you're right. I do. Listen, if you're not busy, I'm about to pay a visit to Preston's grieving widow. Funny thing is, she's got a boyfriend who looks vaguely familiar."

"You're shitting me."

"I shit you not."

"Gimme the address. I'm there."

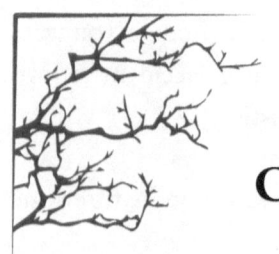

Chapter Eleven

ON HER WAY HOME, DEANNA took the scenic sidewalk that ran along the concrete seawall bordering Tampa Bay. Both the sidewalk and seawall stretched for miles, outlining the entire eastern edge of downtown St. Petersburg before finally curving inland to frame the edges of Coffee Pot Bayou.

On a clear day like today, Deanna could make out the clump of skyscrapers marking downtown Tampa over fifteen miles away on the opposite shore. Tampa Bay was massive. A crescent-shaped inlet of the Gulf of Mexico, it lapped the shores of nearly forty miles of Florida's western coastline.

To Deanna, the view of Tampa Bay was one of her favorite things about the city. In the crisp December sunlight and with a glass of chardonnay warming her insides, it shone like an endless sea of shimmering blue diamonds.

Waves gently slapped the seawall. Twenty feet offshore, a bottlenose dolphin blew out a steamy breath. Deanna stopped for a moment to take it all in.

This is starting to feel like home ... again, she thought.

The beep of a horn startled Deanna out of her daydream. She turned to see a familiar face waving at her through the window of a battered old Geo Metro. It was her half-sister, Jodie Havenall.

"Hey! Aren't you the lady who—" Jodie called out.

"No!" Deanna yelled back, then laughed.

Jodie grinned. "You don't even know what I was going to say."

Deanna smirked. "Knowing you, I've got a pretty good idea."

Jodie laughed. "Wanna ride?"

Deanna shook her head, even though Jodie lived right next door. "It's only a few more blocks. I could use the exercise."

"Okay. See you back at the ranch."

Jodie took off and disappeared around the corner where Beach Drive met Coffee Pot Bayou. Deanna turned back to enjoy the view of Tampa Bay for a moment.

Yes. This is my home, she thought, then turned and continued along the sidewalk.

As she rounded the corner where the wide-open bay met the narrow bayou, the water quickly turned from salty blue to brackish brown. An army of private docks jutted out from the sidewalk into the inlet's inky waters. Most sported an expensive pleasure boat at the end.

On the opposite shore of the bayou sat Snell Island. The miles-long chunk of land had been dredged up from the sea and developed by a Kentucky pharmacist named C. Perry Snell over a hundred years ago. Most of the stately homes he built still stood proudly along either shore of Coffee Pot Bayou. Each was a unique treasure—a throwback to an era of luxury and craftsmanship rarely matched in modern construction.

As Deanna admired the beautiful mansions all decked out for the holidays, she tried to imagine her own house restored to such grandeur. But as the second story of the crumbling pink behemoth slowly came into view above the overgrown Ligustrum hedge, reality set in again.

Deanna's enthusiasm evaporated in the breeze as she trudged toward it, a blonde moth to a pink flame.

As she drew near, Deanna looked both ways down the street, then sprinted across it to the sidewalk in front of her house. Embarrassed to be seen, she quickly squeezed through the narrow entry passage in the hedge and nearly tumbled into her neglected front lawn.

Deanna regained her footing just in time to see a bundled-up figure step out of the weedy shadows and walk toward her.

"Jodie!" Deanna yelled. "You scared the daylights out of me!"

Jodie grinned. "Hiya, sis. How'd it go with Count Dracula?"

Deanna laughed despite herself. "Remind me not to ask you for any more favors. What's with the parka? You look like you're heading to the North Pole."

"It's in the sixties," Jodie said. "I'm not a hardened New Yorker like you."

"Oh. That's right. I forgot," Deanna said, and skirted past Jodie.

She climbed the steps and wrestled with the pile of advertising flyers secured with a rubber band to the doorknob of the screened porch.

The band broke. Half of the ads slipped out of her hand and went flying in the breeze.

"Crap!"

"Got 'em," Jodie said, and went chasing after the flyers.

"Thanks," Deanna said, and fished around in her purse for the keys to the front door as Jodie scooped up the flyers.

Jodie grabbed one and waved it at Deanna. "Hey! Just what you need, Dee. A party pizza for twelve."

Deanna crinkled her nose. "I'll pass."

"Okay, more for me." Jodie tucked the flyer under her arm and followed her onto the porch. She studied another one. "Oh! This one's perfect! It says, 'We buy ugly houses in any condition.'"

"Right," Deanna said, pushing open the front door. "If they saw the inside of this place, they'd run for their lives."

Jodie shot her a look. "You mean like you just did?"

Deanna blushed. "You saw that, heh?"

Jodie's right eyebrow arched over her smirk. "It's almost like you're *ashamed* of the place or something."

Deanna winced. "My house is the neighborhood eyesore!"

Jodie shrugged. "Hey, nobody's perfect."

Deanna groaned. As she watched her half-sister make herself comfortable amid the squalid stacks of newspapers and garbage left behind by her hoarding mother, Deanna felt herself relax a notch.

Jodie's family, now, she thought. *Actually, Jodie's my* only *family now*.

Although the two women looked nothing alike—Deanna was shapely, stylish and blonde, Jodie was stick thin, preferred tie-dyed hippie wear, and had a head of bushy black hair—they still had a lot in common.

For one, they had the same father, Warren McMasters, who had died before they were old enough to remember him. They'd also suffered similar neglect from self-absorbed mothers, both of whom had been suspected of murder, though only one was ever charged.

And, early on, both Jodie and Deanna had adopted the warped sense of humor so often used as a coping mechanism by those left to raise themselves without the security of parents or the power to change their situation.

Jodie unzipped her light-blue parka and flopped into the tattered arms of an upholstered chair in the living room. Her usually good-humored face grew serious. "I really want to know, Dee. How'd it go with Count Cecilia?"

Deanna shrugged. "That woman's parents must've been nearly as bad as ours."

"Really?" Jodie's eyes twinkled with mischief. "Is she psycho, too?"

Deanna laughed. "Not as bad as we are. She's just—wound up tight. Actually, in some ways, I can relate."

Jodie shook her head. "I can't. But hey, who am I to judge? She likes my paintings and her checks don't bounce. That's sane enough for me." She shot Deanna a lurid grin. "So, when do you start shrinking her head, Doc?"

Deanna rolled her eyes. "I can't discuss it."

Jodie pouted in mock offense. "Not even with your dear ol' sis?"

Deanna smirked. "*Especially* not with you. However, she did say you were pretty tight-lipped."

Jodie eyed her curiously. "And that surprises you?"

"I dunno." Deanna glanced around at the junk piled up all over the living room and threw her hands up. "Ugh! I can't think straight in all this mess!"

"Don't let it get to you."

Deanna looked Jodie in the eye. "Easy for you to say. Your mother was a neat freak."

Jodie grinned devilishly. "Yeah. But her need for control was pretty *suffocating*."

Deanna blanched.

Jodie grinned. "Too soon?"

Deanna shook her head. "Little bit."

Jodie laughed and looked around the room. "So, why don't you just hire someone to get rid of this junk?"

"My mother wasn't right in the head, Jodie. Who knows what she might've stashed away amongst all this stuff? I'm afraid I'm going to need to go through it piece by piece. I don't want to lose anything important."

Jodie grinned evilly. "You mean like some more handwritten love letters?"

Deanna shot her a *don't go there* glare.

Jodie held up her hands. "Okay. Switching topics now. Have you decided to keep the place or sell it?"

"Keep it," Deanna blurted, then backtracked. "At least for now—until I can wade through this mountain of junk. Besides, who would want to buy a place tainted by ... you know."

Jodie sighed and sorted through the advertising flyers in her hand. "Maybe The Rescue Squad would, Dee." She jabbed a finger at a flyer. "It says right here, 'Any house, any condition.'"

Deanna's nose crinkled. "Right. If I'm willing to give it away."

Jodie wagged her eyebrows. "Who knows? Maybe you'll get a proposal to turn this place into a house of horrors."

Deanna's lip curled slightly. "Been there. Done that." She eyed Jodie. "Too soon?"

Jodie grinned. "Never." She laid the flyers on a side table atop a pile of old magazines. "So, are you really going to work with the Count?"

"No. Yes." Deanna chewed her lip. "Maybe."

Jodie leaned forward in her chair. "What's the hesitation?"

"I'm meeting Ms. Count at her house tomorrow. But after that ... I'm kind of stuck. I need an office, Jodie. I lied and told her mine was being refurbished. I might be able to stall her another time or two, but if I don't find a space—"

"Hold it!" Jodie interrupted. "I know! I've got plenty of room. Why don't you set up your office at my place? You have to admit, you can't beat the commute."

Deanna's eyes teared up. "Really?"

Jodie shrugged. "Sure. The front room would be perfect for it."

Deanna hesitated. "Won't it interfere with your ... *lifestyle?*"

Jodie smirked. "No. I keep my 'lifestyle' confined to other locales."

Deanna nodded, warming to the idea. "What's the rent?"

Jodie grinned. "Seeing as how you saved my life, I think we can work out something."

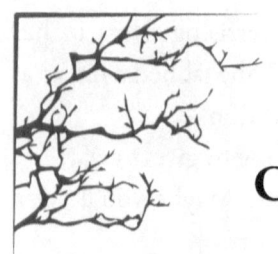

Chapter Twelve

A SCRUFFY ORANGE CAT missing half an ear scurried out from under the broken skirt of a trailer and made a beeline for Blatch's sedan. Like most of his fellow felines, he knew a sucker when he saw one. When Smalls drove up in his black SUV a few minutes later, Blatch was leaned up against his sedan, scratching the purring tomcat under its threadbare chin.

Smalls snorted. "What's new pussycat?"

Blatch groaned and set the tabby down. He nodded to his left. "That's Preston's trailer over there."

Smalls gave it the once over. His nose crinkled. "You ready?"

"Waiting on Davidson."

Smalls scowled. "That cop with the bad intel on the arsonist?"

"The same."

"What for? We don't need him."

"Don't worry. He's not getting a piece of the fee."

Smalls snorted. "What fee? A cut of the fifty bucks you're making on this?"

Blatch shook his head. "I read over the contract. If we prove Preston's alive, we get a percentage of the 'conserved death benefit payout.'"

"What kind of percentage?"

"Five grand's worth."

Smalls' face perked up. "Why didn't you say so in the first place? This'll be the fastest money we've ever made."

"*If* it's Gary Lee Preston. And *if* we bring him in alive."

Smalls nodded. "I guess if we killed him that would kind of blow the 'conserved death benefit payout.'"

"Exactly."

Smalls lifted his fedora and scratched his bald head. "So what's Davidson's angle on this?"

Blatch shrugged. "Vengeance. He swore to me it was Preston's prints on the gas can. But Castleberry told him to take a hike. The kid's itching to prove him wrong." Blatch looked over at the road. "Speak of the devil ...."

A light-blue Chevy Impala pulled up. Davidson stepped out with a pizza box in his hand. He was wearing his police department blues.

"Shit," Blatch muttered. "I told him no uniform."

Davidson sprinted over to the waiting pair. Blatch gave him a hard look. "What the hell—?"

"Sorry," Davidson blurted. "I didn't have time to change."

Smalls shot him a sour look. "What's with the pizza? No time for lunch, either?"

Davidson blushed. "Uh ... no. It's empty. I just thought maybe you might want to use it as a decoy. You know, a reason to come knocking at their door."

"We're not here to play games, kid," Smalls grumbled. "Toss it."

Davidson glanced around. "Into somebody's yard?"

Smalls shook his head. "No. Into the recycling bin. Ugh! Look around you! In this place, who would notice?"

Davidson hesitated. Blatch grabbed the box from his hand and Frizbee'd it into the hedges.

"This is *our* operation," he said to the young cop. "*Our* rules. You're here as a courtesy. Follow our orders or hit the road. Understood?"

Davidson's face sobered. "Understood."

Blatch eyed Davidson's badge with disdain. "Since you're in uniform, I want you out of sight. Work your way around that fence over there and into the backyard, in case he tries to flee. No firing weapons unless it's life or death."

"You got it," Davidson said, and took off for the fence line.

Blatch turned to his partner. "Ready?"

"Yeah. Just one question. What's this guy look like?"

"Oh." Blatch pulled a mugshot out of his jacket pocket. "That's our guy. Last seen wearing a NASCAR cap and an Ozzie Osbourne wig."

Smalls eyed him sharply. "You're in good humor for a guy about to face down death."

Blatch shrugged. "If you gotta go, might as well go happy, right?"

Smalls grinned. "Damned straight. Let's get this *dead*beat."

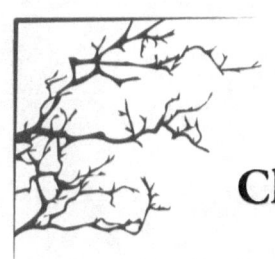

Chapter Thirteen

THE ANGELS WERE BACK on the ceiling again.

A holy multitude of fists, hammering out their decree.

Obey. Obey. Obey. Obey. Obey. Obey.

He stared up toward heaven and chewed his lip until the coppery taste of blood blended with his determination.

I can't be a scaredy-cat.

I must answer God's call.

He stared at the phone on the wall.

It began to buzz.

He winced, then slowly leaned toward it.

Chapter Fourteen

IT TOOK A SECOND ROUND of hard pounding before Tandy Preston cracked open the rusty door to her trailer. With one dark eye, she peered at Blatch and Smalls through the narrow slit afforded by the security chain.

"You guys cops?"

"No," Smalls said, his face and tone that of a man who'd just been insulted.

From the greyish gloom inside the trailer, Tandy's eye moved up and down in its hollow socket, taking in the men. "I ain't seen any in a while, but you still look like cops to me."

Blatch shot her half a smile. "I assure you, we're not. You are Tandy Preston, widow of Gary Lee, aren't you?"

The one eye narrowed. "What do you want?"

Blatch made the pretense of searching his pockets, then shook his head good-naturedly. "Shoot. Must've forgotten my cards. Ms. Preston, we're here on behalf of Mutual Peninsular Life Insurance. We're here to verify a few things—to ensure the death benefit on Mr. Preston can be paid promptly."

"Oh." The eye below the hank of frizzy brown hair softened. The door closed. The security chain rattled. Then the door squeaked open to reveal a thin, gaunt, white woman of indeterminate age. Her body said thirties, but her face was at least a decade ahead of it.

"Come on in," Tandy said. "You guys want a beer?"

Blatch grinned. "I would, but they frown on that back at the office."

Tandy smiled, revealing a missing eyetooth.

Blatch shot his partner a quick glance. The game was on.

Blatch's role was to keep Tandy Preston occupied. Smalls' role was to sneak away and search the trailer.

Blatch grabbed a ball cap from atop an old VCR. "Wow! Is this a genuine Dale Earnhardt cap?"

Tandy nodded with a modicum of pride. "Yep."

In a matter of seconds, Smalls had determined the living room and kitchen were clear. The hallway, too. He heard a slight creaking noise from a back room. Smalls cocked his head slightly. "You got company, Ms. Preston?"

Tandy's smile faded. "No." She bit her lip. "Look, you got papers for me to sign or what?"

"Yes, of course." Blatch reached inside his pocket and pulled out an envelope. It was a piece of junk mail he'd scrounged from his car to use as a makeshift prop. He held it up with the front facing him and shook it at her.

"Yes, ma'am. Just a few statements in here to verify. But first, let's start with the obvious one. It may seem silly, but I have to ask, Ms. Preston. Are you sure Gary Lee is dead?"

Tandy eyed Blatch with astonishment. "Pretty sure, yeah."

Blatch smiled wanly. "And, for the records, how are you sure?"

Tandy's face grew a shade darker. "I identified the body, okay?"

Blatch nodded somberly. "I see. My condolences."

A muffled thump emanated from the back room. Blatch exchanged a quick glance with Smalls.

Smalls cleared his throat. "Ms. Preston, mind if I use your lavatory?"

Tandy bristled. "What? No! There ain't no lavatory in here. We ain't meth heads!"

Smalls didn't skip a beat. "My apologies for the confusion, ma'am. By lavatory I meant bathroom."

Tandy softened a bit. "Oh. Well, uh ... I guess so, then."

"Thank you."

As Smalls headed down the hall, Blatch did his best to block Tandy's view of his partner. Lousy at small talk, Blatch stepped in front of Tandy and asked, "So tell me, how long have you owned that awesome Earnhardt cap?"

SMALLS EDGED DOWN THE scuffed hallway of the trailer toward the bathroom and slowly turned the handle.

The door was unlocked.

Smalls drew his gun from his side holster and flung open the door. He was immediately assaulted by the odor of stale urine. He pushed the ragged shower curtain to one side.

The pungent, yellowed bathroom was empty.

He closed the door and sidled down to the end of the hall where two cheap panel doors faced in opposite directions.

Both were closed.

Smalls was about to try the left one when he heard the thump again. It came from the room on the right. He tried the doorknob.

It was locked.

Smalls put his finger on the trigger of his Glock, then reared back and kicked the flimsy panel door near the doorknob. His boot splintered open a hole big enough for his hand.

In one quick motion, Smalls reached in with his left hand, unlocked the door, and flung it open. He rushed into the dim room.

"Hold i—" he got out before a shoe slammed into his cheek.

Smalls stumbled backward, bracing for another blow.

Then a quick assessment of the situation nearly made him laugh.

The foot that had struck him was attached to a pair of anonymous legs. They were flailing about, trapped within the frame of a small window. The upper half of the body was outside, out of view.

"Hang on," Smalls yelled at the legs. "Stop kicking!"

"Nugh," the man answered, and kicked furiously.

Smalls edged to the side of the window and grabbed the guy by the belt loop of his jeans. He shoved his gun barrel into his assailant's crotch.

"Kick me again and you might live, but it won't be nearly as much fun anymore."

The man stopped flailing. His legs went limp. "Okay."

Smalls pulled him back inside the trailer.

One look at Smalls' Glock and the guy raised his hands in the air. "Hey! Be cool, man. I don't want no trouble!"

Smalls rubbed his eye. It was already beginning to swell. "Well, it's a little late for that. Come with me."

Smalls enticed the man down the hallway with helpful prods from his gun barrel. When the two reached the living room of the trailer, Smalls gave his partner a nod. "Look who I found."

Blatch nodded at his partner's captive and pictured five grand in his checking account. "Well, hello there." He turned to Tandy Preston, who he was holding back by both of her skinny arms. "I thought you said you were alone."

Tandy scowled. "You asked if I had company. Timmy ain't company. He's family."

"Timmy?" Blatch said.

Tandy winced. "Gary Lee's brother."

Blatch nearly choked. The men were nearly identical. *Brother?* He let loose of her arms. "Why was he wearing a disguise when he followed you in?"

Tandy hung her head. "We didn't want our mothers to find out we was together."

Timmy nodded. "Prying eyes talk, you know."

"Shit." Smalls blew out a breath and put his gun away.

"Wait," Tandy said. "Were you guys *spying* on me?"

"No, ma'am," Blatch said. "We came to talk to you about the insurance and saw that man follow you inside. He looked suspicious, so we decided to make sure you were okay."

"Oh." Tandy brightened. "Well, that was nice of y'all. But I'm fine, as you can see." She went over and put her arms around Timmy.

Blatch hid his disappointment behind a tight smile. "So, how long have you two been together?"

Tandy shrugged. "Coupla years."

"Did Gary Lee know?"

Tandy bit her lip. "If he did, he took it to his grave."

Blatch eyed her. "You don't seem too upset about losing your husband, ma'am."

Tandy's face grew fierce. She stuck her chin out at Blatch. "Mister, did you *know* Gary?"

"No ma'am."

"Then you got no business telling me how to feel about him. Gary Lee was no good from the get-go. He was mean to everybody. And he couldn't hold a job for nothin'."

"He was the black sheep of the family," Timmy said. "And her momma thinks I'm the same. But I ain't."

"You sure aren't, sugar," Tandy said, and kissed Timmy. She laughed bitterly. "Remember that time Gary was gonna be an electrician? He weren't there a whole day before he come back home with his clothes scorched and the hair in his ears burned up! Or that time he tried to sell shit door to door? With them crazy eyes of his, wouldn't nobody answer the door!"

"So I take it you and Gary were no longer in love," Smalls deadpanned.

Tandy's smirked. "You got *that* right, mister."

"Is that why you're glad he's dead?" Blatch asked.

Tandy studied Blatch's face, then rolled her eyes. "Look. If you think I wished old Gary Lee dead a time or two, yeah. I sure did. But I didn't kill him, if that's what you think. Truth is, I didn't even know he had that life insurance policy until it come in the mailbox. Gary was done gone a good month when the policy come from ... uh ... what'cha call it? Mutual of Pencils?"

"Mutual Peninsular."

"Yeah. That's it," Tandy said.

Blatch sighed. Both his payday and his hot lead had just fizzled out. "Well, thank you for your time, Ms. Preston. I was just doing my part for the company to confirm that Gary Lee Preston truly is dead."

Tandy nodded. "I understand. And you know, I'm glad you did. 'Cause lately, I'd been wonderin' myself."

Blatch's shoulders straightened. He and Smalls exchanged a quick glance. "What do you mean?"

"I dunno," Tandy said. "It's kinda weird, but I think Gary was on-to me and Timmy right before he died."

"Why do you think that?"

"I remember. It was back around Easter, wasn't it Timmy?"

Timmy nodded.

"I started getting weird calls on our old landline," Tandy said. "You know, just hang-ups. Like somebody was checking to see if I was home. I figured it was Gary 'cause it only happened when he was gone. And sometimes, at night, I'd get that creepy feeling someone was watching me through the windows. I figured it was Gary trying to catch me and Timmy together."

"Did he?" Blatch asked.

"Catch us? If he did, he never said nothing to me about it. Anyway, I thought it was all over with. But then I got another hang-up call last week."

Blatch glanced over at Smalls. He knew one call wasn't much of a reason to keep pursuing the case. But a chance at five thousand dollars was a whole lot better than a chance at fifty. Smalls read his thoughts and gave him a nod.

"Well, that does open up a small possibility that Gary's still alive," Blatch said to Tandy. "The only way to be certain would be to exhume his body. Would you be okay with that?"

Tandy pursed her lips. "Well, I dunno ...."

Blatch gave her a fatherly smile. "Final proof would certainly speed up getting your insurance check."

Tandy's face cleared of uncertainty. "Well, then, sure. Knock yourself out. There's a shovel out back by his grave marker."

Blatch sucked in a breath. "He's buried in the backyard?"

Tandy shrugged. "Well, I couldn't have him staring at us while we're sitting on the couch, could I?"

"Lemme get the metal detector," Timmy offered. "It'll make it easier to find him."

"Metal detector?" Smalls asked.

"Yeah," Tandy said. "To find his urn thing. We had him cremated."

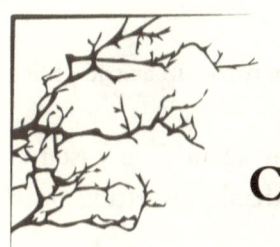

Chapter Fifteen

SMALLS KICKED THE TIRE of his black SUV and nearly slid down in the mud along the shoulder of the crumbling asphalt road. "Geeze! On top of *this* fiasco, it's raining, for crying out loud."

"Quit bitching and get in my car," Blatch said, rolling up his driver's side window.

Smalls reached for the sedan's front passenger door. His hand collided with Davidson's.

"What the?" Smalls said.

Davidson had seen the men leave Tandy Preston's trailer and walk toward their cars. The young cop had come out of hiding and sprinted over. He was soaking wet from guarding his surveillance post behind the rundown trailer.

Smalls swatted Davidson's hand away. "Age over beauty, kid," he said, and climbed into the front seat.

Davidson took the backseat. For a moment, the three men sat in silence, watching rivulets of rain drain down the sedan's windshield.

"You should try RainX," Davidson said. "Water beads up and rolls off like marbles."

"Thanks for the life tip, kid," Smalls quipped. Through the foggy side window, he stared at Tandy Preston's trailer. "Well, I guess that's the end of that."

"Why?" Davidson asked. "What happened?"

Blatch blew out a breath. "The guy turned out to be Gary Preston's brother, Timmy."

Smalls sneered. "Gary's sleeping off eternity in an urn in the backyard. Cremated beyond recognition."

"Oh." Davidson paused. "So, that's it?"

"'Fraid so," Blatch said. "Unless Gary Lee turns up at the police station, he's officially dead."

"Shit," Davidson said. "Castleberry wins again. The bastard." Davidson kicked the back of the seat. "Well, thanks for letting me in on this."

"Sure," Blatch said. "But listen, if for some reason we end up working together again, don't show up in uniform. Keep a change of clothes in your trunk."

"Or come naked," Smalls quipped.

Davidson blew out a frustrated breath. "Will do." He reached for the handle and cracked opened the car door.

"Davidson," Blatch said. "Sorry we couldn't prove Gary Lee was your arsonist."

Davidson leaned back toward the men. "You haven't heard?"

"Heard what?"

"This morning they recovered a body from Mercer Arms. We're not just looking for an arsonist. We're looking for a murderer."

"WHAT DO YOU THINK OF him?" Blatch asked as they watched Davidson climb into his Chevy Impala and take off down the road.

"Sketchy," Smalls said, staring at Davidson's blurry brake lights through the fogged-up windshield. "Doesn't follow orders. Hot-tempered. Self-righteous." He looked over at Blatch. "I like him."

Blatch smiled. "Me, too."

Smalls smirked. "So, who do you think's really in that urn out back?"

Blatch's smile faded. "What do you mean?"

"Tandy could've had someone else's body cremated."

"Not likely. I talked to her while you chased down Timmy. The woman's not smart enough to pull off anything that complicated." He grinned at Smalls. "Nice shiner, by the way."

"Thanks," Smalls said, touching his cheek. "Okay. Maybe it wasn't another *human* body. Hell, that urn could've been full of Chihuahua ashes for all we know. We should've gotten a sample."

Blatch's brow furrowed. "Say we did, and the ashes weren't Preston's. What would that prove? That urn's been in Tandy's backyard for months. Anybody could've opened it and contaminated the evidence. At this point, the only way we could prove Gary Preston isn't dead is to find him alive and haul him in front of the cameras for a press conference."

Smalls conceded with a grunt. "I guess you're right. But what about if Tandy helped her dear hubby meet his maker? Would that policy of hers pay her then?"

Blatch sighed. "I doubt it."

"That's what I thought," Smalls said. "So, would Mutual Peninsular pay *us* if we proved she murdered him?"

Blatch locked eyes with Smalls. "Yeah. I'm pretty sure they would."

Smalls grinned. "So, what say we go for it? We've already established Tandy doesn't have the brains to commit fraud alone. If she did it, she had help. Who does she know who'd help her get rid of her husband and cash in? That pothead boyfriend of hers?"

Blatch shook his head. "I can't see him having enough ambition. Plus, he'd be killing his own brother."

"What about Tandy's mother? She said it herself that the woman couldn't stand Gary."

"It's a possibility," Blatch conceded. "But it seems like a lot of people couldn't stand Gary. According to his neighbor, the guy owed money to everybody. And I've seen his police records. He was no humanitarian. The guy tortured animals for fun."

"What a charmer." Smalls crinkled his nose and winced at the ache. He touched his swollen eye.

Blatch shook his head. "I keep thinking about those hang-up calls Tandy used to get. Maybe they were from someone trying to find Gary Lee and collect their money. Tandy said the calls stopped after he died."

"So, what's your point?"

Blatch turned to face Smalls. "What if this was a loan shark situation? What if they stopped calling because their client, Gary, was dead? They had to eat their losses. But then the sharks get wind of the insurance payout, and now they're calling again and hanging up. You know, keeping tabs on Gary's widow until the money shows up in her bank account."

Smalls chewed the idea over for a moment. "Maybe. But loan sharks usually make it pretty damned clear to their clients exactly when and what they're looking to get paid. They'd be threatening her pretty hard by now. Charging interest by the minute. I dunno. To me, Tandy didn't seem that anxious to get her money."

Blatch bit his lip. "Maybe they don't want to spook her."

"Or maybe someone just dialed a wrong number."

Blatch nodded. "It's a long shot, I'll give you that."

Smalls sighed. "I say let's call it quits on this one. Gary Lee's dead. Check the little box for Mutual Peninsular. Hand in the papers. Get your two hours pay."

"You're probably right, chief. But since we've both got a little time on our hands, what have we got to lose by playing this out a bit longer?"

Smalls shook his head. "You know, I'd like that five grand as much as the next guy. But what's our angle with Tandy or the loan sharks? To play against those stakes, we've got to be holding some high cards."

Blatch smirked. "Without my little check in the insurance box, Tandy gets no big check in hers."

Smalls leathery face cracked into a grin. "Well, look at you. Looks like you're a player after all."

Chapter Sixteen

THE RAIN CAME TO AN end just before dawn, coloring the early-morning clouds as red as any sunset. Deanna smiled at the sky through her front blinds, and then set about getting ready for her big day.

Too antsy for anything more than coffee for breakfast, Deanna was both excited and nervous about meeting Conrad Count this morning. The young boy would not only mark the beginning of her new psychological counseling practice in St. Petersburg—he would also be her first juvenile client.

Deanna had spent yesterday evening next door, measuring Jodie's front room and figuring out what she'd need to transform the space into her new office. Jodie had called her a snob for turning her nose up at Mrs. Havenall's prim, austere furnishings, but Deanna was keen to make the space her own.

That couch was blue plaid, for godsakes, Deanna thought as she applied pink lipstick in the bathroom mirror. *I need my patients to relax, not have an epileptic attack.*

Creating the correct patient environment was one of the many things Deanna had learned during her eight years under the mentorship of Dr. Laurence Filbert. The psychiatrist had served as her manager, friend, and father figure the whole time while she was in New York. He'd also helped Deanna hash out the psychological problems that plagued not only her patients, but herself as well.

And he'd taught her that even little things matter.

Like the fabric on a couch.

Through Larry, Deanna had become aware of the psychology of colors and shapes. Some were soothing. Others could evoke angst or even violence.

In order to set the right tone for her patients, her office needed to feel safe and caring, yet also professional. And Deanna, too, needed to present herself as caring, yet also an authority figure. Figuring out just how to form that balance wasn't always a clear path.

Deanna had spent years creating the perfect office for her New York practice. But her move to Florida after the death of her mother three weeks ago had been such a sudden, knee-jerk reaction that Deanna had yet to make arrangements for the things she'd left behind.

Deanna puckered her lips in the vanity mirror to even out her lipstick. *Why not just have it all shipped down?* she thought.

An image of Larry flashed in her mind. The fact that he looked a lot like Smalls made her smile. Both men were short, balding, and sixtyish. But where Smalls was hard-faced, street-worn, and unrepentantly grumpy, Larry was plump, intellectual, and had maintained a perpetual twinkle in his eyes that could still be seen despite his thick glasses.

Both men had also saved Deanna's life, though in very different ways.

I should call Larry, Deanna thought. *My old office is just down the hall from his. He'd be happy to help me get it packed and moved.*

Still, as Deanna applied a light pencil to her sandy-blonde eyebrows, she hesitated. *What if Florida doesn't work out?*

She finished lining her eyes and checked the time. Six-forty-eight. Larry would be up. She took a chance and gave him a call.

"Well hello, early bird," he said.

The sound of Larry's voice made Deanna grin. "Good morning. You up?"

"Of course. No rest for the wicked."

Deanna laughed. "How are you?"

"Good. Yourself?"

"I need my furniture."

Larry's voice sounded pleasantly surprised. "So, you've decided to stay for good?"

"Maybe."

Larry laughed. "You do like to keep your options open, don't you?"

Deanna cringed. "I know. What does that say about me?"

"That either you're fully embracing the bounty of options set before you in this magnificent, loving world ... or you don't trust stability because you never had it. Your pick."

Deanna grinned and shook her head. "Sometimes I wish you didn't know me so well."

"You don't really mean that, do you?"

Deanna bit her lip. "Sort of."

Larry laughed. "So what else is going on in your brave new world?"

"I've got a kid."

Larry's voice cracked. "What? You're pregnant?"

Deanna nearly choked. "No!"

"Adopting?"

"No. I've got a new client. He's six years old."

"Oh. Wait. I thought you didn't want to work with children."

"I don't. I didn't. I ... I'm trying something new here."

"Good. I'm glad to hear it."

Deanna's face lined with worry. "I have to admit, I'm a bit afraid. I know children aren't just miniature adults."

"No, they're not," Larry said. "They're a lot smarter."

Deanna laughed.

"I'm serious," Larry said. "Kids know what they want. They haven't yet learned how to analyze away their hearts' desires in the name of sensibility. And if you're not careful, those little suckers can see right through you."

Deanna cringed again. "That's what I'm afraid of."

"Why?"

"That this child will call me out as a phony. I second-guess myself all the time, Larry."

"You're not the only adult who does that, Deanna."

"I know. But my own childhood was so screwed up. I wouldn't want to project any of that onto this boy."

"You won't. The sense of self-awareness is strong in you."

"Thanks, Yoda."

Larry laughed. "What I'm trying to say is, you judge yourself too harshly. You're stronger and healthier than you think."

"Thanks. But sometimes I—"

"Look, you're not gonna throw spiders at the kid, are you?"

Deanna blanched, then laughed. "No. Of course not!"

"Then just relax, Dee. Keep things simple and honest. And if you can, make it fun."

"Fun?"

"Get on the boy's level. Play. Make a game of it. Earn his trust and a kid will bear his soul to you quickly. That is, if he hasn't learned deceit already. Has he got any presenting problems?"

"I haven't met him yet. But his mother is wound up pretty tight. Major control freak."

"So, what else is new?"

Deanna sighed. "True."

"So, on another note, how's your love life?"

Deanna laughed. "Nonexistent, as always."

"I thought you and Blatch had a thing going."

"No. If you taught me anything, it's to not shit where you eat."

"How romantic."

Deanna frowned. "I've got enough to worry about right now without him in the mix."

"You can't run from love forever, Dee."

"I'm not running. And I'm not anti-relationship. I've just ... I don't know. I guess I've just never figured out how to stay *me* in one."

"What do you mean by 'stay me'?"

Deanna sighed. "I don't know. I ... I can't seem to stop editing myself into what I think the other person wants me to be. And, inevitably, I end up becoming some resentful nag that even *I* don't like."

"Why do you think you need to change to be likable?"

Deanna shook her head. "Oh, no you don't. I didn't call so you could psychoanalyze *me*."

Larry laughed. "I just want you to realize that you're the only one who thinks you're not enough. Well, the only one *still alive* who thinks that."

Larry's reference to Deanna's unrepentantly disapproving mother made Deanna laugh. "Good one. I can see Melody rolling around in her grave now, wishing she could tell me what a mistake I'm making coming back to Florida."

"Is that what you think?"

"No. I mean ... it's too soon to tell, right? I'm taking the chance for a new start, like you suggested. I just wish I could be like Jodie. She seems so comfortable in her own skin. Nothing bothers her—not even when her mother used to call her a 'fringe person' to her face."

"The fringy edge is where the new discoveries lie, Dee. If you want to change, you need to step out into the unknown. Nobody ever had an epiphany regurgitating the same old lines."

Deanna smirked. "Says the Jewish man."

Larry burst out laughing. "Hey, the Torah doesn't count."

Chapter Seventeen

THE JAGGED MIRROR FRAGMENT cast a warped reflection in the dim light.

"Eat it," the voice demanded.

"I ... I don't want to," the small voice whimpered.

"If you don't, you'll die."

"But ... I don't want it ...."

A finger dipped into black grease, then smeared another mark on the wall.

"Fine. Don't eat it. In two more days you'll be dead."

Chapter Eighteen

SMALLS SNUCK DOWN THE hallway Tuesday morning and tried the knob on the office door.

It was unlocked.

He grunted, undecided whether to be impressed or angry.

Blatch had finally beaten him.

Smalls smiled sourly, pushed open the door, and winced at the bell clanging above his head. But its rude warning was instantly forgotten when the smell of acrid smoke filled his nostrils.

Somewhere in the office, something was burning.

Shit! Smalls thought as he raced down the hall, following the thin blue haze of smoke. As he reached the breakroom, he noticed a faint, white fog was seeping underneath the closed door.

I knew that damned coffee machine was a fire hazard, he thought. He felt the doorknob. It wasn't hot. He cracked open the door and peered inside.

Through the thin veil of bluish smoke, Smalls heard something crash, then a voice rang out.

"Cripes, Smalls!" Blatch yelled. "You scared the crap out of me!"

Smalls nosed his way into the breakroom. "What the hell's going on in here? I thought the place was on fire!"

"No. I just .... I burned some coffee or something. Crap!" Blatch glanced down at the floor and cringed. "And now I've broken one of Deanna's cups. Shit! I was only trying to—"

"Get away from that thing," Smalls barked. "Let me have a look at it."

Blatch didn't argue. He stepped aside and let his partner pass. Smalls hunched over the kitchenette counter and peered angrily at the chrome workings of the cappuccino machine.

"You got this all wrong," he grumbled. "You're supposed to put the milk in *here*, and the water in *there*." He crinkled his nose. "Sheeze. You really did a number on this thing."

"Shit." Blatch hovered over him. "Did I break it?"

"I dunno yet. It's all gummed up. Let me see what I can do. In the meantime, if Deanna shows up, don't let her in here. She already thinks we're a couple of imbeciles."

Blatch smirked. "Well, you're half right on that one."

Smalls shot him a look. "You want my help or not?"

Blatch grimaced. "Yes."

"Then shut up and get out of here. And while you're at it, get the air freshener out of the john. We need to spray the place down."

SMALLS WALTZED INTO the conference room with a tray of cappuccinos in his hands. He eyed Blatch and smirked. "Who's the old dog now?"

Deanna's eyes darted from Blatch to Smalls, taking in his black eye. "Did I miss something?"

"No!" Blatch said before Smalls could speak.

Deanna studied both men for a second and let it drop. "Okay." She smiled at Smalls. "I see you figured out how to use the Willy Wonka contraption."

Smalls smirked and shot Blatch a look. "That makes two of us."

"So, how'd it go with your new client?" Blatch blurted, trying to divert Deanna's attention.

She shrugged. "I made it through the screening process. I have an appointment at her house today at eleven."

"Good for you. Is it in Tampa or St. Pete?"

"Actually, it's right in our neighborhood. At the corner of 11th and Oak."

Blatch's eyebrow shot up. "The big white house with columns? Looks like a scaled-down version of the White House?"

Deanna's face registered surprise. "Yes. I walked by it this morning ...you know, just out of curiosity. How did you—"

Blatch looked over at Smalls. "That's Cecilia Count's house."

Deanna's face crinkled in confusion. "Uh ... yes. How did you know?"

"Aww, shit," Smalls grumbled. "Dee, you've gone and planted your ass on either a goldmine or a landmine."

Deanna rankled. "What do you mean? Jodie said she was well-connected. But—"

"She's not *well*-connected," Blatch interrupted. "She *is* the connection. Her husband is Charles Count, the city planning commissioner. He controls what goes on in St. Pete, and, if rumors are right, Cecilia Count controls him."

Deanna shrugged. "So?"

Smalls locked eyes with her. "No pressure, Dee. But if you screw this up, all three of us might as well cut our losses and leave town."

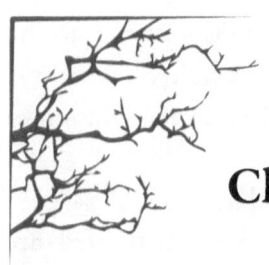

Chapter Nineteen

"I HOPE SHE KNOWS WHAT she's getting into," Smalls said after Deanna left.

Blatch frowned. "Why?"

"You ever had any personal dealings with Charlie Count?"

"No."

"Then count yourself lucky."

Blatch gave Smalls a sideways look. "Was that supposed to be another bad joke?"

Smalls shook his head. "I wish. The guy's a shark. He screwed my cousin out of a city contract and gave it to one of his cronies."

"Isn't that called politics?"

Smalls grunted. "Maybe. But it still stinks. So, what's on the agenda today?"

"Not much. I'm waiting on a call-back from the medical examiner's office from the guy who signed Gary Preston's death cert."

"Sounds riveting."

"Well, we could go stake out Tandy's place. See if we get lucky with any new suspects."

Smalls smirked. "I love the smell of trailer park in the morning."

"You got any better ideas, chief?"

"Not at the moment."

"Then get your jacket. Let's go."

Blatch grabbed his sport jacket from the coat rack by the front door. As he did, the junk-mail envelope he'd used yesterday as a prop with Tandy Preston fell out and landed on the floor.

Blatch reached down to pick it up, but Smalls beat him to the punch. The older man snorted with laughter as he read what was printed on it. "Forty-Plus Sexy Singles Online. We're the solution to your dating dilemma."

Blatch grabbed for the envelope. "Gimme that!"

Smalls jerked it out of his reach. "You really that hard up, Blatch?"

"It's junk mail, Smalls. Ever heard of it?"

"Says here they can find a date for anybody. Who knows, maybe even junk like you."

SMALLS' FOOT MASHED the imaginary brake pedal on the passenger-side floorboard a few seconds before Blatch stepped on the real thing. "That was cutting it close," he grumbled.

"Life in the fast lane, control freak," Blatch said as his sedan came to a stop at the red light.

Smalls shook his head. "I still don't get why you need to check with the coroner who did the autopsy on Preston. Wouldn't they have confirmed his identity back then with a DNA test?"

"Not necessarily. Those tests are bloody expensive. Since they had Tandy Preston to positively ID his body, there's a chance they could've let it go at that."

Smalls grunted. "What about your testimony. You said you saw him get hit by a car. You absolutely positive it was Gary Lee Preston? You know as well as I do that half the time, eyewitness accounts are shit."

Blatch shrugged. "I saw the body after the car had run over him. Would I bet my life it was Preston? No. But I picked his wallet up off the street. I compared the guy's face to his driver's license photo. It looked like him to me."

"Huh." Smalls thought for a moment. "You were still on the force then. Anybody come up missing around that time who bore a striking resemblance?"

Blatch scowled. "No. Not that I recall. But then, I wasn't exactly looking for it. You have any idea how many missing person reports we get?" Blatch blew out a breath. "I mean *got*."

The light turned green. Blatch hit the gas and headed west on 54th Avenue.

"You miss being a cop?" Smalls asked as they passed by dozens of uninspired, rundown strip malls lining the busy road.

Blatch shrugged. "I miss being in the know. And the action. Nothing beats the feeling of putting away the bad guys."

"We put away a couple bums last week, if you recall."

Blatch glanced over at Smalls and smiled. "You're right. I guess I just miss the comradery. We were a unit."

"Not much cohesion there, from what you've said about Castleberry."

Blatch conceded with a nod. "Yeah. But besides the captain, it was actually a pretty good group of guys."

Blatch's phone chirped. He glanced at it. "It's Davidson. I'm gonna pull over and get this."

"Sure. I'm in no hurry to see that ass-end of a trailer park again."

Blatch grabbed his cellphone from the console. "Davidson? Hold on a sec." He pulled the sedan into the parking lot of a convenience store and spoke into his phone. "Davidson. What's up?"

"You let me in on what you knew, so I'm returning the favor," Davidson said. "The body they found in the fire was female. No ID yet, but it's looking like it belongs to a tenant living at the place. Regina Krous. She was last seen by a neighbor walking home the evening of the fire."

"In the rain? How'd the neighbor know it was Krous?"

"Said she always carried a red umbrella."

"That's not much to go on."

"No," Davidson admitted. "But like I said, Krous hasn't been seen since the day of the fire, and so far the body matches enough to not be able to rule her out."

"Thanks," Blatch said. "Any determination on the cause of the blaze?"

"Definitely arson. Someone poured a can of four-cycle in an open side window and lit it. Like I told you, we found the can at the scene."

"You said it was a *gas* can."

Davidson hesitated. "Yeah. I didn't know you then. It was a quart tin of small-engine fuel. The kind they use in lawnmowers, chain-saws, stuff like that."

So, you lied to me, Blatch thought. He wondered if the young cop could be lying again. "Okay. Thanks for coming straight with me."

"Yeah, sure."

"Anything else I should know?"

"Nothing really. Except ... well, something weird that's been bothering me."

"What's that?" Blatch asked.

"The thumbprint we found ... it was on the bottom of the can. Right in the middle. No other prints. I don't know, it just seemed odd to me."

"Hmm," Blatch said, but offered no further response.

After a pause, Davidson said, "Okay, later, man."

"Later." Blatch clicked off the phone.

Smalls eyed his partner curiously. "What did *he* want?"

"Nothing. He said the Mercer Arms victim was a woman."

"I don't get it," Smalls said. "Why is Davidson still helping you?"

"Like I told you. He thinks Castleberry gave me the shaft. And now he's trying to do it to him."

Smalls shook his head. "The enemy of my enemy is my friend. Not the best basis of trust."

Blatch raised an eyebrow. "I hear you."

"So, what else did he have to say?"

Blatch chewed his cheek. "The kid might not know it, but he just gave me an interesting tidbit about that thumbprint on the fuel can they found at the scene."

"The one that he said was supposed to be Preston's?"

"Yeah. Davidson's still convinced it's Gary Lee's. He said the print was right in the center of the bottom of the can. It just strikes me as an unlikely spot—unless you were planting evidence."

Smalls' brow furrowed. "Are you saying somebody killed Preston, then pressed his thumb on a can to frame him for the fire?"

"That's one possibility. Or Gary Preston could've done it himself. Either way, someone wanted to make sure his clean print got found. One that wouldn't get smeared by anyone picking up the can."

Smalls shook his head. "I don't buy it. It doesn't make any sense. Preston already has the perfect alibi. He's dead."

"Unless he isn't. Maybe something happened with his plan to fake his own death, and now Gary suddenly decided he wants everyone to know he's alive. Or maybe someone else found out he's alive and wants the world to know it, too."

"Like who?"

"Someone who had something to gain from exposing his faked death. Or maybe Preston himself."

Smalls shook his head. "You're giving me a headache with all this crap. If Preston was still alive, why go through all this cloak-and-dagger stuff? Why wouldn't Gary just show up someplace? You know, go home and say, 'Look Ma, I'm back.'"

Blatch pursed his lips. "Maybe because if he did, he might really end up dead?"

Smalls grimaced and shook his head. "My money's on Preston being dead. But then, that would mean someone was playing around with a dead guy's corpse. Who'd do such a thing?"

Blatch shook his head. "I don't know. But maybe Deanna would."

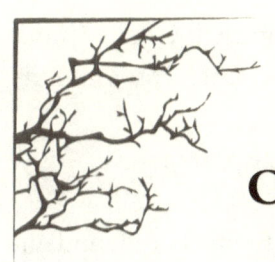

Chapter Twenty

TOO RESTLESS TO WAIT any longer, Deanna left early and arrived eight minutes ahead of her appointment with Cecilia Count. Rather than park in front of her client's huge, white house, Deanna drove around the block a few times.

She told herself the aimless driving was to assess the neighborhood and therefore the possible environmental influences on her new client, Conrad Count. But deep down, she knew it was more than that. She needed to steady her nerves. If Conrad was anything like his mother, she would be facing a cold, hard mountain of denial.

At two minutes to eleven, Deanna finally parked in front of the behemoth of a house and stared at it through the window of her Corvette. Like a foreboding fortress, the sterile, white house seemed to reflect its owner's hard, angular countenance.

Surrounded by a wrought-iron fence, the lawn and hedges were trimmed to perfection. No holiday decorations marred the perfect order of the lawn or house. To Deanna, instead of feeling like a home, the gleaming-white house had the look and feel of a well-managed office building.

Deanna climbed out of the car and stepped up to the spikey, iron gate that barred entry into the yard. She rang the intercom button and waited.

She expected to have to identify herself. Instead, without a word, the intercom buzzed and the gate swung open. Deanna quickly skirted by it and walked up the straight line of precision-cut pavers bisecting the immaculate lawn.

As she reached the white front door, it opened. Cecilia Count appeared, wearing a crisp, white suit that looked as if it cost a month's salary.

"Come in. You're right on time. I appreciate promptness."

Deanna smiled. "Thank you. So do I."

Cecilia Count nodded once, and Deanna stepped inside and onto the gleaming white tile floor. White couches, white walls, white rugs. She blinked against the glare.

"Conrad," Cecilia said in a calm, even tone. "Come down. I want you to meet a friend of mine."

Deanna followed Cecilia's line of sight up the staircase. At the top landing stood a slender, doe-eyed boy in blue short pants and matching jacket. The white gift bag in Conrad's hand coordinated perfectly with the home's décor—as did his white-blond hair.

"Yes, Mother," the boy said, and began descending the stairwell, pausing at each step like a bridesmaid on a wedding march.

Deanna studied Conrad as he descended. She tried to ascertain any tell-tale clues about him from his demeanor. But other than his obvious wish to delay this encounter, she came up empty.

Slowly and deliberately, Conrad walked up to Deanna and offered her a smile. To Deanna, his grin appeared genuine, but something about his ice-blue eyes didn't match the sentiment.

What lurks behind those baby blues? Deanna thought. *Frustration? Anger? Fear?*

"Give our new friend her gift," Cecilia prompted, an edge of impatience in her tone.

Apparently, Conrad forgot his lines, Deanna thought.

Conrad stiffened and held out the gift to Deanna. "For you, Miss Young."

Deanna smiled. "Why, thank you, Conrad."

"Open it!" he squealed, and giggled once before a quick glance at his mother silenced him.

"I like presents," Deanna said, mirroring his enthusiasm. She shook the bag and grinned. "Oh! What can it be?"

"Open it! Open it!" Conrad said and began jumping up and down with excitement.

Deanna laughed and took a playful peek inside the bag.

"Open it!" Conrad squealed.

"What is it?" she teased, and reached in the bag. She pulled out a jar and held it up to the light.

Inside, dozens of flies crawled around a lump of gray meat.

"Aghh!" Deanna cried out.

She dropped the jar.

It hit the tile floor and shattered.

Conrad squealed with delight.

"Conrad!" Cecilia screeched, her hands flying to her face.

Deanna did likewise, bracing against an oncoming swarm of flies.

But after a moment, none came.

Deanna dropped her hands and looked down at the floor.

Dozens of flies limped aimlessly around on the gleaming white tiles.

They hadn't flown away because they couldn't.

All their wings had been torn off.

Chapter Twenty-One

"CONRAD!" CECILIA SCREECHED as her son scrambled around on hands and knees, grabbing at the flies crawling amongst the shards of glass and gray globs on the shiny white tiles.

"Stop it!" she demanded. "What have you done?"

"I didn't do it!" Conrad protested. He stopped and stared up at his mother, his eyes as icy-blue as hers. "Freddie did it!"

"Stop lying! Go to your room!"

"But—" Conrad's face crumpled. He balled his fists and ran up the stairs.

"My apologies," Cecilia said coldly. "See what I have to deal with? He's incorrigible!"

"No need to apologize," Deanna said. Compared to facing down psychotic adult patients in New York, the incident with Conrad had only mildly startled her. "Who's Freddie?" she asked in a calm, practiced tone.

Cecilia sneered. "Nobody. It's what he calls the mangy cat next door."

"Oh."

Cecilia threw up her hands. "What did I tell you? You just saw him in action. He's completely out of control! I assure you he'll be punished for this—and don't worry. I'll pay you for the full hour."

Deanna nodded. "I appreciate that. But I'm not ready to throw in the towel yet. Believe me, I've dealt with much worse."

Cecilia studied Deanna with surprised curiosity. "But the way you reacted, I thought—"

"Conrad just caught me off guard. If you don't mind, I'd like to go up and see him in his room alone. It might help me establish a rapport with him."

Cecilia's eyebrows raised slightly. "Well ... yes. Of course. Thank you."

"Wait here," Deanna said, then ascended the stairs.

IT WAS EASY TO LOCATE Conrad's room from among the half-dozen doors lining the ostensive hallway. It was the only door that had been left cracked open slightly.

Inviting me in, Deanna thought as she put her ear to the door.

She heard the boy sniffle, and tapped lightly on the gleaming white wooden panel. "Conrad, may I come in?"

"Yes, Miss Young."

Poor kid, Deanna thought. *Even when he's distraught he doesn't dare forget his manners.*

She opened the door and smiled at the boy. He was sitting on his bed, propped up by half a dozen decorative cushions that coordinated with his designer-selected bedspread and curtains. There wasn't a single garish toy in sight.

"Hi," Deanna said. "You okay?"

"Yes, ma'am." He reached under one of the cushions and fished out a scented candle. He held it up. "Here's the present Mother wanted me to give you."

Deanna walked over, took the candle, and sat on the edge of the bed. She opened the lid and sniffed. Then she made a sour face. "Phew!"

Conrad grinned and crinkled his nose. "It stinks!"

"Shh!" Deanna nodded and whispered, "I'll pretend I like it."

Conrad chewed his cherub lip and studied Deanna for a moment. His eyes locked on hers with such intensity she had to will herself not to look away.

Suddenly, Conrad broke his staring contest and said, "I'm sorry. I was only trying to have some fun. I thought you'd like it."

Deanna shot him a playful, dubious look. "You thought I'd like *flies* for a present?"

Conrad's small face pinched with worry. "Yes."

Deanna leaned closer to him and whispered, "I'll tell you a secret."

Conrad's eyes widened. "What?"

"That was the silliest present I ever got!"

Conrad's worried expression edged toward hopeful caution. "It was?"

"Yes! Tell me. How did you catch them all?"

Conrad shrugged. "I didn't. Freddie did."

Deanna cocked her head. "He did?"

"Yes. He likes to leave me presents."

"Oh. That's neat. What else has he given you?"

Conrad bared a line of square, even baby teeth. "A rat head. It was gross!"

"Eeew!" Deanna said playfully. "What else?"

Conrad sat up in bed excitedly. "A blackbird with his eyes poked out!"

Deanna put on a look of astonishment. "He didn't fly away?"

"No," Conrad said, suddenly pensive. "I tried to help it, but it couldn't fly anymore. It was dead."

"How did you know it was dead?"

"He smelled bad." Conrad pinched his nose closed with his fingers. "Like frog farts!"

Deanna giggled. "Frog farts! Frog farts!" She blew a raspberry. "Bbbbllllppp!"

Conrad giggled hysterically. He reached out and grabbed the candle from Deanna's hand and opened it. He held it to her nose. "Smell it!"

Deanna took a whiff. "Peeeeww!"

"What's it smell like?" Conrad asked.

Deanna sniffed the candle again and crinkled her nose. "Flowers and frog farts."

Conrad squealed with delight. He sniffed the candle and pretended to fall over dead on the bed.

"Are you dead like the bird?" Deanna asked.

Conrad opened an eye. "No. Not yet."

"Not yet?" Deanna asked, hiding her surprise at his answer.

Conrad sat up and shrugged. "Everything dies. I learned that in school."

Deanna nodded. "That's true. Do you think it hurts to die?"

Conrad chewed his lip and shrugged.

"Hey, I know!" Deanna said. "Can you show me where Freddie gave you the bird?"

Conrad shrugged again, his enthusiasm gone. "Yes, ma'am."

"Race you down the stairs?"

Conrad looked horrified.

Deanna whispered, "I'll tell your mother it was my idea."

Conrad grinned and jumped off the bed. As he ran out the door, he yelled, "Last one down is a dirty old frog fart!"

Deanna got up and raced him down the hallway. As she flew down the stairwell after Conrad, she spied Cecilia Count standing, arms crossed, at the bottom of the stairs. Deanna waved at her. Cecilia seemed to catch her message. She stepped aside and she let her son pass.

"Thanks," Deanna whispered as she passed her, then continued chasing Conrad through the living room and kitchen, then out the back door.

But when Deanna stepped out into the sunshine, Conrad was nowhere to be seen.

"Where are you, Conrad?" Deanna called out from the bottom step.

"Over here," he yelled from the side of the house.

Deanna grinned. The chase was still on.

She sprinted through the yard and around the corner of the house.

Suddenly, her smile evaporated.

She stopped dead in her tracks.

Conrad was caught up in the arms of a scraggly-looking man.

The stranger turned and ran toward the front of the house, Conrad kicking and screaming in his grasp.

Chapter Twenty-Two

"I THINK I'M GOING TRAILER-blind," Smalls grunted. He shifted his weight and stared through the windshield of Blatch's dark-blue sedan.

The men had been staking out Tandy Preston's trailer for the past three hours, hoping for anything that might bring a fresh lead on Gary Lee. But so far, not a single creature had stirred, and the rusted red Camaro parked in her front yard had remained untouched.

Blatch took a sip from his paper cup of cold, convenience-store coffee and grimaced. He poured it out the driver's side window. "Trailer-blind? What have you got against trailers, anyway?"

"Nothing," Smalls said. "I just haven't stared at one this long since I was in high school."

Blatch rolled up the window. "You grew up in a trailer?"

"I wouldn't call it growing up. More like surviving."

Blatch frowned. "At least you had parents and a place to call home. I'd take that over foster care any day."

Smalls grunted. "You made out all right in the end."

Blatch thought about Deloris and Dave and nodded. "You're right about that. But I still did thirteen years in the trenches before I got adopted. I've got the scars, if you need proof."

"No," Smalls said. "I can tell."

"Tell?" Blatch shot him a hard look. "Tell what?"

"Takes a tough kid to know one. I did eighteen years, myself."

Blatch turned to Smalls, surprised. "In foster care?"

"I wish."

Blatch laughed bitterly. "No, you don't. Despite the nice-sounding name, I didn't find much 'care' in the foster place I lived at."

Smalls scowled. "You think growing up with your real parents guarantees tender loving care?"

Blatch looked down at the steering wheel. "No. I've seen enough to know that I got lucky with Dave and Deloris."

"Yeah. I guess you did." Smalls shook his head. "But did they get you in time or not?"

Blatch's eyebrow angled angrily. "What do you mean?"

Smalls sighed. "I ... I guess what I'm trying to say is, if you grow up without love, it's like growing up without money. When you're young, you don't know what you're missing, but you know damned well you're missing *something*."

Blatch pursed his lips. "I never thought about it like that. But, yeah. I can see that."

Smalls stared at the floorboard. "I got this theory. I think if you don't get love as a kid, you don't know what it is when it comes along later. Much less what to do with it."

Blatch eyed his partner. "Wait a minute. Is this about me and Deanna?"

"No!" Smalls crumpled his paper coffee cup. "It's about ...." He looked out the windshield, then spoke in a softer tone. "It's about you and Deanna and me and all the people in the world who got screwed up by parents who didn't give a damn."

Blatch sat in stunned silence. He'd never seen Smalls let his guard down, and wasn't sure what to make of it. Before he could respond, Smalls began to speak again, his words a mixture of condemnation and confession.

"Who am I kidding?" Smalls sneered. "Even if you give a damn, it doesn't always turn out." He let out a heavy sigh. "I screwed up with Edith and Brandon." He glanced over at Blatch. "I messed up my own wife and son."

"You don't know that," Blatch said. He knew nothing about Smalls' family, but wanted to comfort him nonetheless.

"Yes, I do," Smalls hissed.

Smalls shook his head and stared out the passenger window. "I got married young. Edith was the first girl to say she loved me. We were young. Stupid. We didn't know what we were doing. Of course, she got pregnant. And me? I worked two jobs to make ends meet. I spent twenty years angry at both of them. I thought I'd been tricked. Trapped by her and our child. I was a bastard, Blatch. I'm *still* a bastard. I wouldn't know love if it hit me over the head with a shovel."

"Smalls," Blatch began.

Smalls stomped the floorboard. "It was my fault Brandon started taking drugs. Edith blamed me. She was right. When he died, she wouldn't even talk to me. I don't blame her."

"How long ago was it?" Blatch asked.

Smalls stared at the glove compartment. "Not long enough to stop feeling the knife in my gut."

"Smalls, you can't change the past, but—"

"Save me the platitudes," Smalls hissed. "'Time heals all wounds' and all that. Bullshit! More like time wounds all heels. And I was a heel. I deserve my wounds."

Blatch opened his mouth to speak, but no words formed in his mind or on his tongue. When his cellphone rang in his jacket pocket, he jumped at the chance and answered it.

"Marcus Blatch. How can I help?"

"Walker here. County coroner. You called about verifying some records relating to Gary Lee Preston?"

"Yes." Blatch eyed Smalls and whispered, "It's the coroner."

Smalls nodded. Blatch spoke into his phone, "Thanks for returning my call, Mr. Walker."

"Blatch? Your name sounds familiar. Are you with the police?"

"I was. Now I'm a private investigator. Working for Mutual Peninsular. Just looking to double-check that the man you signed the death certificate for really was Gary Lee Preston."

"Why wouldn't it be?" Walker asked indignantly. "Are you doing some kind of undercover investigation here?"

"No, sir. Just paperwork. I need to check off a few boxes so the man's widow can get her death benefit from the life insurance policy."

"One last hope they don't have to pay, is that it?"

"You got it."

"Okay. What do you want to know?"

"Were any DNA tests run to verify the identity of the body?"

Walker flipped through some papers. "No. No need. Widow ID'd the body. So did a police officer. Marcus Bl—*you*. All right, what's this really about?"

Blatch cleared his throat. "I'm being upfront. I swear. I quit the force six months ago. Now I'm doing investigative work. Mutual Peninsular hired me because I'm familiar with the case."

"Right. You need me to verify *your* existence while you've got me on the line?"

Blatch laughed weakly. "No. I really don't mean to be wasting your time. I'm just trying to do my job, like you are."

"Huh. Anything else?"

"Yes. Who handles the bodies after you're finished with them?"

"Post autopsy? They go to the mortuary for transport and disposal."

"Can you tell me where Preston was shipped?"

"Looks like his body was bagged and sent to Bentley's crematorium."

"Who would've had access to his body during that process?"

"Mortuary staff. Transport driver. Whoever was doing cremations that day. Look, I've got to get back to work."

"Thank you. You've been really helpful."

"Think you can tick that box and let the poor widow get her money?"

"Yes, sir, I think I can. Goodbye."

Blatch clicked off the phone and turned to Smalls. "You feeling up to a drive to your friendly local mortuary?"

Smalls blew out a breath. "If it means I don't have to sit here and watch that trailer mutt lick its balls anymore, I'm in."

"LET ME CHECK MY RECORDS," the manager at the county mortuary said, and pecked a few keys on his computer. "When was it? Six months ago?"

"Yes. June twenty-second," Blatch said.

"Right. Summer. The time this place always smells its best."

Smalls snorted.

"Sorry for the morbid humor," the man said.

"No need to apologize," Smalls said. "It comes with the territory for us, too."

The manager smiled. "Right." He peered at the screen. "I'm afraid mortuary assistants buzz in and out of here like flies. I don't understand it. What's not to love about ten cents over minimum wage, and the chance to clean up overripe bodily fluids?"

Blatch cringed out a laugh. "Thanks. I don't feel so bad about *my* job anymore."

The guy looked up from the screen. "Here it is. A guy named Peter Conrad."

"Is he still working here?" Blatch asked.

"Oh, no. I fired him myself."

"Why?"

The manager's nose crinkled. He looked around quickly. "You can imagine that this kind of job ... well, it attracts a certain kind of person."

Smalls' eyebrows rose. "Care to elaborate?"

The man shook his head. "Not really. Let's just say, in a truckload of creepy dudes, this guy stood out."

Blatch's brow furrowed. "In what way?"

The manager fidgeted. "I don't know. He seemed to *enjoy* his work. The grosser, the better."

Smalls grimaced. "Lovely."

"Especially washing the bodies for bagging," the mortuary manager added. "Maybe I was wrong to let him go, but everything in me said this guy was getting off on it. A real necropheliac."

Blatch swallowed as if he'd tasted something vile. "When was his last day?"

The man glanced back at his computer. "Huh. Looks like it was two days after your friend was shipped to Bentley's. June twenty-fourth."

Blatch wrote the date down in a small notebook. "Thanks. Hey, could you describe what this Peter Conrad guy looks like?"

"I can do you one better. We took a photo of him. For his employee badge. Let me pull it up." He tapped a few keys on the computer. "Here it is. You want me to print a color copy?"

"That'd be great. Along with his last known address."

"You got it."

The printer hummed to life and spit out a piece of paper.

"So," Blatch asked. "You do a criminal background check on your assistants?"

The mortuary manager shot him a look. "If I did, I wouldn't have any."

Blatch nodded. "Fair enough."

"I mean, what can you do to someone who's already dead?" the manager asked. He handed Blatch the printout.

Blatch glanced at the paper and shook his head. "Geeze. Full beard and moustache? This guy's hairier than an ape. He could be anybody."

The manager raised an eyebrow. "Yeah. Poor hygiene. Just another part of his charm."

Smalls took the photo from Blatch and scowled. "You recall anything that made this guy stand out? Tattoos? Accent? Missing teeth?"

The manager's brow furrowed as he thought. "Yeah. One thing. He stunk worse than our clientele, and that's really saying something."

Blatch blew out a breath. "Thanks. I appreciate the intel."

Blatch reached out to shake the manager's hand. For a moment, the man looked taken aback. Then he smiled and held out his hand. "Thanks. Usually, nobody wants to touch me."

Smalls laughed and nodded at Blatch. "This guy here's got the same problem. You ever try Forty-Plus Sexy Singles?"

Chapter Twenty-Three

"STOP!" DEANNA SCREAMED as the thin, scraggly-haired man disappeared around the front of the house with Conrad Count squirming in his arms.

To her surprise and horror, the stranger did as she'd commanded.

He stopped, turned around, and leered at her, his sharp-looking teeth glinting in the sun, encircled by an unkempt, dirty-blond goatee.

Deanna froze with uncertainty. *Dear God! What do I do now?*

She had no weapon—no way to fight off the man other than her bare hands.

The stranger took a step toward her.

Conrad screeched and wriggled in his arms.

With no other option, Deanna did the only thing she could think of.

She turned and ran.

"CONRAD'S BEING KIDNAPPED!" Deanna screamed as she flung open the back door of the Count house. "Cecilia! Mrs. Count! Call the police!"

Deanna's voice echoed in the empty house. No one answered.

Deanna's mind raced. *Has Cecilia been kidnapped too?* Deanna wondered as her heart pounded in her throat.

She grabbed a knife from the wooden block on the kitchen counter and ran into the living room. Through the front window, she saw the stranger carrying Conrad across the lawn toward a white van.

My purse—my phone, she thought. *It's upstairs in Conrad's bedroom!*

The man was now mere steps away from the van.

There's no time to call for help!

Deanna ran for the front door and fiddled desperately with the locks. *Please, for the love of God, open!* she thought as she flipped the last deadbolt.

She flung the door open and brandished the knife in the air. "Stop right there!" she screamed.

The man froze.

"Turn around!" Deanna commanded.

The man turned to face Deanna. He spied the knife. His eyes grew wide, and he dropped Conrad.

The boy came running toward her.

"What's going on?" Cecilia Count asked from behind Deanna, startling her so badly she nearly collapsed.

"You're okay!" Deanna said, turning her head to face her. "I thought you were ...."

Cecilia stared at Deanna, horrified. "What are you doing with that knife?"

"That man ..." Deanna stuttered, and nodded toward the stranger by the van. "He's—"

"That's Peter," Cecilia said. "Peter!" she called out. "Come here!"

"What?" Deanna gasped, trying to catch her breath. "He's who?"

"Conrad's au pair."

"I ... I thought Conrad ... I thought he was in danger."

Cecilia studied Deanna. "Not that I'm aware of, unless you were planning on teaching him to play with knives."

Deanna suddenly remembered the knife in her hand and lowered it sheepishly. "No. I ... never mind." She handed the knife to Cecilia as the young man with long, sandy-blond hair approached.

"Ms. Young, meet Peter Steiner," Cecilia said.

The scruffy man smiled at Deanna, bowed slightly, and spoke with a slow, stilted accent. "Hallo. I am very happy to make your acquaintance."

"Oh. Yes ... likewise," Deanna said, recovering some of her composure. "My apologies. I didn't know Conrad had an au pair."

Peter nodded. "Sorry. We only play a little game—"

"You're dismissed, Peter," Cecilia said sharply. "Do something with the boy?"

"Yes, as you wish," Peter said. His eyes met his bare feet, then he glanced sideways at Conrad and offered the boy his hand. "Come. Let's go to my room. We make fun, yeah?"

Conrad grinned. "Yeah!"

Peter took Conrad's hand and led him around the side of the house.

"Peter lives here?" Deanna asked, careful to hide her frustration. *It would have been good to know Conrad had an au pair, for crying out loud.*

Cecilia inspected the knife blade in her hand, making Deanna wonder if the woman was hoping to charge her for any damage it might have sustained. Finally, Cecilia looked up and said, "We made a place for him in the garage."

Deanna did her best to suppress her astonishment. "He lives in the garage?"

"It has a bathroom," Cecilia said unapologetically. She opened the front door to her gleaming mansion and motioned for Deanna to go in. "I'm not a monster. Peter has a side entrance. He can come and go as he pleases."

Deanna's brow furrowed. "But you have this huge house. Why not let him used one of the spare rooms?"

"Good lord," Cecilia said indignantly. "I'm not going to let a stranger roam around freely in my house!"

No. Just with your child, Deanna thought as she followed Cecilia inside. In the living room, a short Hispanic woman was waiting by the stairs. She held a white garbage bag in one hand.

"I think this is the last one," she said to Cecilia, and held out her fist. When she unfurled her fingers, a wingless fly crawled around the center of her palm.

Cecilia crinkled her nose. "That will be all, Consuela."

As the woman left, Deanna asked, "And she would be?"

Cecilia bristled. "What is this? An interrogation?"

Deanna stood firm. "If I'm to help Conrad, I need to know who his influencers are."

Cecilia's eyebrow arched. "Influencers?"

"People who have enough contact with him to shape his thoughts and ... beliefs."

Cecilia sighed. "Consuela's the housekeeper. She comes three times a week. Unless there's an ... uh ... emergency or something."

Deanna nodded. "And how much time does Conrad spend with Peter?"

Cecilia shrugged. "Peter walks him to and from the bus stop, and takes care of him until I get back from work."

"So, three or four hours a day?"

"More or less. Depends on my plans for the evening."

"Where's Peter from?"

Cecilia's blood-red lips pursed to a fine line. "From Lithuania. Or Croatia. Someplace like that. He came recommended from a dear friend. He's on a student visa, and he works cheap."

"Cheap?" Deanna asked. *Incredible! The woman probably did more research on the Prada shoes she's wearing than on her son's care-taker!*

"I never discuss business terms with anyone not involved in the actual arrangement," Cecilia said curtly. "But it's above minimum wage, if that's what you're asking. I mean, it's well above it when you include room and board." Cecilia sighed. "And God knows Peter takes advantage of it. He puts away enough groceries for two."

Deanna could barely contain her anger. Cecilia was complaining about how much Peter ate when the woman didn't pay him enough in a month to purchase one of the pointy-toed pumps on her feet. She took a breath to calm herself. "You said Peter came recommend-ed. What are his credentials?"

Cecilia's eyes narrowed. "He's a student working on his college degree. What kind of credentials does he need to take care of a six-year-old boy?"

"I was just trying to learn more about him. What can you tell me? Like, for instance, why did he leave last job?"

Cecilia's lips curled slightly. "My dear friend's husband caught her with Peter in, shall we say, an *awkward situation*."

"What kind of situation?"

Cecilia winked. "Let's just say it involved one of the Ten Com-mandments."

Astonished, Deanna offered a tight smile. "I see."

Cecilia Count was not going to make this easy. She'd already sent Conrad off with Peter, thwarting Deanna's plans to spend time with the boy. Now she was being obtuse with information about his main caregiver, Peter.

Deanna decided it was time to regroup and fight this battle an-other day. She gave Cecilia a polite nod. "I think we should call it a day. It was a short session, but I believe I've established a thread of trust with Conrad."

Cecilia looked Deanna in the eye. "I believe you have."

She walked over to the kitchen counter and lay the knife down, then reached into her purse. She pulled out a check and offered it to Deanna. "Same time tomorrow? I'd really like to take advantage of the school holidays to see what you can do with the boy."

Deanna took the check. "Yes. Eleven tomorrow works for me. The holidays have freed up my schedule as well."

Cecilia smiled coolly. "Glad to hear it."

Deanna reached out and shook Cecilia's hard, boney hand. But when she tried to let go, Cecilia held it tight. She squeezed Deanna's fingers and locked her ice-blue eyes with hers.

"Just one thing, Dr. Young," she said through gritted teeth. "I hope you don't plan on winning Conrad over with cheap shortcuts. And I'd appreciate it if you didn't try to undermine my authority ever again."

Chapter Twenty-Four

DEANNA DROVE AWAY FROM Cecilia Count's house feeling both angry and guilty. On one hand, Cecilia was a brutally frank woman. On the other hand, she appeared to delight in withholding important information, then watching her victims blunder and stumble from being blindsided by her omissions.

Does that make Cecilia a sadist or a bitch? Deanna wondered. She sighed. *Who says she can't be both?*

Before she left the Count house, Deanna had considered dropping the case and handing Cecilia back the check she'd doled out to her like a charity gift. Who did the woman think she was?

Deanna couldn't care less if Cecilia Count was a big shot or not. No. It was something altogether different that made her hang onto the case.

Deanna couldn't abandon Conrad.

She knew his pain all too well.

When a parent's love has to be earned, the poor child in question can never live up to the task, she thought as she pulled away from the cold, white mansion.

And if Conrad's begun venting his frustration by torturing animals, he needs my help.

And fast.

THE WIND CHILLED DEANNA'S red cheeks to ice, making her wish she'd put the top up on the Corvette. As she slowly cruised down the brick streets of the posh, Old Northeast neighborhood, Deanna wondered what kind of impression she'd made on Cecilia and Conrad.

Childhood insecurities, it seemed, never died. They just got transferred from generation to generation.

Deanna felt certain she'd at least partially won over Conrad. But Cecilia was another case altogether. Her stony poker face had been nearly impossible to read. The only thing Deanna was sure of was the woman's reaction to her automobile. There had been no mistaking the look of envy in Cecilia's eyes when she'd watched Deanna climb into her cherry-red, 1961 Corvette Cabriolet.

The car had belonged to Deanna's mother. But due to Melody Young's increasing agoraphobia, the Corvette had remained in the garage un-driven for the past twenty years. A little tinkering by Marcus Blatch had gotten it up and running, but from the occasional backfire, Deanna knew it was in dire need of a real tune-up.

As Deanna turned left onto Beach Boulevard, a sudden thought caused her to chew her lip.

Cecilia Count and Melody Young had several traits in common. But the most obvious one was also the most hurtful; Things seemed to matter to them much more than people.

Deanna's heart pinged with pain. As a clinical psychologist, she knew that type of deep detachment usually had its roots in early infancy. Sometimes, as early as in the womb—if the mother and environment were stressful enough to cause withdrawal from all stimuli.

How Deanna's own mother had become so detached from the world, she still had very few clues on which to base a diagnosis.

Melody Young had never allowed any talk of her past.

Deanna shifted into second gear, said a quick prayer for her mother, then let the pinging anxiety in her chest go. There was nothing she could do to help her mother then, and certainly nothing she could do for her now.

But Conrad Count was another story.

If this is going to work, I'm going to have to break through Cecilia's defenses, Deanna thought. *I need to help her find a way to be the kind of mother she really wants to be.*

Projection.

The word crashed into Deanna's mind like a kamikaze pilot.

She cringed.

Is this about Conrad and Cecilia, or about you and Melody? she asked herself.

Good question, she thought as she steered the Corvette along Northshore Park. Her mentor, Larry Filbert, had taught her to be wary of projecting her own feelings and motivations onto her clients.

Yet feelings were as inevitable as death.

Deanna was painfully aware that part of her would always long for a mother who loved her. She could change neither her childhood circumstances nor her adult feelings about that.

But with the patient counsel of Larry, her good friend and therapist, Deanna had learned not to blame herself for wanting a caring mother. She'd also learned not to focus on changing the past, but on changing what was possible.

The future.

As she hit the gas and turned onto Coffee Pot Boulevard, Deanna knew she could use the insight she'd gained from her own situation to help people like Conrad and Cecilia process their feelings, and, if not change, at least find a way to move beyond their painful past.

But for Conrad to have a chance at a better future, she needed to get Cecilia on board.

Despite what Cecilia had said, this wouldn't be a quick fix. In order to make real progress, Conrad would require more than a couple of counseling sessions over the winter holidays. He needed long-term stability and the security of someone's love. Without them, any help she could offer would be nothing more than a Band-Aid on a gaping wound.

Deanna pulled the Corvette into the alley that ran behind her house and parked it inside the detached garage. As she climbed out of the car, she realized she hadn't eaten all day.

Hunger gnawed at her throat.

So did her need to speak with Larry.

Deanna sprinted to the back door and into the kitchen. She pulled a TV dinner from the freezer and popped it in the microwave. Then she busied herself making a glass of iced tea while it cooked. A few minutes later, she was standing at the kitchen counter washing down a mouthful of gummy pasta when the doorbell rang.

Deanna padded to the front of the house and peeked through the small glass pane in the front door. Outside the screened-in porch, a man was standing on the steps, looking off to his left.

Deanna cracked open the front door. "Can I help you?"

The man peered through the screened door. "Hi! Sorry to bother you. I was just driving by and saw smoke coming from your yard. I stopped and ... well, I found this."

He held up what looked like a can of motor oil. "It had a piece of cloth in it. It was ... smoldering."

Deanna's eyes widened. "You're kidding!" She stepped onto the porch and looked at the oil-smutted can. "Oh, my! Thank you."

The man shook his head. "No need to thank me. I'd hope anyone to do the same for me."

Unsure what to say or do, Deanna fumbled for words. "Can I re-pay you in some way?"

"No. Just doing my part to be a good neighbor." The man glanced at his watch. "Oh! I've got an appointment and I'm already late! Here's my card. If you ever need my services, just give me a ring."

Deanna opened the screen door and took the card. "Thank you. I will."

She looked up from the card. With the screen no longer blocking her view, she noticed the man was wearing a cheap toupee. He gave her a quick smile and nod, revealing a horsey set of dentures. Then he turned and sprinted down the walkway and through the hedgerow.

Deanna looked down at his card again and grimaced.

A realtor. That figures.

After all the flyers and calls she'd gotten from various firms looking to list her house for sale, Deanna wondered for a brief second whether the man had staged the whole thing—just to stand out in the crowd.

Chapter Twenty-Five

DEANNA TOSSED THE REST of her gummy pasta in the trash and searched the cluttered kitchen for a bottle of wine to wash away the taste in her mouth. She was sipping a glass of pinot grigio when her cellphone rang.

"Hey, Dee," Larry said when she answered the phone. "You never gave me an address where to ship your office furniture."

Deanna smiled, genuinely happy to hear her old friend's voice. "I was just going to call you. You must be a mind reader."

"If I was, I wouldn't need a degree in psychiatry, now, would I?"

Deanna laughed. "No, I suppose not. And to answer your question, my new office is next door."

"What? You're kidding."

"No. Jodie's living there now. She moved out of that art commune in Kenwood and invited me to use her front room for my office. That is, at least until I can get my act together."

Larry's voice went dry. "Wow. Talk about returning to the scene of the crime."

Deanna nearly winced. "I know. But I think it might be healing—for both of us."

"Huh. You surprise me, Dee. In a good way, I mean. I'm proud of how strong you've become."

Deanna shrugged. "Thanks. But I have to give my finances more credit than my so-called bravery. Jodie could use the money, and I could use the cheap rent."

"Don't discount your accomplishments. You've come a long way."

Thanks, Dad, Deanna thought. But she wasn't being snide. Over the years, Larry had become the kind, supportive father Deanna wished she'd had growing up. "I appreciate you—gallows humor and all."

Larry laughed. "Life shapes our sense of humor. Mine just happens to be in the form of a noose. It was inescapable, really."

"Don't tell me. School of hard knocks?"

"No. Genetics."

"Genetics?"

"Yes. Like any good Jew, I grew up learning that when life doesn't give you much to laugh about, you have to improvise. Anyway, sick humor's not a crime. It's the totally humorless you have to watch out for."

"That's what I'm afraid of." Deanna sighed. "Cecilia Count's sense of humor is totally MIA."

"Who?"

"The boy I told you I'm counseling. She's his mother."

"Oh. Right. So, tell me. How did your first session go?"

"I don't know, Larry. The situation seems wrong on so many levels, I don't know where to start."

"That's easy. Start with the mother. What are our parents for if not to blame everything on?"

Deanna let out a jaded laugh. "Thanks for putting it all in perspective."

Larry's jovial tone sobered. "Okay. Seriously. What did you learn about her that's so disturbing?"

"Nothing specific. Just a feeling. Cecilia Count is so ... prim and proper. And wound up tighter than a broken clock. She actually accused me of trying to undermine her authority when I was trying to build Conrad's trust."

"Conrad? The boy?"

"Yes."

"And were you?"

"Was I *what?*"

"Undermining her authority."

Deanna chewed her lip. "Only in a small way. I agreed with him that the candle she gave me smelled like frog farts."

Larry laughed. "You co-conspirator, you."

Deanna smiled. "Maybe. But it was funny. And harmless, right?"

"Yeah, sure."

"That's what I thought." Deanna's tone went somber. "But Cecilia took it deadly seriously. Honestly, I don't think the woman even knows how to laugh."

"Reminds me of someone I used to know. Tell me about Conrad. Why is she concerned about him?"

"Like I told you earlier, she caught him playing with a dead bird."

"That's not as unusual as you might think, Dee. Kids are highly curious creatures, and still haven't adopted a lot of human society's odd values."

"Like playing with dead things?"

"Precisely."

"I don't know. I was prepared to give Conrad the benefit of a doubt for not knowing it was wrong. But then ...."

"What?"

"He gave me a jar of flies."

Larry laughed. "He's a boy. That means he likes you."

"I don't think so. Their wings were torn off."

Larry's tone changed. "How old is this kid again?"

"Six."

Larry paused. His voice grew serious. "Okay. Any more presenting problems?"

"Conrad claimed he didn't tear their wings off. He said the neighbor's cat did."

"So he's got an imagination. That's actually a good sign. Is he physically healthy?"

"Yes. As far as I can tell. According to Cecilia, he's slightly autistic. I think he's a bed-wetter, too. I felt plastic crinkle when I sat on his bed."

"Hmm," Larry said. "How's the family dynamic?"

"Parents separated. Apparently, they hate each other. And Cecilia is an emotional iceberg. She's hired a young man barely in his twenties to watch Conrad while she's not there."

"What do you know about him?"

"Not much. His name is Peter Steiner. He's a student—a European here on a student visa. He looks rough, but maybe that's just his style. He seems polite and caring enough. And Conrad seems to like him immensely."

"And the mother?"

"Cecilia calls Peter her 'live-in au pair,' but she has him stowed away in the garage like a used car."

"Huh." Larry paused. "So, nurturer of the year, she's not."

"No." Deanna sighed. "Cecilia's definitely on the defensive emotionally. She's got enough walls up to keep out anyone who tries to get close. I'm afraid that includes Conrad. I feel like the poor kid has no stable, caring adult in his life."

"What about the father?"

"I haven't met him yet."

"Conrad's at a vulnerable age, for sure," Larry said. "He hasn't yet reached seven, the age of reason. So the difference between right and wrong is still a malleable concept to him. He's working more from imagination than information. And, from what it sounds like, he lacks anyone to lend a real guiding hand in that regard."

Deanna sighed. "Yes. I'd say that sums it up."

"That's a powerful set of circumstances, Dee. Conrad is vulnerable. He could swing either way."

Deanna's brow furrowed. "What do you mean?"

"Imagination can work for you or against you, depending on your perception of the world at large."

"What do you mean?"

"Take kids like Conrad. At his age, they either fear or love the tooth fairy, depending on how safe they feel in their little worlds. I, personally, loved the tooth fairy. I knew I'd get a quarter under my pillow."

"I feared it," Deanna said. "I always woke up with a spider in my bed. I thought the tooth fairy was a monster who hated me."

"Exactly my point. As a kid, if you feel unsafe, you imagine all kinds of horrors. Daddy's snoring down the hall at night becomes a fire-breathing monster coming to get you. With no one to turn to for comfort or answers, anxiety and anarchy can take over and rule your world."

"Yes, it can," Deanna said.

Larry sighed softly. "That reminds me of a case I had once. A little girl. On the first day of school, she was ordered to sit at a desk that had another girl's name on it. A healthy child would have simply pointed out the error. But this little girl's self-esteem had been crushed by her insensitive, unreliable mother. So, rather than tell the teacher of the name mix-up, the girl sat at her desk and chewed her fingernails to the quick, wracked with fear over what would happen when she was finally outed as an imposter."

"Larry—" Deanna began.

"Don't interrupt me. I'm making a point. Scared silly, the little girl concocted a story in her head about the girl whose name was on her desk. By midday, she'd convinced herself that she'd been placed at that awful desk by the door because that's where they put children they wanted to get rid of. In her mind, the other girl had already been snatched away. Now, it was just a matter of time before they came to get *her*. As I recall, the little girl suffered in misery for weeks, waiting for the monster behind the door to come and grab her away."

Deanna chewed her lip. "That was a long time ago."

"I know," Larry said softly. "I just wanted to remind you what it's like to feel powerless and afraid in a world run by adults whose rules don't make any sense."

"Like Conrad might be feeling now." Deanna sighed. "I want to do my best for him, Larry. I really do."

"I know. And you will."

Deanna nodded. "Oh. Thanks for your suggestion to make a game out of talking with Conrad. I think it really helped bring him out."

"Then keep that up. If he's engaging with you, that's a really good sign that he's not beyond help."

Chapter Twenty-Six

I'M A GOOD BOY. THEY'LL see.

His dirty finger traced the secret marks on the wall.

One. Two. Three. Four ....

Only one more chance remained.

If he could do it, they would see he was trying.

And he would be redeemed.

Or, if he wasn't brave enough, he would die.

He took the knife and stabbed at the metal edges of the can.

Blood began to flow ....

Chapter Twenty-Seven

DEANNA POKED HER HEAD into the conference room at Blatch & Smalls. Inside, the two private eyes were locked in a heated discussion. Both men clammed up as soon as they noticed her.

"What's going on?" Deanna asked. "A break in your case?"

"No," Smalls said. He nodded sharply at Blatch. "You tell him, Deanna."

Deanna's brow furrowed. "Tell Blatch what?"

Smalls folded his arms across his chest. "Tell him it's his turn to make the cappuccinos."

Deanna nearly snorted. "You're kidding. That's what this is about?"

Smalls straightened his shoulders. "I like to think of this place as an equal-opportunity establishment."

Her older partner's convenient burst of modernism caused Deanna to smirk. "He's right, Blatch. It's your turn."

"Fine." Blatch pushed away from the table. "I'll be right back."

As Blatch disappeared down the hall, Smalls leaned toward Deanna and grunted, "I hope he doesn't burn the place down."

"What do you mean?"

"Nothing."

Deanna shot Smalls a look that compelled him to elaborate.

"Okay. Let's just say, Blatch isn't the most mechanically inclined person I've ever known."

Deanna raised an eyebrow. "I don't know. He got my Corvette running in no time."

"Huh," Smalls grunted. *I bet he did.*

"Did you see the wreath I hung on the door?" Deanna asked. "Nothing too Christmassy. I kept it simple. Classic holly and poinsettias, so as not to offend anyone's sensibilities."

"I thought the holidays were all about offending people's sensibilities," Smalls said.

Deanna laughed. "I suppose you have a point—"

"I do. And here it is." Smalls reached under the conference table and pulled out a Santa Claus doll that stood about a foot high. He set it on the table and flipped a switch on its boot.

The cheesy figure in red velvet began to gyrate salaciously to the tune of *I Saw Mommy Kissing Santa Claus*.

Dumbstruck, Deanna watched as Santa Claus finished his routine, then leaned over and dropped his pants, revealing his bare buttocks. His left cheek was imprinted with a pair of red lips.

"Kind of sums up *my* holiday sentiment," Smalls said. "Ho ho ho."

Deanna shook her head. "Thanks for sharing."

Blatch walked in and set down the tray of cappuccinos. He spied the Santa Claus figure and both pairs of his rosy red cheeks. "Well, seeing as how we're all in a festive mood, I'd like to take the opportunity to invite you both to Christmas Eve at my place."

Smalls shot Deanna a quick glance, then looked Blatch in the eye. "Did you okay it with your mommy, first?"

"Ha ha," Blatch sneered. "Watch it, Grinch, or you'll be uninvited."

Smalls opened his mouth to say something snide, but the image of watching *Scrooge* alone with a turkey TV dinner made him think twice. "So, what should we bring to the festivities?"

Blatch grinned. "I'd say a covered dish, but in your case, Smalls, just stick with a bottle of wine."

"Mind if I do the same?" Deanna asked. "My place is still a disaster."

Blatch shrugged. "That's fine. You know, I don't know how you come to work looking so put together when your house could make the cover of *Hoarder's Weekly*."

Deanna shrugged. "I got my training at college. I had to share a dorm room with two other girls."

Smalls turned his nose up. "You school-educated people." He stabbed his chest with his thumb. "I made my way in this world *without* college. I'm a self-made man."

Blatch smirked. "So, why'd you give up before you were done?"

Smalls sneered. "If you didn't make such good coffee, I'd tell you both to take it on the arches."

Deanna smiled to herself, wondering if this was what it was like to have brothers. A twinge of melancholy pinched her heart. Relatives could be such a mixed bag.

"Okay, so everybody's in for Christmas Eve?" Blatch asked.

"Count me in," Deanna answered.

"Yeah, me too," Small grunted.

Blatch smiled. "Good. I'll let Mom—Deloris know. So, down to work. Anybody got anything new to report?"

"I got my first check," Deanna said, and fished it out of her purse. She held it up for the guys to see.

"A hundred and fifty bucks?" Smalls said, shaking his head. "Maybe I *should've* gone to college."

Deanna smirked. "Even better, I'm still on Cecilia Count's good side. At least, I think I am. I've got another appointment with her today."

Blatch smiled. "That's great. Good for you."

"Thanks." Deanna tucked the check away. "What about you guys?"

Blatch winced. "We're working a few angles with the Preston case.

"*Obtuse* angles," Smalls said.

Blatch shot him a look. "At least I'm bringing something to the table."

"Yeah. Maybe you can serve up some of that wild goose your chasing at your party." Smalls picked up a copy of *The Tampa Times* newspaper and unfolded it. "Now *this* is something really interesting."

Blatch turned to Deanna and rolled his eyes. "Usually, when anyone starts a sentence with, 'this is really interesting' it never is."

"Hilarious," Smalls deadpanned. He turned the newspaper to page two and held it up for Blatch's and Deanna's inspection.

At the top of the page was an article Smalls had circled in red. As his partners strained to read the small print, Smalls raised a bushy eyebrow and said, "Well, boys and girls, looks like we got us another naughty little fire in the Old Northeast."

Chapter Twenty-Eight

BLATCH NEARLY DROPPED his cappuccino. "*Another* fire?"

"Yeah." Smalls arched a gray eyebrow. "Not far from your house. *Again*. Fenton Place."

Deanna's back stiffened. "I know that building. It's just a few blocks from Mercer Arms, isn't it?"

Blatch nodded. "Yeah. Another tenement house."

Deanna's eyes widened. "You think we've got a serial arsonist on the loose?"

"Could be." Blatch scowled. "I wonder why I didn't hear about it from Davidson."

"Davidson?" Deanna asked.

"A cop we're working with on the Preston case."

Smalls shrugged. "Probably because there *is* no Preston case. Besides, there wasn't much to this one. The article said it was a small, self-contained fire. One of the residents doused it with a beer." Smalls peered at the article. "Says the fire was 'extinguished without incident.'"

Blatch glanced over at Deanna. She looked stunned. "What is it?" he asked.

Deanna's lips pursed to a taught line. "Do you think someone might be targeting old buildings in the neighborhood?"

Smalls' eyebrow shot up. "It's possible. I mean, what's an empty lot go for in Old Northeast anymore? Quarter mil?"

Deanna arched an eyebrow. "More like three-fifty."

"Huh," Smalls grunted. "No better way to clear away an eyesore than a good bonfire. You get the work done for free, and the insurance payout to boot."

Deanna bit her lip. "I guess I should tell you guys about something that happened yesterday."

The two men glanced at each other, then back to Deanna. "What? Something to do with Cecilia Count?"

"No. It may be nothing, but a man rang my front doorbell yesterday afternoon. He told me he was driving by and saw smoke, so he stopped to investigate. He showed me a can of oil he found smoldering by my front porch."

Deanna locked eyes with Blatch. "My place is an eyesore, too. Do you think it might've been targeted? Was I was supposed to be next?"

"Geeze," Blatch said, shaking his head. "It sure doesn't sound like a coincidence. Did you get the man's name?"

"Yes! I mean, I got his card."

Deanna reached for her purse, then pulled back her hand. "I left it at home on the kitchen counter. I remember that he was a realtor."

Smalls grunted. "What did he look like?"

Deanna shook her head. "Older. White guy. Bad toupee. Really bad dentures."

Smalls blew out a breath. "We're talking realtors, Deanna. That description doesn't narrow things down much."

Blatch shot Smalls a look, then turned to Deanna. "What was he driving? Did you get a tag number?"

"No. The hedge blocked my view. And, to be honest, I didn't look. I ... I figured it was just someone tossing garbage out their car window. I didn't think that much about it."

Smalls' leathery brow furrowed to the top of his bald head. "Somebody tries to firebomb your house and you don't think much about it?"

"I ... I guess I've just been living in New York City too long."

Blatch put his hand on Deanna's arm. "What did you do with the oil can?"

Deanna winced. "It's in the garbage bin in the back alley. I threw it away."

BLATCH, SMALLS, AND Deanna arrived in Blatch's sedan just in time to see a garbage truck dump the community container behind her house into the back of its huge bed.

"Shit." Smalls grumbled. "If there were any prints on the can, they're history now."

Deanna winced. "I'm sorry. I didn't think—"

Smalls' face softened. "Don't worry about it. I know you didn't make the connection."

Deanna climbed out of the sedan and hung her head like a scolded child. "I'll go in and get the man's business card."

While Deanna headed off toward her back door, Blatch and Smalls stayed in the sedan. As Deanna reached the door, it flew open. Jodie Havenall came tumbling out with a garbage bag. She beamed proudly at Deanna. "Surprise! I cleaned up a little."

Deanna blanched. "You didn't!"

Jodie shot her a sideways look and held up a hand. "Don't worry. I can put all your precious garbage back just where I found it, Melody, Jr."

Deanna shook her head. "No, it's not that. I just. Well, I need to find a realtor's card I left inside somewhere."

Jodie frowned. "You decided to sell?"

"No," Blatch said, stepping up to join them. "But it just may be that someone's trying to persuade her to."

"WHERE DID I PUT THAT stupid card?" Deanna said as she pilfered through the stacks of mail, empty jars, and plastic food containers piled all over her kitchen counters. She glanced at the clock on the wall. "It's quarter till eleven. I've got to go meet my client."

"It's okay. We can take it from here," Jodie said.

"Lovely," Smalls cracked. "Go ahead. Leave all the fun stuff to us."

Deanna bit her lip. "Sorry. Look, just save anything you come across that has to do with a realtor. If we can't find his business card, maybe we can find something else with his picture on it."

Smalls sneered. "What's this *we* business? *You're* leaving."

"She's got her job to do," Blatch said defensively. "And we've got ours."

"Sorry," Deanna said again and turned to leave.

Blatch took a step toward the door. Smalls barked at him. "Where do you think *you're* going?"

Blatch turned and glared at him. "Outside for a minute. I need to call Davidson. See if he knows anything about the new fire that the press doesn't."

Blatch sprinted across the kitchen and opened the door for Deanna. "You need a lift?"

"No. I'll take the Corvette. It seems to impress Cecilia Count, even if I don't."

Blatch studied Deanna's face. "I'm not buying that. There's no way you can't make an impression."

Deanna pursed her lips into a smirk and headed out the door. "I meant a *good* one."

Blatch smiled and followed after her. "Now *that,* I refuse to believe. Probably just sour grapes."

"Yeah, right."

What woman wouldn't want to be you? Blatch thought, watching Deanna climb into her Corvette. As she disappeared out of sight, he pulled out his cellphone and punched a number. It rang once.

"Officer Jerry Davidson speaking."

"Hey, Davidson."

"Blatch."

"I read about the Fenton Place fire in the news. Think it's related to Melton Arms?"

"I don't know. You got an angle on it you care to share?"

Blatch hesitated a moment. "Just a theory. Maybe a real-estate developer looking to force sales on neglected properties? With no cash flow, selling might look more profitable than rebuilding."

"Huh," Davidson grunted. "Interesting. I can't comment on *that*. But I *can* tell you that whoever tried to set the Fenton fire used a suspiciously similar MO. Same kind of incendiary device—a four-cycle fuel can with a torn cloth wick. Only in this case, a well-timed Budweiser doused the arsonist's plans."

"Right," Blatch said. "Did you get a look at the actual incendiary device?"

"Yeah. In fact, I'm looking at it now."

"What brand of fuel is the guy using?"

"Hold on. I'll .... Aww, shit!"

"What?"

"I tipped over the damned can .... What the fuck!?"

"Are you okay?" Blatch yelled into the phone. He listened for a reply, but the line remained eerily silent. "Davidson?" he asked repeatedly into the void.

Suddenly, the young cop returned to the line, his voice shaky. "Holy shit, Blatch."

"What? You find another thumbprint on the bottom?"

"No. This time, I found the whole thumb."

Chapter Twenty-Nine

DEANNA DROVE TOWARD Cecilia Count's house with one goal in mind. This time, she wouldn't let the woman thwart her efforts to spend some real time assessing Conrad.

Her talk with Larry reminded Deanna that Conrad was in a very vulnerable stage of personal and moral development. Through the age of six, children's brains and minds were basically information sponges, soaking up whatever their environments offered them, with little discernment about what was right or wrong.

As Deanna steered her Corvette onto Cherry Street, she was determined to unearth every possible influence that could be affecting young Conrad. She needed to get at the root of what was inspiring his unusual behavior.

Somehow, the poor boy has surmised that torturing and killing animals is okay. But from where? she wondered. Given the easy access to such horrific things on TV and the internet, Conrad's influencers didn't have to live nearby. Or even be real, for that matter.

His odd actions were proof that Conrad's young, susceptible mind was being over-stimulated, perhaps even already laying down faulty wiring in his brain. But how bad was the damage? Was it still reversible? Deanna needed to get into the boy's head if she was going to ascertain what beliefs he'd already formed.

I need to find out if Conrad has unsupervised access to the internet, she thought as she shifted gears. *I also need to interview Peter, the au pair. Maybe some game or video he's exposing him to might be too much for Conrad to discern from reality.*

But when Deanna pulled up to the Count house, her thoughts evaporated.

A tall, dark-haired man in an expensive business suit was milling about in the front yard, peeking in the windows.

Deanna watched him for a moment, engine idling, wondering whether she should take off and call the police. Then she realized the man had something in his hand. It looked like a large knife.

Her heart leapt in her throat.

Deanna grabbed blindly for her phone, her eyes locked on the strange man. As she fumbled for her phone, the man turned, saw her, and stood up straight. Deanna realized he was holding hedge trimmers.

"Can I help you?" he called out.

Deanna eyed him suspiciously, her phone gripped tightly in her hand. "I'm here to see Cecilia Count." She poised her foot on the gas pedal, ready to peel out and escape, if necessary. "Who are you?"

"Charles Count," the man said. His handsome face was red, either from bending over, high blood pressure, or embarrassment.

"Cecilia's husband?"

"Temporarily," he said bitterly. "Now I'm just the handyman, here to fix things for free. Unclog the sink. Repair a broken hinge. Fix a tripped breaker."

Deanna shut off the Corvette's engine and climbed out of the car. She walked over and offered him a sympathetic smile. "I'm Deanna Young. A ... friend of Cecilia's. Divorce can be tough for the whole family."

The man sighed. "You're right. Sorry." He switched the hedge trimmers to his left hand and reached out to shake her hand. "Let's start over. I'm Charles Count, the soon-to-be ex-husband. Cecilia's had to take Conrad to the doctor. She'll be back any minute."

Deanna's eyes widened with concern. "Is something wrong with Conrad?"

Charles made a sour face. "Only in Cecilia's mind. Conrad seems to come down with something every time it's my turn to have him for the weekend."

"Oh."

Charles shook his head. "The only time I get to see him is when I come here to fix something. I used to mow the lawn, but she got a service. And now that she's got her little boy toy in the garage, I guess I'm out to pasture for good."

Charles glanced at the garage door with disgust. "She calls him Conrad's 'European au pair.' I guess that sounds fancier at her bridge club than her 'fuck-buddy.'"

Deanna winced. "I don't know what to say."

Charles shook his head. "Sorry. I don't know why I just said that. To be honest, Peter seems like a decent enough kid. It just bothers the hell out of me that some stranger gets to spend more time with my son than I do."

"I can understand that."

Charles' angry face softened. "Look, I don't mean to dump my issues on you. You want to wait for Cecilia in the backyard? I'd let you in the house, but she's changed the locks."

"Well ..."

"Oh." He fished in his coat pocket and pulled out a business card with his photo on it. "Don't worry. I really am Charles Count." He glanced back toward the road. "Cecilia will see your car and know you're here. Nice 'Vette, by the way."

"Thanks."

"Follow me."

Charles led Deanna around the side of the house. She noticed he shot an angry glance at the side door to the garage—Peter's entry door. She could barely blame him. As Charles passed by a metal garden shed, he shook his head.

"See that?" he said. "By the time I moved out, that stupid tool-shed was the only place I had left I could call my own. You've seen what she did to the inside of the house? The woman made it into a freaking showcase. A designer hospital! I'm afraid to sit on the couch. If I left a mark on it, I'd never hear the end of it."

Deanna nodded, but said nothing. She didn't want to interrupt the man's insightful monologue.

"She thinks she's better than me," Charles spat, and kicked the shed in frustration.

A car horn sounded from around the front of the house.

Charles sneered. "Looks like the snow queen is back. You go ahead. Let Her Majesty know I'm around back fixing the sprinklers."

Deanna nodded. "Okay. It was nice to meet you, Mr. Count."

Charles stopped his tirade. His face softened and he offered Deanna half a smile. "You too, uh ... I've forgotten your name. Mrs?"

"Ms. Deanna Young."

Upon hearing the word "Ms.," Charles' smile grew a little brighter. He gave Deanna an appreciative glance up and down.

The horn honked again.

"I better go," Deanna said.

Charles' face hardened again. "I know. Her Majesty doesn't like to wait."

Deanna turned to go. Charles called out behind her. "Be careful. Cecilia loves to win—even more than she hates to show her cards."

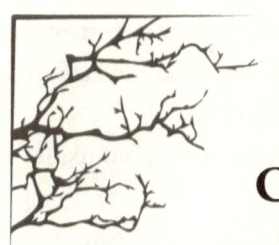

Chapter Thirty

"WHAT DID CHARLES SAY to you?" Cecilia asked, studying Deanna as she followed her inside the house.

"Nothing. Only that he's fixing the sprinkler system out back."

"In *that* suit? I doubt it. He's probably setting up some hidden camera to spy on me. Or he went through my mailbox."

Deanna took her notebook from her red leather satchel. "I think he'd like to see Conrad more often."

Cecilia blew out a breath. "Right. That's why he's leaving without saying hello to the boy."

She nodded sharply toward the front window. Charles Count was marching across the lawn toward a red Mercedes convertible.

"Where's Conrad?" Deanna asked, watching as Charles climbed into the Mercedes and took off.

"He ran up the stairs," she said. "See? He didn't want to see Charles, either."

"I did, too!" Conrad called from the top of the stairs. "I wanted to show him this." He struck an angry pout and held up a soup can.

"Come down here right now!" Cecilia demanded.

Conrad slunk down the stairs.

She snatched the empty soup can from his hand. "What are you doing with this ... *garbage?* And why would you want to show it to your father, of all things?" She glared at Conrad. "Wait a minute. Charles! That bastard! Has he asked you to go rummaging through my trash cans?"

"No!" Conrad shouted. "And Father's not a ...." His voice trailed off. "Freddie—"

"Not that stupid cat again!" Cecilia screeched. She turned to Deanna. "Take him out of here. I need a drink." She marched toward the kitchen. "Talk some sense into him, would you?"

Deanna took Conrad's hand. "Come with me. Let's go outside."

"Why?"

"I want you to show me where you found your special can."

Conrad lowered his eyes. "It's not special."

Deanna squeezed his hand. "It is to me."

"SO, WHERE DID YOU FIND the can?" Deanna asked after she'd settled Conrad into the pillows on the covered swing in the back yard.

"You promise you won't tell Mother?"

"Yes." Deanna winked. "Unless, of course, you committed some kind of crime."

Conrad's face grew ashen. "I did. I stole it."

"From who?"

"From the kitchen."

"Why?"

"I knew he needed it."

"Who?"

"Freddie."

"Oh. Freddie likes chicken soup?"

Conrad shrugged. "I guess. He ate it, didn't he?"

"How do you know *Freddie* ate the soup?"

"Because he had to."

Deanna envisioned Conrad holding the cat's head down in the broth, forcing it to eat the soup. She shook the thought away. "He *had* to?"

"Freddie was hungry, so I stole the soup and put it on the back step for him last night. When I got up this morning, it was empty. So he *had* to eat it, right?"

"Oh." Deanna felt relief course through her body. "Yes, I guess so. Well, that was nice of you, Conrad." Deanna took the chance to dig a little deeper. "What about the dead bird? Freddie didn't want to eat it?"

Conrad crinkled his nose. "No. It was too stinky. Besides, Mother made me throw it away."

Deanna nodded. "Can you show me where you found the dead bird?"

Conrad pointed toward the back door. "There. On the steps. Freddie always leaves me presents on the back steps."

Deanna crinkled her nose playfully. "Is that where you found the gross rat head?"

Conrad snickered. "Yeah. And the dead lizards, too."

"Lizards?"

"Yeah. Freddie chews their feet off and pokes their eyeballs out with sticks. It's so gross!"

"Ew!" Deanna would've made a pretense of pretending to be disgusted, but she didn't have to. Her inner alarm bells were ringing. Could the beautiful, blond boy in front of her actually enjoy blinding lizards and biting off their feet? She tucked her disgust behind a playful grimace. "Yuck! That's really gross!"

Conrad laughed. "If I could catch a frog, I'd squish him till he farted!"

Deanna grimaced again, and dropped some of the playfulness in her voice. "It sounds like Freddie likes to kill things. Is that true?"

Conrad bit his lip and giggled. "Yeah. Maybe."

Deanna studied his face. "What does it feel like to kill something?"

Conrad's ice-blue eyes lit up. "Squishy! Like worms!"

"Eww!" Deanna managed to say without revealing her rising concern. She needed Conrad to trust her if she could get deeper into his imaginary world.

"I have a secret," she whispered.

Conrad's blue eyes grew wide. "What?"

"I ate a worm once."

Conrad's face scrunched in delighted disgust. "Really?"

"Yeah." Deanna leaned closer and whispered in his ear. "It tasted like dirt."

Conrad squealed with delight.

Deanna studied him with a practiced grin. "Now *you* tell *me* a secret!"

Conrad glanced up at the house to see if anyone was watching through the windows. "Okay," he said, then leaned in closer to Deanna. He whispered, "Freddie tries to be good. But he gets so mad sometimes. He has bad thoughts. He doesn't want to be like our Gustus."

Deanna nodded. "Who's Gustus?"

"A bad boy. He died."

The hair on the back of Deanna's neck stood on end. A chill ran through her body. Had Conrad actually killed another boy? "How did Gustus die?"

Conrad studied Deanna for a moment. He opened his mouth to speak. A plop of rain landed on Deanna's nose.

Conrad shut his mouth and held out a palm. A raindrop splashed on it. "Uh oh!" Conrad said. "Robert's coming!"

"Robert?" Confused, Deanna looked in the direction of Conrad's gaze and saw Peter coming around the corner of the house.

Conrad's au pair looked up at the sky, then grinned at Conrad. "You ready for a rainy-day story, little Conrad?"

"Yeah!" Conrad squealed. He jumped off the swing and ran toward Peter.

"Cecilia says your time up," Peter said, scooping Conrad into his arms.

Deanna watched the two disappear around the side of the house, then picked up the empty soup can Conrad had left behind. It was the only tangible evidence she'd gathered from the boy's twisted, imaginary world.

Freddie. Gustus. Robert. Either Conrad has an overactive imagination or he's deeply disturbed, Deanna thought as she got out of the swing and headed for the back door. *Could the poor boy be suffering from a dissociative disorder? Schizophrenia?*

Conrad had surprised Deanna with how quickly he'd revealed himself. He'd basically confessed to being Freddie, yet he'd shown no remorse for his behavior—just calm, even *playful* detachment. Had he somehow been shattered enough to invent multiple personalities in order to cope with the trauma? Was he now projecting his unvented rage through imaginary personas?

Deanna looked up and was startled to see Cecilia Count staring at her from the back door.

"I thought we might have a chat about Conrad's progress," she said, shaking the ice in the empty highball glass.

Deanna hid her concern behind a neutral face. "It's a little early for that. I'm still gathering information."

Cecilia's face grew dark. "Don't lie to me. It's bad news, isn't it?"

Chapter Thirty-One

HIS HEART POUNDED IN his throat.

Still as a statue, he dared not even blink as the door creaked open, squealing like pigs at a slaughterhouse.

From within the blinding light emerged a monstrous hand. The horrible, cutting claws of the Scissor Man.

His heart sank. His sacrifice hadn't been enough.

As the hand clawed at the air mere inches from his face, he began to pray.

Let me live, and I promise I'll find a better sacrifice.

Something fresher.

Maybe even something still alive ....

Chapter Thirty-Two

"A THUMB?" BLATCH GASPED into his cellphone. "Davidson, what are you talking about?"

"I knocked over the freaking fuel can," Davidson said, his voice shaking with rage and disgust. "The rag this monster used for a wick ... it fell open. Inside was a damned—"

Blatch heard a gagging sound. Then retching. When Davidson returned to the line moments later, he struggled to get the words out between dry heaves. "It's a thumb, man. A fucking human thumb."

Davidson clicked off the phone.

Blatch stood in stunned silence for a moment. In the quiet oasis of Deanna's backyard, he numbly observed the acrobatics of a squirrel as it deftly scampered across an electric line overhead. As his heart thrummed in his ears, he wondered what kind of sick monster was roaming his neighborhood setting fires, and now cutting off people's thumbs.

A thought struck him suddenly, and he sprinted for Deanna's back door.

Blatch had to get to Fenton Place before the cops did.

And he needed Smalls' help.

"NOT EVEN A LOUSY POLICE tape," Smalls said as they pulled up to Fenton Place in Blatch's sedan. "So much for preserving the integrity of a crime scene."

"Until Davidson found that thumb, it was just a case of petty vandalism," Blatch said. "Come on, let's take a quick look around. When word gets out what Davidson found in that can, this place'll be swarming with cops."

The two men climbed out of the car. Smalls hesitated before closing his door.

"What?" Blatch said. "We can't compromise the scene any worse than it already is."

"No. That isn't it."

"Then what?"

Smalls shook his head and stared at Fenton Place. "I was just wondering where to start."

Blatch followed his gaze, and for a moment, the men stood in silence, taking a long look at the building before them.

Fenton Place was a modern-day ruin. The two-story, Spanish-style, flat-roofed apartment building was about the size of two office buildings put together. In the center of the boxy structure, an arched, open-air entryway sagged, roundish and dark, like a gaping, toothless mouth.

Painted that not-quite-right shade of pink favored by low-rent addresses, Fenton Place had been built in the 1940s as a holiday let/boarding house. From the looks of its tired, crumbling exterior, the old building had seen the last of its glory days.

"I think we should start in the open lobby," Blatch said. "Easy access."

"That, or a stairwell," Smalls said.

The two men entered the dim entryway and discovered two sets of stairs, each one leading to a separate side of the building.

"You guys reporters?" a young man asked, coming down a stairwell on the right.

"Yes," Blatch said. "Who are you?"

"Brent Smith." The man gathered his dirty blond hair and fastened it into a man-bun on top of his head.

"You know anything about the attempted fire yesterday?" Blatch asked.

He nodded proudly. "Sure do. *I'm* the one who put it out."

"I guess somebody owes you a beer, heh?" Smalls joked.

The kid smiled. "Wanna see where it happened?"

Blatch shrugged as if disinterested. "Sure."

The young man led them into the center of the open-air lobby up to a decorative niche inset into the faded stucco wall. In days past, the niche probably housed an urn or statue. Now, however, it was empty save a torn spider web. Greasy-looking stains ran down the wall underneath the niche, like syrup down a stack of pancakes.

"Up there," Smith said, pointing to the niche.

Blatch nodded. "How high is that?"

The kid shrugged. "I'd say about six, seven feet?"

Blatch reached over his head and took a few photos of the niche with his camera, careful to get it from all angles. He turned to the kid. "How long you think the fire was burning before you put it out?"

"No idea. It was blazing pretty good. Maybe a foot high?"

"Did you see anybody hanging around at the time?" Smalls asked.

Smith shrugged. "Naw, man. Just some kids playing in the street."

"Thanks," Blatch reached out to shake Brent's hand. "You did a good thing. You probably saved lives."

"That's what I figure," he said, full of himself. "You want my photograph?"

Blatch looked at him oddly.

"You know, for your article?"

"Oh. Yes, sure." Blatch raised his cellphone and focused the camera on the outline of the scruffy young man, trying to avoid including his ragged T-shirt with the inscription, *Do your curtains match your vape?*

"Say cheese," Blatch said, and snapped the shot. He glanced at the kid again and wondered, *Whatever happened to shaving, clean clothes, and basic human dignity?*

"That's Brent Smith," the young man said, and grinned like a politician. "B-R-E-N-T."

"Got it," Blatch said. "Thanks again."

"No problem, man." The young man grabbed a scooter leaning against the wall and shuffled off down the sidewalk.

Blatch turned to Smalls. "How tall are you?"

Smalls scowled. "Tall enough to get chicks, if that's what you mean."

"No. I .... Come here. Reach for that niche."

Smalls walked over and grunted as he raised himself on tiptoe under the niche. He barely managed to get his fingertips on the bottom ledge. He gave up and shot Blatch a look. "Satisfied?"

"Yeah. So our perp has to be at least taller than you."

Smalls glanced around the lobby at the beach chairs and bicycles leaning against the walls. "Or he had a ladder, a chair, a step-stool, or one of those damned scooters."

Blatch looked toward the street. "Shit."

"What?" Smalls turned to look.

A police cruiser had pulled up in front of Fenton Place. The passenger door flew open and a familiar face climbed out. The ruddy jowls and red hair belonged to Captain Anthony Castleberry.

He didn't look happy to see them.

"What are you doing here?" Castleberry barked at Blatch as he marched toward them. "This area is restricted to official police personnel only!"

Blatch wanted to punch Castleberry in the nose. But his years with his adoptive parents had taught him to at least *try* to use his words first. "Last time I looked, there was no law against walking around in my own neighborhood."

"This is a crime scene, you imbecile!"

Blatch slapped on his best *I don't give a fuck* face. "Oh. I must need glasses. Smalls, do you see a crime tape?"

Smalls smirked. "Not even a sticker."

Castleberry's red face twisted like an angry, spoiled child. "Get your asses out of here!"

"What are you gonna do? Call the cops?" Smalls quipped.

Blatch nearly flinched. "Well, I guess we'll just be leaving you to it, then," he said to Castleberry. "Come on, Smalls. We've got somewhere else to go."

Castleberry shot Blatch a bulldog scowl. "Yeah. *Down.*"

"GEEZ DOES THAT GUY ever hate you," Smalls said as they climbed into the sedan. "What'd you do? Sleep with his wife? Oh yeah. Even worse. His girlfriend."

Blatch frowned and cranked the ignition. "Can it, would you?"

Smalls caught the pain on Blatch's face and stopped ribbing him. "What happened to Cathy isn't your fault. You know that, don't you?"

Blatch blew out a breath, ignoring Smalls' remark. He shifted into drive and hoped the subject of his last love would disappear, along with his painful memories of her.

"While we're out annoying the hell out of people, let's pay a visit to that fired morgue assistant," Blatch said. "The one the morgue manager said was working when Gary Preston's body went through."

"The creep who got off on cleaning cadavers?" Smalls said.

Blatch sighed and glanced in the rearview mirror. "At least *some-body* enjoyed their job while they had it."

Smalls snorted, then leaned forward and picked up the manila folder lying on the floorboard. "The address is in the file. It's on 1ˢᵗ Avenue South. Take a left—"

"I know how to get there," Blatch growled.

"Touchy today, aren't we," Smalls said.

When Blatch didn't respond, Smalls knew not to pester him. Not when his mind was clouded with memories of Cathy. He kept his trap shut, and the two men rode the rest of the way in silence.

"IS THIS IT?" BLATCH asked as he pulled up to the address of a rundown halfway house called The Acorn Seed.

"'Fraid so," Smalls answered.

"Another dump. Figures."

The two men got out of Blatch's sedan and spent twenty minutes passing around a picture of the beard-covered face of Peter Conrad. None of the derelicts milling around the building recognized him.

"Great," Blatch said. "The guy's got no face, no job, and no residence."

"The trifecta of obscurity," Smalls quipped.

Blatch shook his head. "Screw this. We might as well be chasing a ghost."

"You mean *two* ghosts." Smalls put a hand on Blatch's shoulder. "Let's face it. Gary Lee Preston is dead."

Blatch sighed. "Okay. You're right. Let's go back to the office. I'll check the box on the insurance form and be done with it." Blatch pulled his cellphone from his jacket pocket.

"Who you calling?" Smalls asked.

"Aanya Gill. Just want to let her know she can pay the claim."
Blatch punched in her number. As the phone began to ring, he got
another call.

"Shit." He poked his phone at Smalls. "You know how to put this
on hold?"

Smalls' face crinkled. "You nuts?"

"Argh!" Blatch ended his call to Gill and picked up the incoming
call. "Blatch here."

"Blatch. It's Davidson. You're not going to believe this."

"What?"

"We lifted a print off that thumb."

"The one in the fuel can?"

"Yeah."

"Geez. Don't tell me it's ...."

"Okay. I won't tell you. But it is."

"You mean it's Preston's?"

"That's exactly what I mean."

Chapter Thirty-Three

DEANNA WAS JUST PULLING away from the Count house when Blatch rang her cellphone. She pulled back to the curb and answered it.

"Marcus. What's up?"

"Deanna. We've got a new development in the Preston case. We could really use your help. Could you meet us at the office?"

"Sure. I'm on my way."

"CAN I REMIND YOU WE'RE not getting paid for any of this?" Smalls grumbled from his seat at the head of the conference table.

"We will if we can prove Gary Preston's been murdered," Blatch said.

"Murdered?" Deanna's eyes grew wide. "I thought he died in an accident."

"Maybe he did," Blatch conceded. "Or he might've been murdered for his life insurance. Hell—while we're at it, there's even a chance Gary Preston could still be alive."

"Yeah," Smalls grumbled. "And there's a chance I'm Frosty the Snowman."

"I don't understand," Deanna said.

"Blatch thinks the two fires might be related, and that Preston is involved," Smalls deadpanned. "Did I mention they found one of his body parts at the last one?"

"What?" Deanna locked eyes with Blatch. "What's going on?"

Blatch shot Smalls a dirty look. "It's true. They found Preston's thumb at the Fenton Place fire. The same kind of incendiary device was used as at Mercer Arms. It's pretty obvious there's a serial arsonist at work."

"What about the incident at Dee's place?" Smalls said, nodding at Deanna.

"It may be related or it may not," Blatch said. "That's part of why I want us to sit down and sort this whole thing through."

Deanna chewed her lip. "Okay. So, what have we got so far?"

Blatch picked up a marker and drew a square on a dry-erase board. Inside it, he wrote the initials MC. "We've got fire number one. The burned-down tenement building, Mercer Arms."

"Right," Smalls said. "And that fire claimed one arson victim, Regina Krous."

Blatch put a circle inside the Mercer Arms square. He drew an X over it and marked it with the initials RF. "Gary Lee Preston's thumbprint was on the bottom of the fuel can that lit up Mercer Arms." He drew a can next to the building and marked it with GLP.

"We've got a hundred-grand life insurance policy payable to the widow, Tandy Preston," Smalls said.

"Right." Blatch went to the other side of the board and drew a rectangle with wheels.

"What the hell's that?" Smalls said.

"A trailer, okay?" Blatch put the initials TP inside, along with $100K.

"Don't forget Timmy," Smalls said.

"Who's Timmy?" Deanna asked.

"Tammy Preston's boyfriend. He also happens to be Gary Lee's brother."

Deanna's eyebrow arched. "Oh."

Blatch drew a heart inside the rectangle and squared the initials TP.

"Cute," Smalls said.

Blatch shot him a look. "What else have we got?"

"The urn in the backyard with Gary's supposed ashes in it," Smalls said.

Blatch drew a cross next to the trailer, and the initials RIP GLP. He turned back to face Deanna and Smalls. "And now, we've got one of Gary's thumbs."

Deanna nearly choking on her cappuccino. "Where was it found?"

"Davidson found it in the fuel can the perp used to try and burn down Fenton Place," Smalls explained as Blatch drew another square for a building and marked it with the initials FP. He drew a crude thumb inside the square.

Smalls eyed Blatch's handiwork and quipped, "Rembrandt, you ain't." He turned to catch Deanna laughing at his joke. She wasn't. Instead, her face was ashen. "What's wrong?" he asked.

Deanna cringed. "Do you think ... the can I threw away at my place ... do you think it had a thumb in it, too?"

"There's no way to know," Blatch said. "But I brought in something I want you to look at." He hoisted a plastic shopping bag onto the conference table.

Deanna cringed.

"It's not body parts," Blatch said.

Deanna sighed with relief. "Thank goodness."

Blatch opened the bag and pulled out three different brands of small-engine fuel. "Do you recognize any of these as the kind you found at your place?"

Deanna nodded. "Yes." She pointed at a black can with a red devil on it. "That one."

"Bingo," Blatch said. "Same brand as the other two fires. So, chances are, we're talking about the same perpetrator in all three instances."

Deanna's eyes grew wide. "So, what does that mean? Is this person targeting old buildings ... or the people inside them?"

Blatch shook his head. "I don't know. That's where we're hoping you can help. We need you to get inside the head of the arsonist, Deanna. What kind of person would set fires and cut off body parts?"

"I know," Smalls quipped. "A real whack job. Get it?" He held out a thumb and karate chopped it with his other hand. "Whack!"

Deanna and Blatch locked eyes and shook their heads.

"Huh," Smalls grunted. "Tough crowd."

Deanna kept her eyes on Blatch. "When you said 'cut off body parts,' do you mean someone else's, or their own?"

Blatch's eyebrows shot up. "I never thought about someone cutting off their *own* limbs. Is that a real thing?"

Deanna nodded. "Actually, yes. It's called body integrity identity disorder."

Smalls cringed. "Why the hell would someone want to cut off their own body part?"

"I know it sounds incredible," Deanna said. "But they feel that the offending limb is alien somehow ... that it doesn't belong to them. They consider it 'flesh without a soul.'"

Smalls shook his head in disgust. "What kind of lunatic would do such a thing?"

Deanna locked eyes with Smalls. "Usually, it's a middle-aged white male, and the most common request is for amputation of the left leg."

"The most common?" Blatch asked, grimacing. "Does it happen a lot?"

"No," Deanna said. "But cases have been reported for hundreds of years."

"What would make someone do it?" Blatch asked.

"Two reasons. One is body integrity identity disorder, and the other is apotemnophilia—the desire to be an amputee."

"That's fucked up," Smalls said.

"Smalls!" Blatch scolded, but the look on his face showed he felt the same.

"Psychiatrists used to think it was some kind of fetish or perversion," Deanna said. "But new studies show it may be linked to brain mapping."

"Brain mapping?" Blatch asked.

"Yes. It happens while the brain and body are being developed in the womb. In rare cases, it appears that the body part develops normally in a physical sense, but it isn't 'mapped out' or accepted by the brain. Therefore, it seems foreign to it."

"I don't get it," Smalls said.

"You've heard of phantom pains in amputated limbs, right?"

"Yeah."

"Well, this is kind of the other side to that coin. With phantom limb pain, the brain sees the body part as still there. But in the case of body integrity identity disorder, the brain thinks the healthy limb isn't supposed to be there."

"How do you know this?" Blatch asked.

"I had a patient once who cut off their 'bad' hand."

"Jiminy Christmas," Smalls spat. "You think our arsonist might be one of these ... you know, identity disorder freaks?"

"I don't know," Deanna answered. "But arsonists are usually middle-aged white males, too."

"Are these people dangerous?" Blatch asked.

"Not typically," Deanna said. "I mean, only to themselves."

Blatch chewed his lip. "Okay. What if the perpetrator was cutting off other people's limbs? What would we be looking at then?"

Deanna crinkled her nose. "Dismemberment usually involves an act of insanity, either temporary—like a burst of rage or passion—or persistent, like full-blown psychopathy."

Blatch nodded. "Which one do you think is more likely?"

Deanna pursed her lips as she thought. "How much planning was involved in the fires?"

"Why?" Smalls asked.

"Many psychopaths start out as arsonists," Deanna explained. "They're usually pretty intelligent, so they're capable of planning intricate crimes. But other mentally ill individuals, like schizophrenics, are typically opportunistic. Like people committing crimes of passion, schizophrenics and individuals with dissociative disorders are driven by impulse. They act on the spur of the moment, not thinking about the consequences, or even about leaving incriminating evidence behind."

Smalls scowled. "How much planning does it take for some jerk to open a can of fuel, shove a wick in it, and set it on fire?"

Blatch's brow furrowed. "Not much, I'd say."

"It depends," Deanna said. "If the materials were already at hand, there's a chance a schizophrenic could pull it off. But if he had to buy the fuel and opener, and procure a lighter, it may be too much for him. And it seems unlikely, unless he got lucky, that he'd get away with the crime undetected and unhurt."

"I don't think the fires are what you call 'a crime of passion,' Dee," Smalls said. "Too many disparate addresses."

"I agree," Deanna said.

"So, if I'm hearing this right, we're most likely dealing with a psychopath?" Blatch asked.

Deanna bit her lip. "Either that, or someone who hated Gary Lee Preston enough to dismember him."

"So you don't think Preston could've done this to himself?" Smalls asked.

Deanna shook her head. "I didn't say that. But if he did suffer from body integration identity disorder, it would probably be in his records somewhere. These people can be quite persistent in their pursuits to rid themselves of their offending limbs."

Smalls winced. "I'm not too happy with myself sometimes, but I've never thought about cutting off my body parts."

"Count yourself lucky, then," Deanna said. "The ability to dismember someone usually requires a level of psychopathy stemming from severe childhood trauma."

"How severe?" Smalls asked.

"Very. And usually repeated, either from a relative or a stranger."

Deanna thought of Conrad and shook her head. "Being powerless against an abuser can invoke a deep-seated rage. A child can repress it for years. But then, slowly, it will find expression."

"Expression?" Blatch asked.

"Yes. Acting out. Often, it starts small at first. Passive-aggressive sabotage. Damaging property. Then, if the child gets away with petty crimes, he gains more confidence. He can then move on to torturing and killing small animals. Vandalism. Setting fires. Any number of other crimes. If he's successful with those, then he often graduates to burglary, rape, acts of sexual depravity, and, finally, murder."

Blatch held up a manila folder. "What you just described reads like Gary Preston's rap sheet. Except for the murder."

Smalls grunted. "Maybe he just graduated."

Deanna chewed her lip. "Or, maybe someone else just did."

Chapter Thirty-Four

HE STOOD IN THE DARKNESS for hours, silent and still.

Scissor Man did not return.

Still, as darkness descended on the day, he knew his time was running short.

Scissor Man would find him. Cut him to pieces ....

I need another sacrifice. Before it's too late.

His mind spun with panic.

Where can I turn now?

Then an idea sprouted in his mind like a disease-ridden seed.

He retrieved the knife from its hiding place, and set his plan in motion ....

Chapter Thirty-Five

SMALLS CHEWED ON A slice of pepperoni pizza and studied Deanna from across the conference table. "That's pretty impressive."

"What?" Deanna asked, wiping her greasy fingers on a paper napkin.

"How you get into the mind of a perpetrator."

Deanna shrugged. "It's not magic. It's part of my training. To be honest, the information I shared with you and Marcus came from decades of psychiatric studies conducted on actual murderers and serial killers."

Smalls stared down at his pizza. "I set my parents' yard on fire when I was a kid. You know, playing with matches."

Deanna stifled a smirk. "I don't think that makes you a psychopath, Smalls."

Deanna wasn't surprised when Smalls' leathery face registered a slight hint of relief. Most sane people worried once in a while if they were abnormal. Abnormal people, on the other hand, never seemed to question their sanity for a second, as far as Deanna knew.

"Okay, pizza party over," Blatch announced as he stepped back into the conference room. "Let's get back to work." He handed Deanna a photo. "Recognize him?"

She crinkled her nose at the image. "Who is it?"

"The morgue attendant who was working the day Gary Lee's body was processed. Does he look familiar to you?"

Deanna shook her head. "No. But with that beard and all that wild mane ... are you sure there's a person underneath all that hair?"

Blatch snatched the photo back. "Exhibit A. Useless."

Smalls grunted and picked a glob of melted mozzarella off his shirt.

"What's Exhibit B?" Deanna asked.

Blatch passed her his cellphone. "Pictures of Fenton Place, the scene of the other attempted fire."

Deanna's brow furrowed as she stared at the screen. "What am I looking at?"

"Spill patterns." Blatch turned his back to her and began taking books from a shelf just above his head. He turned around again and set the volumes on the conference table.

"What are you doing?" she asked.

"I want to try to recreate the marks left on the niche and wall at Fenton Place."

Smalls got up and hovered over Deanna. They both peered at the pictures on the cellphone.

"Sorry. What exactly are we looking for?" Deanna asked.

Blatch pointed at the screen. "See the scrape marks on the lip of the niche's ledge? To me, it looks as if the fuel can was shoved up and over it. I think the perpetrator was too short to reach the ledge without being on his tiptoes."

Blatch grabbed one of the fuel cans to demonstrate. He stood in front of the empty shelf, then bent his knees until he had to reach over his head to put the can on the shelf. "See how I'm holding it? With my thumb on the bottom of the can for support? That would explain Gary Preston's thumbprint."

Smalls snorted. "Only one problem with that theory, boy wonder. How could Preston do that if he didn't have a thumb?"

Blatch blew out an exasperated breath. "Maybe it was his *other* thumb."

"And maybe Elvis was abducted by aliens."

"Geez, Smalls!" Blatch said. "At the moment, anything *could've* happened. What I'm trying to determine is what *most likely* happened."

"Yeah, okay," Smalls conceded. "But at the angle you held the can, you'd be spilling fuel all over yourself. Lit fuel, I might add."

"If the can was full, sure," Blatch agreed. "But if he dumped some out, he could've avoided that. Look at the photo of the floor under the niche. There's a trail of drip stains, like the can was leaking, or fuel had sloshed out over the sides."

Smalls studied the photo. "Right. So the guy was on the short side, and he spilled some fuel either on purpose or by accident."

"Right," Blatch said, putting down the can. "I know it's not much, but it's a start. And I think you're right, Smalls. We can probably rule out Gary Lee Preston as the perp. At least in *this* fire."

Smalls grinned. "Just following the rule of thumb."

"Arrgh!" Blatch groaned. He reached over the table and snatched his phone from Smalls' hand. He was slipping it back into his pocket when it rang.

Blatch looked at the display. "It's Ms. Gill from Mutual Peninsular. I better take this."

"Ms. Gill?" Blatch said as he walked out of the conference room.

"Mr. Blatch? Yes, it's Aanya Gill. I saw you tried to call earlier?"

"Yes. How are you? I've been working on your case."

"Good. Any confirmation on whether Gary Lee Preston is deceased?"

Blatch leaned against the wall and chewed the cuticle of his index finger. "It's looking likely that he *is* dead, but nothing definite yet. I hope to have a solid answer for you in the next few days."

"Good. But that's not really why I'm calling. I have another case for you."

Blatch stopped leaning against the wall. "Okay."

"It's another suspicious death in your area. The woman whose remains were found in the Mercer Arms fire. Regina Krous."

"Yes. I'm familiar with the name."

"Good. I'd like you to investigate her death."

"In a way, I already am."

"I figured as much. That's why I called you. I think the cases may be related."

"How so?"

"Regina Krous also had a hundred-thousand-dollar life insurance policy issued by us."

"Huh. That's interesting."

"It gets more interesting."

"How so?"

"The beneficiary on her documents is none other than Gary Lee Preston."

Chapter Thirty-Six

"SO NOW OUR OLD PAL Gary Preston's got *two* reasons to live," Smalls said. "Or should I say two-*hundred-thousand* reasons."

"Right." Blatch drew a line connecting the initials for Regina Krous and Gary Lee Preston on the white board. "Somehow, they've got to be connected."

"How?" Deanna asked. "Lovers? Co-conspirators? You know, like Bonnie and Clyde?"

"If so, Clyde killed Bonnie for the money," Smalls said.

Blatch drew a question mark on the board. "Or a third party killed them both for a double payout."

"Must've been some party," Smalls quipped. "I wonder if they served ladyfingers."

Blatch groaned. "Is there no end to your bad jokes?"

Deanna ignored the pair, lost in her own thoughts. "Why would Regina willingly name Gary Preston as her beneficiary? She must've either cared about him or she owed him something."

"Like what?" Blatch asked.

Deanna chewed her lip. "I don't know. What if the two were lovers and Preston was trying to save her from the fire at Mercer Arms? What if he was with her the night the place burned down? Suppose he went downstairs to investigate, found the place on fire, and picked up the fuel can, leaving his thumbprint. But by then, it was already too late. The building was too engulfed in flames to go back in and rescue her."

"Huh," Smalls said. "If the place was that far ablaze, that can would be too hot to pick up, don't you think? I'd say it's more likely

Gary Lee planned the fire in order to murder Regina for the insurance payout, but somehow ended up dead himself before he could cash in."

"You may be right," Deanna said to Smalls. "Gary could've been pretending to woo Regina for the money."

Blatch drew a question mark on the board and circled it. "Either one of those scenarios would require that Gary Lee Preston still be alive."

"So we're back to square one?" Deanna asked.

"Right now, it's the only square we've got," Blatch said. "I think it's time we dig into Gary Lee's past a lot deeper than his rap sheet."

"Agreed," Deanna said.

Blatch glanced over at Smalls. "I guess that means it's time to go back to the trailer park, chief. Let's see if that nosy neighbor I talked to a few days ago knows whether Gary Lee was cheating on Tandy with Regina Krous."

Smalls didn't reply. His eyes were fixed on a distant point to his left.

"Smalls?" Blatch said a little louder. "You need a *nap* or a *hearing aid*, old man?"

Smalls turned his head and locked eyes with Blatch. "Fuck you. I was thinking about a cold case from around ten years ago."

Blatch sighed, barely managing to stop himself from rolling his eyes. "And?"

"Remember that guy who was found dead with his thumbs cut off?"

Smalls had Blatch's attention now. "No. Was it local?"

"Yeah. Some old grandpa type, as I recall. Bled out in the bathtub. Fingers chopped off with hedge clippers. Never found his thumbs."

Blatch looked over at Deanna. "What do you think? Could there be a connection?"

"Possibly. Psychopaths' first victims are often their abusers." Deanna's brow furrowed. "And similar patterns of abuse can be handed down from generation to generation."

"Like grandpa like son like grandson," Smalls said.

Deanna nodded. "Yes."

"So there may be some connection between that cold case and our thumb cutter," Blatch said to Smalls. "Good catch. Why don't you see what you can find out? In the meantime, I'm going out for a minute."

"You got a lead you're not telling us about?" Smalls said.

"Yeah. Pepperoni. It gives me heartburn." Blatch put a fist to his chest. "I'm gonna run down and get some TUMS from the shop around the corner. Anybody need anything?"

"Yeah," Smalls said. "See if they've got another one of those dancing Santa things." He turned and grinned at Deanna. "Just trying to spruce the place up for the holidays."

Deanna smirked. "Ho ho ho. How'd you get the shiner?"

"Wouldn't you like to know."

AS HE LEFT THE DRUGSTORE, Blatch popped a TUMS in his mouth. He took a step and nearly choked on the chalky lozenge.

Underneath a blue-and-white umbrella, Officer Davidson was buying a hotdog from a stand on the corner.

Blatch quickly chewed the antacid and swallowed the dusty residue.

"Those things will kill you, you know," he said as he approached Davidson.

The young cop glanced at the roll of TUMS in Blatch's hand. "Pot calling the kettle black."

Blatch laughed. "I was done in by a pepperoni pizza. What are you doing down here?"

Davidson rolled his eyes. "Traffic court."

Blatch nodded. "Ah. The good old days."

As Davidson poured ketchup over his hotdog, Blatch leaned in and whispered, "I don't mean to talk shop, but that was really something—finding Preston's thumb in that can."

Davidson opened his mouth to take a bite of the hotdog, then stopped. "Yeah. I nearly lost my breakfast burrito."

"It must've been quite a shocker."

Davidson sighed. "It was. At first, I thought it was fake—until I saw the bone sticking out." Davidson took a bite of hotdog. Ketchup dribbled onto his shirt.

Blatch handed him a napkin. "What did it look like?"

"The thumb? To tell you the truth, kind of like this hotdog." Davidson held the bit end up for Blatch's perusal. "Kind of pinkish gray."

"Really?" Blatch said. "It looked like a shriveled hotdog?"

Davidson's lip curled. "Yeah. For a guy who's been dead six months, his thumb was holding up pretty good."

Davidson took another bite of hotdog.

Blatch took another TUMS. He chewed the chalky tablet and said, "You must be feeling pretty good. Looks like your theory that Gary Preston is alive may be true."

Davidson licked ketchup from his lips and studied Blatch. "Hey, look. Don't say anything about the thumb, okay? We're holding it out of the papers. It'll be something only the killer—or the freaking amputator, or whatever you want to call the sick bastard—knows."

Blatch nodded solemnly. "No problem. I appreciate the tip."

"Sure." Davidson stuffed the rest of his hotdog into his mouth. "Freaking Castleberry," he mumbled, then dusted his hands and asked, "You got anything for me?"

Blatch shook his head. "Not much. Except the guy's probably a psychopath. It takes a lot of childhood trauma to create a head-case who gets his jollies from cutting off body parts."

"How do you know that?"

Blatch shrugged. "I watch Dexter on Netflix."

"HEY, WHERE'S THE DANCING Santa?" Smalls asked as Blatch stepped back into the conference room.

Blatch shot him a look. "You were serious?"

Smalls shrugged. "Christmas Eve's only two days away."

"It's on Saturday," Blatch corrected.

"I know."

"Today's Wednesday."

Smalls smirked. "Last time I checked it was Thursday."

Deanna shrugged. "He's right. It's Thursday."

Blatch scratched his head. "Huh. For some reason I thought it was Wednesday. Anyway, I ran into Davidson outside. From his description of the thumb, our man Preston could be alive—or he *could've been* alive—not too long ago."

"How's that?" Deanna asked.

"Let's just say the thumb looked fresh."

Blatch popped another TUMS. Smalls crinkled his nose and reached for the roll. "I'll take one of those."

Blatch handed him the antacids. "By the way, Davidson asked me—and now I'm asking you two—don't mention to anyone about him finding a thumb in the incendiary device. They're holding back that tidbit to identify the perp."

"Darn," Smalls said. "I was gonna put it in my holiday newsletter."

Deanna and Blatch shot Smalls a look.

"What?" Smalls said, holding his hands up. "You gotta admit, nothing warms the holiday cockles more than a severed thumb in a flaming fuel can."

Chapter Thirty-Seven

AS BLATCH TURNED INTO Palm Court Mobile Home Park, a tow truck pulled out with its lights flashing. Strapped to the bed was an old Dodge minivan.

Blatch turned to Smalls. "Repo or tow?"

Smalls eyed the worn-out minivan as the tow truck headed down the road to his right. "Thing probably doesn't run. It'd hardly be worth the repo fees. Still, could go either way." He turned back to face the windshield. "I take that back. It's a repo."

Blatch followed Smalls' gaze. Directly in front of them, an obese woman was standing in the middle of the road. She was bent over, hands on her knees, panting so hard it looked as if she might explode.

Smalls snorted. "She'd probably of caught the guy it if she wasn't carrying that frying pan."

Blatch shook his head. "Looks like another lovely day in the trailer-hood."

Smalls laughed. "Nice one. Oh. I meant to mention, while you were chatting it up with Davidson after lunch, Deanna and I did some research on the internet."

Blatch shot Smalls an arched eyebrow.

Smalls scowled. "What?" He folded his arms across his chest. "Okay, *Deanna* did some research. She did a google search on, 'homicide cases with missing thumbs.'"

"And?" Blatch asked.

Smalls chuckled and shook his head. "I'll be damned if it didn't come right up. The old man in that case file I was trying to think of. His name was Donald Reiner."

"Any relation to Gary Lee Preston?" Blatch asked as he drove past a trailer with a blue tarp on its roof.

"Not yet. We didn't get that far. It'd help to get a copy of the police file."

"I'll see what I can do."

"Good. You gonna ask your buddy, Davidson?"

"No. Someone else."

Smalls smirked. "What. You two break up or something?"

Blatch pulled up to the dilapidated trailer belonging to Tandy Preston's next-door neighbor and shifted into park. "No. It's just good not to wear out your welcome."

Smalls eyes the overgrown lawn littered with toys and garbage. "Or put all your rotten eggs in one basket. So who lives at this fine establishment?"

"I didn't ask her name."

"That bad, huh?"

"Mind your manners, chief. She's probably hopping mad."

"Why?"

"Why do you think? I only hope she's cooled off enough by the time she gets here that she doesn't use that frying pan on us."

Smalls winced, then glanced in the rearview mirror at the angry-faced woman stomping down the road toward them. He slunk back in his seat and said, "Great."

"I TOLD HER I'M A FRIEND of Gary's," Blatch said as he shifted into park and waited for Tandy Preston's neighbor to huff her way back to her trailer. "I said that Gary owes me money. He can owe you money, too."

"Thanks," Smalls said.

Sweaty and red-faced, the woman didn't appear too happy about the men parked in her driveway. She marched up to the driver's window, her frying pan swinging.

"What do you—" she began, as she raised the skillet to defend herself. When she recognized Blatch, she let the pan drop. "Hey. You still looking for Gary?"

"Yes," Blatch said. "Tandy's still got my IOU."

"And mine, too," Smalls said.

Blatch shot him an *I've got this* look and turned back to face the woman. "I thought maybe if I could find out more about Gary, it might help me track him down."

The woman eyed Smalls dubiously. "Who's your friend?"

"I'm Smalls," he said, and tipped his fedora.

The woman laughed. "And you admit it? Well, there's something you don't see every day. An honest man."

Blatch's face burst into a grin. He leaned toward Smalls and whispered, "Feel the burn."

Smalls sneered. "Sorry. That'd be you. I don't have any STDs."

The woman laughed, clearly dropping her defenses. "So what do you two want to know about Gary?"

"Did he have an employer?" Blatch asked.

"An employer?" she snorted and shook her head. "He never had a job *that* fancy. At least, not one *I* knew about. Gary mostly just did odd jobs around the neighborhood. Called himself a handyman. Handy. What a crock! That idiot didn't know how to do shit."

"What about a job outside the trailer park?" Blatch asked.

The woman chewed her lip while she thought. "Well, once in a while he worked for some lawn service guy. You know, one of those vans full of mowers and Mexicans."

"You remember the name of it?"

"No. Bluebells. Red Rover. Something like that."

"Right," Blatch said. "Does Gary still work for them?"

"No. Like all of Gary's so-called 'new careers,' it didn't work out for him," the woman said. She shook her head. "I do remember him coming home one day with a push mower. Probably stole it. He told me he was starting his own lawn business. I fell for it and let him mow my yard. Big mistake."

"What happened?" Smalls asked.

"He did a shitty job, that's what happened! He ran over my kids' toys and scared the dog so bad he ran away. Never saw the poor mutt again."

"That's strange," Blatch said.

"Yeah. I thought so, too," the woman said. "But what could I do?"

"You think something else could've happened to the dog?" Blatch asked.

The woman looked around, then leaned closer to the window of the sedan. "Yeah. To be honest, I think Gary killed Buster."

"Why do you think that?" Blatch asked.

"Buster wasn't the first dog to come up missing around here. And, funny thing is, Gary never had no money but he always had meat for his barbeque grill. Of course, we couldn't prove nothing. But it sure did seem like a convenient coincidence, if you know what I mean."

"I think I do," Blatch said. He turned to Smalls. "What do you think?"

"Geez," Smalls grunted. "I think I need another one of those TUMS."

Blatch turned back to face the woman. "Thank you, Ms.—you know, I don't even know your name."

The woman smiled coyly. "Friends call me Candy."

"Of course," Blatch said. "So, Candy, did Gary have any friends that you knew of?"

"No." Candy folded her arms over her bulbous belly. "Not around here, anyways. People don't take kindly to their pets being served up for dinner."

Blatch nodded thoughtfully. "That's understandable. What else do you know about Gary? Did he have any girlfriends on the side?"

Candy's eyes darted left, then right. She took a few steps closer to the sedan and leaned a forearm on the bottom of the open window. "I seen him at Walmart once with a woman. He was buying her all kinds of shit."

Blatch's eyebrow raised up an inch. "You know the woman's name?"

"Yeah. His old high-school sweetheart. Jenny Clark. We all three was in the same class."

"Were they lovers?"

Candy backed off the window and struck an indignant pose. "Why else would he be buying her all that shit? I mean, they had a whole cart full."

"What kind of shit was it?" Smalls asked.

Candy shot him a dirty look. "I don't know. I'm no busybody."

"No, of course not," Blatch said, and shot her a charming smile. "Do you know if Tandy Preston knew about Jenny?"

"No. But I do know this," Candy said. "Tandy's a sneaky devil."

"What do you mean?"

"She's all tight-lipped. Keeps to herself. Always looking over her shoulder. She acts like a woman who's got secrets, if you know what I mean."

"No," Blatch said, and prompted Candy. "What do you mean?"

"I think she's up to something. Always sneaking around like an alley cat. You know. Jumpy. Like somebody's after her."

"How long has she been like that?" Blatch asked.

"I don't know. I guess as long as I've known her."

"And how long is that?"

Candy chewed her lip. "Since I moved here. So, I guess about a year."

"Thank you, Candy," Blatch said. "You've been really helpful. Tandy's lucky to have a good neighbor like you." He reached through the window and gave her a twenty-dollar bill. "I appreciate your help. Can we keep this our little secret?"

"Sure," Candy said, snatching the money from his hand.

Blatch gave her a smile and cranked the ignition.

As he backed down the crumbling driveway, Smalls grumbled, "What'd you give her a twenty for? You just blew half the money you're making on this job. And if you ask me, that woman couldn't keep a secret if her life depended on it."

Blatch turned to him and grinned. "That's what I'm counting on."

Chapter Thirty-Eight

"WHAT ARE YOU HOPING to get out of giving Candy twenty bucks?" Smalls asked as they drove away from Palm Court Trailer Park.

"The old saying goes, you catch more flies with honey than with vinegar."

Smalls smirked. "Yeah. But unless you're an outfielder, who wants to catch flies?"

"Candy may be looking for more where that came from."

"Twenty bucks? More likely she's in on the scheme and she's ringing up her accomplices as we speak."

Blatch shook his head. "If this *is* a case of murder to commit insurance fraud, she's not in on it."

"How do you know?"

"She's too broke to even make her car payments. If Candy was involved in a fraud scheme worth a hundred grand, she'd be applying pressure for some upfront payment by now."

Smalls glanced over at Blatch. "By 'applying pressure' I assume you mean threatening to blow the scheme."

"Yeah."

"Blackmailing a murderer?" Smalls shook his head. "They'd never give her the money."

"Exactly. They'd give her an early grave instead."

Smalls' eyebrow perked up. "With an insurance payout after the funeral?"

Blatch sighed. "Let's hope it doesn't come to that."

"Think we should check Candy for priors?"

"I don't know. But if you want to run her prints, I'm sure she left some pretty good ones on the driver's door panel."

"SO WHERE DO WE GO FROM here?" Smalls asked as Blatch cruised down 1ˢᵗ Avenue South toward their office downtown.

"The way I see it, we've got two main options. Either we work the case as if Gary Lee Preston were alive and involved in insurance fraud, or we work it like he's dead and someone else is trying to frame him for it."

"I say we split the work and each take a different angle," Smalls said. "If you don't mind, I'll take the one that Gary's still alive."

Blatch shot his partner a surprised look. "Why the role reversal?"

"Because of what Deanna said," Smalls said. "You know, about abuse being handed down in families. I've already started digging into the cold case involving the guy murdered ten years ago. If you could get me the original police file, I could run down the relatives. Look for connections, if there are any."

"Okay. That makes sense," Blatch said. "I'll make a call about getting the file. Donald Reiner, right?"

"Yeah. Good thing you've still got a friend or two on the force."

Blatch stopped for a red light and shot Smalls a look. "Sometimes I think that's the only reason you chose me as a partner."

Smalls smiled, but said nothing.

Blatch scowled. "Okay, what about the other angle? Say Gary Lee's dead. That he had nothing to do with the arsons or Regina Krous' murder. If you follow the money, all roads lead back to his widow, Tandy."

"Not every widow is a murderer," Smalls said.

"Are you saying you don't think Tandy's in on it?"

Smalls shrugged. "No. If Tandy knew Gary Lee had a woman on the side, I'd say that'd be pretty good motivation to kill him."

"That's what I'm thinking," Blatch said. "And if Tandy knew about the life insurance policy on Regina Krous, she'd have even more reason to see him dead."

Smalls lifted his fedora and scratched his head. "Maybe she found out about the policy, maybe she didn't. It could just be a lucky bonus."

Blatch pursed his lips and stepped on the gas. "Maybe. But like Tandy's neighbor Candy said about her missing dog and Gary's barbeques—it seems like a 'convenient coincidence.'"

"I'll give you that," Smalls said.

Blatch blew out a breath. "What do you think about what Tandy said? You know. About getting weird calls. And the feeling like someone's creeping around, watching her."

Smalls shrugged. "Could be a total fabrication."

"I don't think so. Candy's description of Tandy seems to corroborate it."

Smalls glanced out the window at the lopsided stadium that served as home to the Tampa Bay Rays baseball team. "Say it *is* true. Who'd be harassing Tandy, and why?"

"Maybe someone who's owed money by her or Gary," Blatch answered. "They could be getting restless. The smell of money brings out the sharks—and the weirdos."

Smalls grunted. "Possibly. Or it could be Tandy trying to build an alibi. Cover her tracks."

"Ugh," Blatch sighed. "So we've basically gone round and round and come back full circle empty-handed."

"Not completely," Smalls said. "We learned from Candy that Gary Preston worked with mowers. That means he had access to small-engine fuel. And, like Deanna says, he fits the profile of most arsonists and serial killers."

"How so?" Blatch asked.

Smalls grinned. "He's like you. A middle-aged white man."

BLATCH AND SMALLS WERE a block from their office building when they noticed the police car parked on the side of the street. As they drove past, the young, blond cop inside waved.

"Davidson again," Smalls said, watching Davidson hop into his car. "It's a pretty 'convenient coincidence' how he keeps showing up, if you know what I mean."

"He works the downtown beat," Blatch said. He glanced in the rearview mirror and noticed Davidson's patrol car pull out. "Davidson's involved in the arson case. No surprise to see him around."

Blatch pulled into the parking garage. A moment later, Davidson pulled his patrol car in behind them.

"No surprise, huh?" Smalls said.

Blatch scowled. "He probably wants to ask about what we've found out so far." He pulled into a parking spot and cut the ignition. As he and Smalls climbed out of the car, Davidson pulled up behind him and rolled down his window.

"What's up, Davidson?" Blatch asked.

Davidson climbed out of the car, his face determined, yet somehow apologetic. "Mr. Blatch, I need you to come back to the station with me."

Blatch's brow furrowed. "For what?"

Davidson's jaw tensed. "For questioning. Your prints have been found at the scene of three recent fires." He lowered his eyes. "And Captain Castleberry seems to think you fit the perpetrator's profile to a tee."

Chapter Thirty-Nine

"YOU SAID YOU FOUND something under Conrad's bed?" Deanna asked as she met Cecilia Count at her front door. The woman's usually stony face was cracked with panic. She appeared utterly undone.

"Yes," Cecilia said, as if getting out the one syllable had taken all her strength and composure.

My God! What's happened? Deanna wondered.

Less than ten minutes ago, she'd received a nearly hysterical call from Cecilia asking for an emergency session with Conrad. Given the dreadful look on Cecilia's face, Deanna began to question whether she would've been better off notifying the police.

"What is it?" Deanna asked, not certain she wanted to know. *Has Conrad killed something more horrendous than birds and lizards? What could make Cecilia crack like this? A severed human head?*

"I ... I'm not sure," Cecilia stuttered. "Consuela, the maid, found something when she was cleaning Conrad's room today. Please ... just ... come with me."

Cecilia turned and headed up the gleaming staircase. When they reached Conrad's closed door, she stopped. Deanna thought she heard the woman fight back a sob.

"Is Conrad inside?" Deanna asked.

"No. He's with the au pair. He doesn't know we've discovered his ... his ...."

"I see," Deanna said. "And Consuela? Where is she?"

Cecilia shook her head. "She ran out screaming. I don't know if she'll be coming back."

Deanna took a deep breath and steadied herself as Cecilia pushed open the door to Conrad's room.

Like a cosmic finger, a ray of sun shone from the window and pointed to a spot on the floor. In the middle of an expensive Turkish rug lay a plastic grocery bag.

Deanna fought hard not to cringe. "What's in it?"

Cecilia opened her mouth to speak, then shut it again. She shook her head and turned away.

Deanna took another step toward the bag, then bent over and opened it to see what was inside.

She gasped.

Greasy wads of human hair clogged the bottom of the soggy bag. Amongst the clumps were dirty fingernail clippings.

Deanna closed her eyes and swallowed hard. Then she stood and turned to Cecilia. The woman's face was ashen. A tear dribbled down her puffy cheek.

"Tell me, Dr. Young," she asked, her voice breaking. "Is my son a monster?"

DEANNA HATED TO ADMIT it to herself, but discovering human hair and fingernails under Conrad's bed had changed the way she felt about the boy.

He was no longer merely a curious child still forming the boundaries of right and wrong.

He was a twisted soul.

And now, it was up to her to save him.

Deanna's gut boiled with concern and trepidation. Where had the hair and fingernails he was hiding come from? Had he attacked someone to get them? Some poor, helpless person?

A sudden thought chilled her to the bone. *Had Conrad gotten the hair and nails from a ... dead person?*

"Hello, Conrad," Deanna said, failing at her attempt to deliver her usual playful tone with him.

From his perch in the swing in the backyard, the boy shot her an angel's smile. But his cold blue eyes didn't match.

"Hello, Dr. Young."

Deanna hid her surprise. "How do you know I'm a doctor?"

Conrad folded his arms over his crisp, ironed shirt. "Peter told me. Is it true?"

Deanna nodded. "Yes."

Conrad scowled. "You lied to me."

"I didn't mean it as a lie. I'm still your friend. I just don't like to tell people I'm a doctor."

Conrad's angry eyes softened with curiosity. "Why not?"

Deanna shrugged and took a cautious position on the edge of the swing. "Because it makes people think I'm going to give them a shot. And that makes them scared of me. Like you are now."

Conrad locked eyes with her. "I'm not scared of you."

That makes one of us, Deanna thought. "Then how *do* you feel about me?"

"Mad!" Conrad kicked at the swing. "You and Mommy hate me. You want to send me away!"

Deanna caught the subtle change in the boy's vocabulary. The fact that Conrad had used the word Mommy instead of Mother meant one of two things. Either he was feeling vulnerable, or he was trying to manipulate her into feeling sorry for him.

The boy is already clearly on the defensive, Deanna thought. *I don't want to shut him down by backing him into a corner.*

Using a tactic she'd learned while counseling adults, Deanna quickly deflected the focus from herself and used the moment to try and uncover the true wellspring of her patient's anger.

"Do you feel mad a lot?" she asked.

Conrad eyed her curiously. "No."

It sounded like a lie, but Deanna nodded anyway. "Does Peter make you mad?"

"No!" Conrad re-folded his arms and pouted. "Peter's my friend. He reads me stories! We play games together."

Pretty defensive reaction, Deanna thought. *Interesting.* "What kind of games do you play with Peter?"

"Fun games. Games where we squish people."

Deanna kept her surprise from her face. "Oh! Does this game have a name?"

"Yes. Candy Crush."

"I thought you crunched candies in that game."

"Yeah. But we pretend they're people."

"Why?"

Conrad shrugged. "It's more funnier."

"Do you like crushing people?"

"Yeah." Conrad smiled tentatively.

His innocent appearance almost unnerved Deanna. "How many people have you crushed, Conrad?"

He giggled. "A thirteen bazillion."

Deanna nodded her head and tried to look impressed. "That's a lot!"

Conrad grinned. "Yeah!"

"After you crush the people, do you ever take pieces of them?"

Conrad looked confused. "Pieces?"

Deanna shrugged casually. "Yeah. You know. Like an eyeball. Or a finger?"

Conrad's nose crinkled. "Yuck!"

Deanna smiled. Either Conrad was innocent, or he was the best child actor she'd ever seen. She leaned a little closer to him. "You want to know a secret?"

Conrad eyed her warily. "Yeah."

"My grandmother used to carry a lock of my hair in a pendant."

"Why?"

"So she could remember me."

Conrad looked up, his blue eyes clear and calm. "What's a pendant?"

"A necklace."

"Oh."

"Do you like to keep hair, too?" Deanna asked.

Conrad shrugged and fiddled with the buttons on his shirt.

"Your Mother found some hair under your bed."

Conrad frowned and looked down at his lap. "I didn't do it."

"Do what?" Deanna prompted.

"Cut it off."

"Who cut the hair, Conrad?"

"Freddie."

"Freddie's not a cat, is he?" Deanna asked.

Conrad's eyes met her eyes for a moment. Then he jumped off the swing and ran into the house.

"WHERE DID CONRAD GO?" Deanna asked Cecilia. She was waiting in the kitchen for her as she entered the back door.

"Up to his room," Cecilia said, then blew her nose into a tissue.

Deanna took a step toward the living room. Cecilia grabbed her by the arm. "Wait. Tell me. What happened?"

"I'm not sure yet, but I think Conrad may be suffering from a dissociative disorder."

Cecilia's eyes grew wide. "What do you mean?"

"I think he may be inventing friends and projecting his acts onto them. Do you know anyone named Gustus or Robert?"

Cecilia shook her head. "No."

"I confronted him about Freddie. That's why he ran inside."

Cecilia chewed her lip. "What do we do now?"

"I'd like to continue with him. Right now. I may be on the brink of reaching him."

"Yes. Okay. But ... I guess I should tell you something." Cecilia stared at the polished white tile floor as she spoke. "I think Conrad scratched up my car. And twice now, I've woken up to find him standing by my bed, staring at me."

Deanna nodded worriedly. "Does Conrad ever come back home with his clothes dirty?"

Cecilia looked up, surprised. "I ... I don't know. I'd have to ask Consuela. But, like I said, she may not be my housekeeper anymore."

"Okay. Listen," Deanna said, taking Cecilia by the arms. "I need to go up and continue with Conrad. Could you call Consuela and ask her about his clothes? Especially if she found any blood, grease, or oil on them?"

"Yes, of course. But I—"

"I'd really like to get back to Conrad. I'll explain later."

Cecilia nodded.

Deanna sprinted up the stairs and knocked softly on the boy's bedroom door. "You okay, Conrad?"

"Yes, ma'am."

He's back to his well-mannered, controlled protocol, Deanna thought. *Shit.* "Can I come in?"

"Yes, ma'am."

Deanna opened the door. A shiver of disgust crept down her spine.

Conrad was sitting on the rug, playing with a wad of greasy hair.

He put the dirty clump up to his chin as if to make a beard, then looked up at Deanna and giggled.

Fighting back revulsion, Deanna laughed along with his macabre game. "And who are you? I'm looking for Conrad."

Conrad laughed. "I'm your grandpa. See? I've got your lock of hair." He held out the greasy handful of hair for her inspection.

"Is that really grandpa's hair?" Deanna asked, her face a mask of happy curiosity.

"No, silly!" Conrad said. "It's Freddie's!"

"Oh! Freddie's! He doesn't need his hair? Is he bald now?"

Conrad found the idea hilarious. He giggled hysterically and rolled around on the floor, oblivious to the ghoulish bag of human clippings beside him.

"Tell me more about Freddie," Deanna said. "Does he like to catch rats?"

Conrad sat up and nodded enthusiastically.

"What else does Freddie like to do?"

Conrad's face grew somber. He chewed a cherub lip for a moment, then whispered, "You promise not to tell?"

Deanna knelt on the floor. "Yes. I promise."

Conrad's face grew anxious and sad. "Freddie's a bad boy. He wants you to help."

"Help?"

Conrad nodded. "He's trying to be good. Honest, he is! But he has all these bad feelings inside him."

Deanna gave him a sympathetic smile. "I think I can help Freddie, if he really wants me to."

Conrad looked up at her with the doe-eyed face of a cherub. "Really?"

"Yes."

Deanna wondered if she was staring into the face of an angel or a demon. Still, she offered the boy the best smile she could muster and said, "Why don't you tell me more about Freddie?"

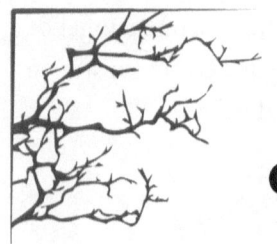

Chapter Forty

"AGAIN, I'M REALLY SORRY about this," Officer Davidson said as he led Blatch into the police station.

"Well, at least you didn't cuff me," Blatch quipped sarcastically.

Davidson winced.

Blatch softened his tone. "Look, I know you're just doing your job."

"Thanks," Davidson said, keenly aware that every cop's eyes were on Blatch as he led him through the office toward his desk.

To Blatch, most of his former colleagues appeared as surprised and concerned as he was. A couple, however, looked disconcertingly smug. Blatch knew he shouldn't take it personally. The officers' reactions simply reflected whichever side they'd been forced to choose in the latest office politics.

When Blatch himself had worked there, he hadn't taken sides. That had been part of his problem all along ....

Davidson walked behind his desk and motioned for Blatch to sit in the hard-backed chair in front of it. "Have a seat."

"Where are your Scooby snacks?" Blatch asked as they sat.

Confusion traced Davidson's brow for a second, then he shook his head. "Damned Castle—" He stopped mid syllable.

Davidson's eyes grew wide.

He stood up so fast his chair rolled across the floor and slammed into the wall behind him. "Captain Castleberry. I apprehended Blatch, sir, just as you asked."

"Apprehended?" Blatch said. "I thought I was just here for questioning."

Blatch turned in his chair to look at Castleberry. The ruddy-faced captain was standing a few feet away, arms folded over his barrel chest. His bulldog of a mug looked pleased to see him—in the same way Hannibal Lector was pleased to see Clarice.

"Appears you've gone back to your evil ways, like I knew you would," Castleberry said.

Blatch studied him with disgust. "What are you talking about?"

"Convenient memory you've got there, Blatch." Castleberry opened a manila file and read aloud from a report. "Exhibits social difficulties, impulsive behaviors, and aggression." He looked up at Blatch. "Punched your roommate in the face, did you? Then you tried to set his room on fire."

Blatch's face sagged.

He recognized the charges.

The incident had happened at a foster home when Blatch was eleven. Somehow, against policy and perhaps even against the law, Castleberry had gotten ahold of his juvenile records.

Those should've been sealed, Blatch thought. Even Deloris didn't know about the incident. She'd never asked about his past.

Blatch stood and faced down Castleberry. "That was a long time ago. What's your point?"

Castleberry grinned. "My point is, you're back to your old ways, Blatch. *You're* the arsonist setting fires in your neighborhood, and I'm going to prove it."

Blatch's eyes narrowed. "You're full of it, Castleberry."

Castleberry laughed. "Am I? Or are *you?*"

Blatch stared him down. "This is about Cathy, isn't it?"

Castleberry's grin evaporated. "We've got a witness who puts you at the scene of the Mercer Arms arson."

Blatch glanced over at Davidson. The young cop looked down at his desk, his face scarlet. Blatch shot Castleberry a sour face. "I heard the firetrucks and ran over to see if I could help."

"Sure you did, model citizen that you are." Castleberry looked down at his notes. "So how do you explain your prints at Fenton Place? We've got a witness who puts you there after the fact. A very *reliable* witness."

"I was there for the same reason you were, and you know it. I was gathering information."

"Or covering your tracks."

Castleberry shook his head. "Face it, Blatch. You meet the profile. White. Single. Somewhat intelligent. Broken home. Childhood neglect in foster homes. Prints at *all three* scenes. What's not to like?"

"*Three* scenes?" Blatch glared at Castleberry. "How do you know about the fire at Deanna Young's?"

Castleberry hesitated. His shoulders broadened and his lips slowly curled. "I didn't. I was talking about Tandy Preston's trailer fire."

Blatch bit down so hard he heard his molars squeak. Tandy's neighbor had mentioned a fire at her place, but nothing had seemed damaged when he and Smalls had searched her trailer. Was Castleberry jerking his chain?

Castleberry grinned. His eyes narrowed with mirthful menace. "Did you hear that, Davidson? I do believe Blatch here just confessed to a fourth crime scene."

The tendons in Blatch's neck twitched. "This is bullshit, and you know it."

"Bullshit, eh?" Castleberry chuckled. "Evidence of you at two scenes? Maybe you could chalk that up to coincidence. Three scenes? Pretty damned unlucky, I'd say. But *four*? Nobody's going to buy anything you have to say to explain that away, Blatch. You're guilty. And you're going down."

Chapter Forty-One

"CONSUELA TOLD ME CONRAD came home with dirty clothes a couple of times," Cecilia Count said to Deanna as she came down the stairs. "Oil and grease, but no blood."

"Thank you," Deanna said. "That may be helpful."

Deanna felt she'd made good progress with Conrad, and had decided not to push him any further today. She needed to gather more facts before she dug in deeper tomorrow.

"Where are they?" she asked Cecilia as she reached the bottom of the stairs.

"The clothes? Consuela said they weren't salvageable. She threw them away."

Deanna nodded thoughtfully. "Did she say how his clothes got dirty?"

Cecilia shook her head. "No. Probably playing with Peter in the garage. There's all kinds of paint and stuff stored in there."

"Of course," Deanna said. "Listen, if you don't mind, I'd like to speak with Peter. And see his room in the garage, if that's all right."

Cecilia's face reddened. "What's *Peter* got to do with anything?"

"Maybe nothing. But he spends time with Conrad, so I need to ask him about what they do together."

Cecilia hesitated, making Deanna wonder if the woman really wanted to help her son, or if she was worried more about her own reputation. As she was earlier, Cecilia still seemed genuinely upset.

But is she simply acting dutiful? Deanna wondered. *Is she merely 'performing' her role as mother to avoid blame? So she can say she did all she could for Conrad? To distance herself from any blame for the child's damaged mental state?*

"I don't think speaking with Peter is a good idea," Cecilia said.

Deanna took her hand. "I'm not trying to pry into your personal business. Believe me, I wouldn't ask if it weren't important."

Cecilia looked down at the floor and whispered, "Okay. I'll let him know."

PETER STEINER'S ROOM in the garage was nothing like Deanna had envisioned. It was no slave dungeon. In fact, it was actually sort of nice.

Half of the two-car garage was crammed with bicycles and shelves full of paint cans, cleaners, and typical household junk. The other half was cordoned off with white sheets. Strung up on hooks from the ceiling, they formed a makeshift fabric wall.

Peter Steiner stood in front of the fabric wall, next to two folds in the material that served as the entryway into his tent-like quarters. His scraggly, dishwater-blond hair was pulled back in a neat ponytail. His clothes, a simple button-down short-sleeved shirt and khakis, were a bit crumpled, but clean.

He looks like a typical college kid, Deanna thought.

"Dr. Young. Hallo," he said with a quick nod. "You want to speak to me?"

"Yes. Hello, Peter. I just have a few questions. Do you mind?"

His lips smiled, but his eyes seemed fearful.

Maybe he does *mind,* Deanna thought as she walked toward him.

"Okay," Peter said. "Yes. Sure. It's just ... I'm sorry. Will it take long? I'm studying for exams."

Deanna nodded. "It won't take long. May I come in?"

Peter's eyebrows raised. "Uh ... of course."

He pulled the sheet back, and Deanna stepped into a foreign, gypsy-like world. The walls were plastered with posters of international music stars. Odd electronic gizmos blinked from a bookshelf. Sandalwood mixed with the faint smell of marijuana ....

Peter quickly lit an incense stick, then offered Deanna the only chair in the room. He, in turn, sat cross-legged on his full-size bed, which took up half the tent.

"I'd like to get your opinion on Conrad," she said, cutting to the chase.

Peter's face registered relief. "My opinion? What do you mean?"

"Well, for one, do you think he's harboring pent-up emotions?"

"Of course," Peter said, as if it were both obvious and expected. "His parents are fighting each other. He is a confused and angry boy." Peter shook his head. "I went through the same thing five years ago. I tell Conrad it's not his fault. But kids ...." he looked down. "We always think it's our fault."

Peter's insight took Deanna by surprise. "What are you studying in school?"

Peter held up a book. "Psychology and criminology."

Deanna nearly blanched. "Oh. Well, good for you. I'm a psychologist, as you know."

Peter nodded, his lips pursed. "Yes."

"You seem upset by my presence in some way. Do you think Conrad doesn't need my help?"

Peter looked her in the eye. "I think he needs help, yes. That's why I am already giving it to him."

Deanna nearly gasped. "You? How? By playing video games and pretending you're killing people?"

Peter looked horrified. "No! You don't understand. It's just a ... how you say it ... *release*. I help Conrad take away his anger on pretend people. So he doesn't do it ... for real."

"That seems like an odd approach," Deanna said. "Unless .... Peter, do you think Conrad is capable of true violence?"

"Of course." Peter blew out a breath and stared at the wall. "We *all* are, if pushed hard enough."

Deanna chewed her lip. She was finding Peter's mixed messages hard to read, and his amateur methodologies of treatment disturbing. "Aren't you concerned that instead of helping Conrad vent his frustrations, your 'games' may actually be teaching him it's okay to kill people?"

Peter's proud, angry face went limp. "But he's so young, I thought—"

"Getting inside someone's head is a tricky business, Peter," Deanna said. "That's why it requires years of study and training. Above all else, we must do everything we can to avoid doing more harm than good."

Peter's face reddened, causing Deanna to wonder if he was embarrassed or angry. He blew out a tired sigh and glanced at a book on his bed. "Are we finished? I really need to study."

"Okay," Deanna said softly. "But you didn't answer my question."

Peter looked up at her sullenly. "What question?"

"Do you think Conrad is capable of violence? Torturing small animals, that kind of thing?"

Peter's eyes shifted to the floor. "I'm not the doctor. You are."

Deanna stood. "Okay. Thank you. If you need help, call me."

Peter eyed her suspiciously. "Help? Me? With what?"

"With your studies," she said. "Or anything else. Here's my number."

Deanna pulled out a business card she'd picked up at a printer's that morning. As she handed it to Peter, she noticed a bookshelf stocked with dozens of books. "Oh. You like to read, I see."

Peter nodded. "Reading is good for the mind."

Deanna smiled. "Depends on the author, doesn't it?"

Peter chewed on her comment for a moment and smiled. "I suppose there's some truth to that."

"YOU KNOW, I DIDN'T used to be like this," Cecilia said apologetically as Deanna came in from the garage. To Deanna's amazement, it was as if some evil spell had been broken. Gone was the ice-cold woman who'd tried her best to stonewall her. In her place was a needy, anxious woman Deanna barely recognized.

"I used to be fun, if you can believe that," Cecilia said, her usually angular face plumped round by tears and worry.

Deanna wasn't sure what to make of the transformation. *Is Cecilia apologizing for Peter? For Conrad? Or something she has yet to confess?*

She gave Cecilia a sympathetic smile. "You don't have to explain anything to me."

Cecilia's pleading eyes brimmed with tears. "You think Conrad's problems are because of me and Charles, don't you?"

Deanna maintained a noncommittal expression. "Divorce is hard for any child."

"It's not like I wanted—" Cecilia's voice trailed away. "You know, sometimes I think Charles only married me because our monograms matched. We're both CC ...."

That's what you're thinking about right now? Deanna thought. "Look, Mrs. Count. I'd like to see Conrad again tomorrow, if that works for you?"

Cecilia's shoulders straightened. "Oh. Of course." She wiped her tears away. "That would be excellent."

"Eleven, then?" Deanna asked.

"Yes, of course! And, well, now that we're kind of friends, why don't you call me Cissy?"

Deanna forced a smile. "That's nice," she said. But at that moment, she couldn't even imagine it.

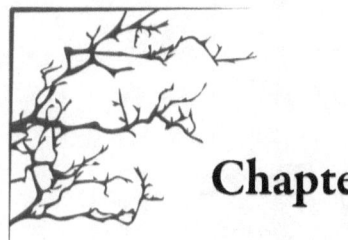

Chapter Forty-Two

A WILD, FRIGHTENED eye ogled the world through the dark slit.

The thunder-makers were back.

It would rain soon.

And then God will call.

He winced at the thought.

How can I show him I've been good?

A sudden movement outside caught his attention.

An angel landed.

It spoke in tongues as it snipped and snipped.

Suddenly, it stopped.

"Ow!" the angel cried, and sucked its thumb.

He watched the blood drip—and finally understood what he must do.

Chapter Forty-Three

"THE HOUSE CONRAD LIVES in isn't suitable for children," Deanna said to Larry over the phone. "Everything's white and pristine—like it's some kind of residential hospital. And his bedroom ... not a pillow out of place. It's so tastefully decorated any kid would hate it."

Larry chuckled. "Wait a minute. You're not blaming Conrad's behavior on the *décor*, are you?"

"Very Funny. No. I just wonder if perhaps the sterile surroundings he's forced to live in cause him to rely too heavily on his imagination for stimuli."

"Interesting," Larry said.

"And maybe that overdependence on his imagination led him to create 'pretend' friends."

"I see where you're going with this," Larry conceded. "But if Conrad really *is* doing these bad deeds and disassociating them as the work of his imaginary friends, there has to be something deeper going on—something that sparked his original need to act out."

"His parents are totally absorbed in their own problems," Deanna said. "The father is never around. And the mother—well, she might as well not be."

"What do you mean?"

"The woman is incredibly *changeable*, Larry. One minute she's a block of ice. The next she's melting with tears. I can't decide whether her cold façade is to hide her neglect, or she's simply a single mother at her wits' end, trying to cope with too many problems at once."

"Parenthood isn't for sissies," Larry said.

Deanna cringed. Larry had lost his daughter and wife in a traffic accident. "I'm sorry. I—"

"Remember, children are willful little animals," Larry said, cutting Deanna off before she went any further. He didn't need to re-open that wound today. "I say give the mother the benefit of a doubt. Offer her a soft shoulder. You never know when a stone wall is ready to crumble."

Deanna sighed. "You're right. As usual. But what about Conrad? Is he your average troubled kid simply trying to get through his parents' divorce, or is he the next Jeffrey Dahmer?"

"You don't see anything in-between?" Larry asked. "Remember what I told you?"

"Yes. People who only see things as black or white are missing their gray matter."

"Exactly. So, what have you got to prove he's a budding serial killer? You've got a dead bird, some flies minus their wings, and some hair and fingernail clippings. Is that it?"

"Yes. Unless you count the soup can."

"The what?"

"Conrad wanted to give his dad an empty soup can."

"Huh." Larry laughed. "I have to admit, that's actually a relief."

Deanna's brow furrowed. "A *relief*? You're kidding."

"No. That could explain how Conrad came across all of this stuff. He's probably been rummaging through someone's garbage."

Deanna's jaw dropped. "Wow. If you're right, that *is* a relief."

"Yes. *If* I'm right."

"I hope you are. Otherwise, you have to admit, his actions point toward an escalation of mental illness."

"Yes. I'll admit they are definitely off the scale of ordinary. But remember, at his age, he's operating more on feelings than intellect. He's more likely modeling behaviors he's picked up from others in his immediate environment."

"That's what I'm afraid of."

"What do you mean?"

"Well, you see, Blatch and Smalls are working on this case where—" Deanna's phone beeped. She checked the screen. "Looks like I've got another call coming in. It's Blatch."

Larry grinned. "Oo-la-la. Better take that one."

"Ha ha. I'll call you back and explain—"

"Give it a few days, Dee. Don't be so concerned about Conrad. Most likely he's just a young boy exploring his boundaries. Something you should take a lesson from."

Deanna frowned. "What do you mean?"

"You need to get a life, my friend. Call me if anything else develops. Talk soon!"

Larry clicked off the phone.

Deanna blew out a breath, then answered the other call. "Blatch?"

"Oh, thank God!" Blatch said.

Deanna's heart leapt in her chest. "What? What's wrong?"

"Deanna, could you ... uh ... do me a favor?"

"Of course! What do you need?"

"Could you come pick me up?"

"Sure. Is your car broken down?"

"No."

"Where are you?"

"Police headquarters. On 1st and 13th."

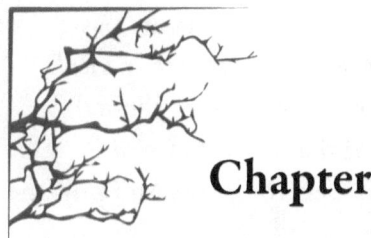

Chapter Forty-Four

BLATCH WAS STANDING with his back to a palm tree when Deanna spotted him a block from the police station, on the corner of 1ˢᵗ Avenue North and 12ᵗʰ Street. She couldn't help but notice he had a trace of that lost puppy look in his eyes when he climbed into her Corvette.

"Thanks for picking me up."

"Of course. Glad to help. But I'm curious. Why didn't you call Smalls?"

"I did. To tell him to stay away. I couldn't trust the old coot not to barge into the station and make matters ten times worse."

"Worse?" Deanna's eyes widened. "What matters? What happened?"

Blatch scowled and stared at the floorboard. "I'm a loser. That's what happened."

Deanna shoved him on the shoulder. "Cut it out. What are you talking about?"

"Castleberry."

"Your old boss?"

"That's the one." He glanced over at Deanna. "He has it out for me. And in a way, I don't blame him."

Deanna stopped at a traffic light and turned to face him. "How can you say that?"

"I'm adopted. I don't know if you knew that."

Deanna shrugged. "Being adopted doesn't make you a loser."

"No, that's not what I meant." Blatch stared out the passenger window. "It takes a lot more than that. And I've got it in spades."

Deanna stepped on the gas. "What are you talking about?"

Blatch sighed and resigned himself that the secret he'd kept for thirty years was a secret no longer. Castleberry knew. And now the world would, too.

"When I was in foster care, I roomed with this bully named Jarod. I was his punching bag for nearly a year until I learned the trade myself."

"Oh," Deanna said as she took a left onto 14thStreet.

Blatch fiddled with his seatbelt. "Anyway, after I'd learned to give back what Jarod was serving, he started picking on this other kid. He was half Jarod's size. I saw him knock the kid to the ground and something just snapped inside me. I lost it and punched Jarod in the head. He went down and didn't get up."

Deanna gasped. "He died?"

"No. But I thought he did. So ... I got some matches and lit the room we shared on fire."

Deanna swallowed hard. "Oh."

"Yeah." Blatch blew out a breath. "I wasn't there when Jarod came to. He got out in time, thank God. Long story short, I was tried as a juvenile or I'd have served time for attempted manslaughter. I did a year in juvenile detention, then I went back on the foster home circuit a couple of days after my twelfth birthday."

Deanna reached over and took Blatch's hand. "I'm sorry that happened."

Blatch's eyes met hers for second, then he looked away.

"Tell me," she asked. "What does that have to do with why you were taken to the police station?"

"Nothing," Blatch said. "Or at least, it shouldn't. But somehow, Castleberry got ahold of my sealed records. It's the perfect fuel for his campaign against me."

"What do you mean, campaign against you?"

"According to Castleberry, I fit the profile of the arsonist we're investigating. And he's right. And now, thanks to my own stupid attempt to track down the arsonist, they've got my prints at every crime scene."

Deanna's face crumpled. "Geez."

"Exactly."

Deanna offered Blatch a sympathetic smile. "But we know you're innocent. We'll figure it out."

"I hope so."

Deanna stopped at a red light, and turned to face Blatch. "Tell me. Why does Castleberry have it out for you so badly?"

"That's a story for another day. Let's just say it was about a woman we both wanted."

"And she chose you?"

"Sort of."

Deanna offered up a smile. "Wise move, if you ask me."

"Right. Always good to bet on a loser."

Deanna shook her head. "You're not a loser, Marcus. If you looked at my history, I wouldn't look that great on paper, either."

"I doubt that."

"It's true." Deanna put her hand on Blatch's arm. "I used to feel a lot like you do. But then a wise man told me, 'If you don't look good on paper, you need to read between the lines.'"

Blatch shot her a sarcastic smirk. "Jesus?"

"No." Deanna smiled. "My own personal Yoda. Larry Filbert."

Blatch let out an unconvincing laugh. Deanna turned to face the road again. As she mashed the gas pedal, she hoped in her heart everything would turn out all right in the end.

But something in her gut wouldn't let her believe it.

"THANKS AGAIN FOR EVERYTHING," Blatch said as he climbed out of Deanna's Corvette. He glanced at the bungalow he shared with his mother. "Look. Mommy left the light on for me."

Deanna smiled. "You're lucky to have Deloris. She's lovely."

"I know. I don't deserve her."

"Yes you do," Deanna said. "Marcus, what do they do with kids who are at risk of turning into criminals?"

"You mean like me, back then?"

"Yes."

Blatch blew out a breath. "If there's enough money, they get counseling. If not, they're just in for more hard knocks. Why?"

Deanna shrugged. "Just curious."

"If you think juvenile detention is easier than prison, you're mistaken." He sighed and clenched his jaw. "Prison. Geez. I'm not looking forward to that."

Deanna offered him a tight smile. "Everything's going to work out. You'll see."

"I wish I had your optimism. *And* your car."

Deanna smiled. "See you in the office tomorrow."

"Right. Goodnight, Deanna."

As Blatch turned to go inside, he saw a light go out at Old Man Melman's place next door.

He shook his head and thought, *Merry Christmas, old man. You're really gonna love this one.*

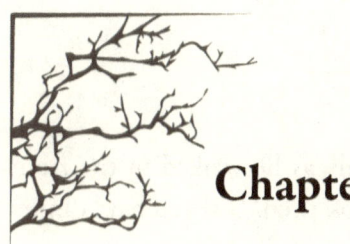

Chapter Forty-Five

BLATCH STOOD ON THE sidewalk in front of his house, trying to get his head together.

He knew Deloris was waiting for him inside. But after facing the blue-and-red flashing lights at the police station, the warm glow of the holiday lights emanating from his mother's windows seemed surreal—the mirage of an oasis he didn't deserve.

How can I face her? he wondered. *She and Dave are angels from another world. How can I tell her they saved a demon?*

His adoptive father had gone to his grave not knowing his terrible secret. But now, Deloris couldn't be spared it. He pictured the tiny woman with a big spirit and cringed. She'd dared to trust him with her heart, with her possessions, with her life ....

How will she feel when she learns the truth about me? he asked himself.

But he could no longer hide it. Fate—in the guise of Captain Castleberry—had forced his hand.

And the hand he'd been dealt was likely to get worse by the minute.

If Castleberry and his cronies managed to cook up any more "evidence" against him, Blatch knew he could be arrested for arson—maybe even murder—before the evening was through.

Nothing would please Castleberry more, he thought. *There's no way this is just going to go away.*

He set his resolve and took a step toward the front door.

Deloris deserves to know the truth. She's going to find out anyway. Better that she hears it from me.

"MARCUS," DELORIS SAID cheerily as he walked in the front door. "I'm so glad you're home. You look tired. Did you have dinner yet?"

Marcus winced. Even with the massive weight of his own problems bearing down on his shoulders, his immediate thought was of Deanna. He wondered if she'd ever received such a caring welcome from her own mother, Melody.

He doubted it. To him, it seemed life could be unfair in the cruelest of ways.

I don't deserve this, he thought. *Deanna's the one who should've gotten Dave and Deloris.*

"I'm not hungry," he said, offering his mother a distracted smile. "But thanks anyway."

"Suit yourself," she said, then put her hands on her hips. "Well? How does the place look?"

Deloris swept her hands around like Vanna White.

Marcus glanced around the living room and offered up a surprised smile. "Good thing Christmas garland isn't a snake, or I'd be a goner."

Deloris laughed, her smile sparkling like the white and silver garlands hanging from every doorframe.

Bobbles and bits of holly dotted the tables and lampshades. And a fresh, fragrant cedar tree stood by the front window, glowing with tinsel and colored lights.

"Did I overdo it?" she asked.

"Not a bit. It looks great."

Deloris beamed. "Good. I wanted the house to look festive for the party tomorrow night. I know you've been busy, so I got a head start. I saved the star for you, though. Will you put it on top of the tree?"

Deloris pressed a fragile, blown-glass ornament into Marcus' hand. It was a family heirloom, passed down in the Blatch family for generations. Her husband Dave had done the honors until his death five years ago. After that, Marcus had been handed the role, performing the task as the latest in a long line of Blatch men.

I'm an imposter, he thought as he looked at the delicate, clear-glass star shot through with stripes of gold leaf. He froze.

"What's wrong?" Deloris asked. Her delicate smile faded with concern.

"I have to tell you something first," Marcus confessed. "Then you'll have to decide whether or not you think I deserve to hang your family's Christmas star."

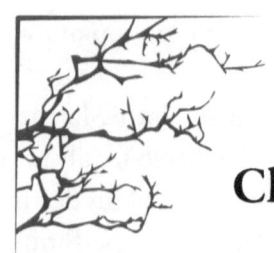

Chapter Forty-Six

MARCUS' HANDS TREMBLED as he reached above his head and into the branches of the cedar, all the way to the tender top.

He carefully placed the delicate, glass star on the green shoot sticking up toward the ceiling, then bit the tip of his tongue to keep his composure as he adjusted the star left and right at Deloris' bidding.

"A little to the right," she said.

Marcus obliged her. He'd confessed both his past and his present predicament to Deloris. She'd sat silently through it, crying softly. Marcus had been certain she would ask him to leave. But after he'd finished, she'd explained that she hadn't been crying from anger or shame, but for the childhood Marcus had been forced to endure.

When Marcus had said all he had to say, the woman who'd taken him into her life had kissed his cheek, given him a long bear hug, and whispered in his ear, "I love you, Marky."

"A little to the left," Deloris said.

Marcus shifted the star again, blinking back the tears brimming in his eyes. "How's that?"

"Perfect," she said, clasping her hands together. "Just like you."

What did I ever do to deserve you? Marcus thought, his breath catching in his throat. He turned to face her. "I love you, Mom."

"I know. Now how about some cocoa?" she asked, as if nothing had changed.

But something had changed.

Marcus had felt it deep within. A shift—an unburdening—as if he'd dropped a heavy stone he'd been carrying since birth.

He knew now that Deloris truly loved him, and she always would.

MARCUS BLEW HIS NOSE for the third time and wiped the tears from his red-rimmed eyes. He flushed the toilet as the final act to perpetuate the ruse he'd told his mother.

He hadn't wanted Deloris to see him cry.

Her unconditional love and acceptance had been both too wonderful and too terrible for him to bear. Unburdening himself of his horrible secret had freed his heart to expand, and he'd been overcome with both grief and relief.

After hanging the star, he'd excused himself calmly, then gone into the bathroom, where he broke down and sobbed.

He was finally free from the prison of his past.

The one looming in his future, however, would be another story.

But somehow, nothing seemed impossible to him anymore.

Marcus splashed some water on his face, dried his hands, and opened the bathroom door. "Is that cocoa ready yet?" he called out, then cleared his scratchy throat and padded into the kitchen.

"Almost," Deloris said, her back to him, stirring a pot on the stove. She turned and laughed. "For goodness sakes, Marcus. Take off your jacket."

Marcus blushed. He'd left his coat on, fearing Deloris would throw him out after learning what he'd done to Jarod all those years ago.

"Right, sorry," he said, then smiled and peeled the jacket off. As he lay it on the kitchen counter, a photo fell out of one of its pockets.

"Who's that?" Deloris asked.

Blatch shrugged. "No one. Just one of my cases."

Deloris smiled. "You're working on a case? See, I told you everything would work out. You're good at what you do. You're doing great, son."

Blatch fought a fresh wave of tears. His heart was still too tender to take in more love and praise.

Deloris handed her son a cup of cocoa, then turned the picture around to study it. Her brow furrowed in thought.

Blatch blew on his cocoa, then looked up, surprised to see his mother still staring at the photo. "Don't tell me you know the guy," he joked.

Deloris looked up. "Yes. I think I do."

Blatch set his mug down. "How?"

Deloris shrugged apologetically. "I didn't want to say anything. You've been so busy this week. And I wanted the yard to look good for our party."

"Mom, what are you talking about?"

She grinned coyly. "Well, this morning, I saw a lawn service crew working on the house across the street. I went over and hired them to mow our front lawn."

Blatch hid his concern. "This guy in the photo. Did he own the business?"

Deloris shook her head. "No. He was the one who mowed the lawn. I gave him a glass of water. He looked so tired and thirsty."

"Did he tell you his name?"

"No. He didn't say a word. He drank the water, then his boss saw him and yelled for him to get back to work."

"Did the boss guy say anything else?"

Deloris shook her head. "No. He wasn't very nice. Wait. He called the man Gone-bad. I think it was a nickname. A mean one."

"What did he look like?"

Deloris cocked her head. "Like this picture?"

"No." Marcus smiled patiently. "I mean, was he fat? Skinny? Tattoos?"

"Oh. Skinny. Poor thing. He was just skin and bones, really. And to tell the truth, he could've used a haircut and shave. And a good shower." Deloris crinkled her nose. "But mowing is dirty work, after all, right?"

"Right. Do you remember the name of the lawn service?"

Deloris chewed her lip. "No. I just gave him twenty dollars and wished him a happy holiday. Oh, wait. I remember the van was white. Does that help?"

"Yes. Thanks, Mom."

She grinned. "You're welcome. How's the cocoa?"

"Perfect, as always." Marcus tucked the photo back into his jacket. When he looked up, Deloris was eyeing him with concern.

"Are you going to tell me who that young man in the picture is? It's certainly not that dastardly Captain Castleberry, is it?"

"No, it's not, Mom. Someone even worse."

Her face went blank. "Oh, dear."

Marcus took his mother's hands in his. "If he comes around again, don't open the door. And call me. Immediately. Promise?"

"I promise. But why are you looking for him?"

"Because the man in the picture has a serious criminal record, Mom. His name is Gary Lee Preston."

Chapter Forty-Seven

"YOU'RE SHITTING ME," Smalls said.

"I wish I was," Blatch whispered into his phone. He glanced around the corner at Deloris. She was out of earshot, setting up a Scrabble game on the kitchen table.

"My mother ID'd him. She seemed pretty sure the man working in her yard this afternoon was Gary Lee Preston."

"Hot damned! So the bastard's alive and working for a lawn service." Smalls laughed. "Looks like our odds of getting that five grand just went up exponentially."

"It appears so."

"You don't sound too thrilled about it."

Blatch sighed. "We don't have him yet. Oddly, my mother said he went by the name 'Gone-bad.'"

Blatch grunted. "Is that supposed to be some kind of joke?"

"If it is, I'm not laughing. I'm just grateful he didn't hurt my mother."

"Oh. I didn't think about that." Smalls' tone grew serious. "Did your mother know the name of the outfit?"

"No. Only that they drive a white van."

"Geez. Seems all of 'em do. What about the neighbors? Did they know?"

Blatch sighed. "No. They're snowbirds. They won't be back for the season until after Christmas. But Deloris told me she'd keep an eye out for both the neighbors and the lawn service, in case they come back early."

"Right. Anything else?"

Blatch chewed his lip. "Oh. Yeah. Mom said the van had a yellow trailer hitched to it. It was full of mowers and rakes and stuff. If these guys work this neighborhood regularly, it shouldn't be too hard to track them down. I'll drive around tomorrow and see if I can spot them."

"Okay." Smalls hesitated. "I got some news on the Donald Reiner cold case."

Blatch nearly slapped his own forehead. "Oh, shit! I forgot about calling to get you the case file."

"Don't worry about it. I know you were a bit preoccupied, getting yourself arrested and all."

"Fuck you."

Smalls snorted. "I got my own sources down at county records. But it doesn't matter. It's a dead end. Apparently, the best suspect in the case was a kid. His name was expunged from the records because he was a juvie."

"Shit. So the lawn service is our best lead."

"Looks like. Listen, I can help you case the neighborhood tomorrow, if you want."

"Sounds good. See you around eight?"

"If that's as early as you can make it."

Smalls clicked off the phone, then walked into his dark, dreary, kitchen. He opened the freezer and stared at the frozen dinners stacked in neat rows. He picked one at random and grabbed a beer from the fridge.

After sticking the prepackaged meal into the microwave, he took a long pull on the beer and stood in the glowing light of the humming oven, watching the frozen food spin as he waited on the dinner bell.

BLATCH SAT AT THE TABLE in his mother's cheerful, green-and-white kitchen, playing Scrabble and drinking cocoa with her. He'd always been grateful to Deloris, but tonight, with all his secrets revealed and her love unchanged, he felt an ease and lightness he'd never known was possible.

"You keep daydreaming like that and I'm going to beat the pants off you," Deloris said, looking up from her playing tiles.

Unbeknownst to her, for a split second, Deloris' words had conjured up recollections of horrific childhood beatings Blatch had endured. But for the first time, he was able to push them away before they had a chance to tarnish his enjoyment of the present.

"We'll see about that," he said, and waggled his eyebrows at her. "Okay. Show me what you've got."

Deloris grinned and laid down five letter tiles on the board. "G-O-N-A-D," she said triumphantly. "Triple letter score. Eighty-five points."

Blatch whistled softly, shook his head, and wrote down her score. "Good one, Mom."

She laughed. "Thanks. I don't know why, it just came to me."

Blatch studied the board a moment and crossed her O with a few letters to spell out NOOT.

Deloris eyed him dubiously. "That's not a word."

"Sure it is. It's a nickname."

She raised a silver eyebrow. "Like Gone-bad?"

"Yes," Blatch said, and shot her a grin.

She sighed. "Okay. I'll allow it. But only because I love you."

They exchanged a smile, then Deloris looked down to study her new letter tiles.

As she concentrated on her next move, Blatch's mind ping-ponged around, struggling to reach some faraway word or forgotten connection.

Nickname.

Gone-bad.

Gone-sad.

Gone-rad.

What am I missing, here?

A sudden, sharp rap on the front door broke Marcus' train of thought. He looked over at his mother.

"You expecting a hot date?" he joked.

She laughed. "No. Are *you?*"

"I wish."

Marcus padded to the door, opened it, and nearly gasped.

Red and blue lights blared in his face.

"Marcus Blatch?" barked a cop he didn't recognize.

"Yes."

"You're under arrest."

Blatch clenched his jaw to steel himself, then turned around to be cuffed. Deloris was standing at the table, her face ashen.

"I'm sorry," he said.

She shook her head. "Nothing to be sorry about."

But there is, he thought. *I'm sorry for hurting you.*

For everything else, he wasn't sorry. He was mad.

Boiling mad.

As the cold, steel bands curled around his wrists, Blatch knew this was Castleberry, up to his dirty tricks.

The bastard had only let him go earlier today so he could arrest him at his home tonight.

For maximum humiliation.

As Blatch was led to the waiting police car, he took one last look back. Next door, Old Man Melman was sitting in his chair on the front porch, staring at him. He could deal with that. But what he saw next nearly broke his heart.

His mother was leaning against the doorframe of her open front door, crying her eyes out.

Chapter Forty-Eight

BLATCH LEANED BACK in the hard, metal chair and stared at the cup of coffee growing cold on the table in front of him. He knew the game. But this time, he was playing for the other team.

Captain Castleberry spat more words at him, making no effort to hide his contempt. "So tell me again, Blatch. What's your relationship with your fourth arson target, Deanna Young?"

Blatch kept his eyes on the coffee cup, weary of Castleberry's smug expression. "I told you. She's a business partner."

"Oh. Right." Castleberry held up Blatch's business card and read it aloud. "Blatch & Smalls Discrete Investigations." He snorted with disgust. "Funny. I don't see your *partner's* name anywhere on your card. Is that you being *discrete?* Because you sure as hell weren't with your fingerprints."

Castleberry threw a report across the table at him. "See for yourself. Your prints are plastered all over every scene except the Young case—the only one you've got half an alibi for."

He crumpled Blatch's business card and tossed it into a trash can. "Pretty shoddy work for a *so-called* PI."

Blatch willed his voice to remain calm and steady. "I told you, I'm conducting an investigation that involves those crime scenes."

"Oh yeah?" Castleberry leaned close enough to fling spittle on Blatch as he spoke. "Who's your client?"

Blatch looked up and shot Castleberry a sneer. "Revealing that wouldn't be too discrete of me, now would it?"

The smug lines on Castleberry's face sharpened cruelly. He chuckled. "Go ahead, smartass. Dig your grave a little deeper. Classic dumbass move returning to the scene of the crime. We've got your prints at Fenton Place, along with a very reliable witness who said you were photographing the spot where you started the fire. What's up with that? Taking trophies?"

Blatch sat up in his chair and glared at Castleberry. "So you found my fingerprints in a few public places. I'm sure you found a ton of others along with them." Blatch blew out an angry breath. "I think we both know why you're not bothering to follow through on any of the hundreds of other possible leads."

Tendons appeared in Castleberry's thick neck. "There's no hundreds of other leads, you arrogant shit. Not in this case." He slammed a picture of a ballpoint pen onto the table. "Remember this little baby here? It only has two prints on it. Yours and Tandy Preston's."

Fuck. How'd he get that? Blatch thought. "So?"

"Ms. Preston told us you were trying to help her get paid by Mutual Peninsular for Gary Preston's death."

Blatch shrugged. "And?"

Castleberry's eyes narrowed in his puffy cheeks. "And why the hell would you want to do that?"

"I've got a soft spot for trailers," Blatch said.

Castleberry's mouth pursed to a white line. "*I'll* tell you why, smartass. You and Tandy got some little scheme worked out, don't you? What's your cut of the hundred grand for murdering Gary Lee?"

Blatch's jaw went slack. Did Castleberry hate him so much he'd set him up for a murder charge? "You've got to be kidding. I was there when the man died. I ID'd his body."

Castleberry grinned. "Yeah. Well, ain't that mighty convenient."

Blatch ground his teeth. "You know I had nothing to do with Preston's death! I went to visit his widow on behalf of Mutual Peninsular. Your man Davidson's the one who sparked the whole investigation in the first place. If he hadn't told the press he found Gary Lee's prints on the incendiary device at the Mercer Arms arson, they never would've hired me to make sure he really was dead."

Castleberry's eyes shifted left. Blatch wasn't sure, but he thought he might've touched a nerve when he'd mentioned Davidson. Maybe the prick really *did* have it out for the kid, too.

Blatch held up his open palms. "Look, you don't believe me, one quick call to a claims adjuster named Aanya Gill will prove she hired me to interview people who might be able to bear witness that Gary Lee Preston was either truly dead or still alive."

Castleberry raised a thick eyebrow and nodded. Then he stood and walked over to the door of the interrogation room. He grabbed the handle and opened the door. Then he turned his head and winked at Blatch.

"I'll check it out," he said. "What with it being the holidays and all, I should have time to get around to making that call sometime after Christmas. In the meantime, enjoy your luxury accommodations here, compliments of the good people of Pinellas County."

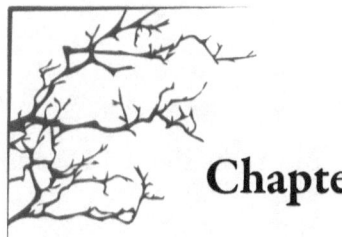

Chapter Forty-Nine

"DID THEY SET BAIL YET?" Deanna asked as she stepped into the conference room Thursday morning. Smalls was standing at the whiteboard scratching his head.

He looked away from Blatch's diagrams and doodles. "No. We should know more by noon."

"How long have you been here?"

"Since three a.m." He sighed. "I couldn't sleep anyway."

"Me either." Deanna flopped into a chair. "Why does Castleberry have it in for Marcus, anyway?"

"The usual suspects," Smalls said. "They wanted the same girl. Cathy Overton."

"I know. But there's got to be more to it than that."

Smalls sighed. "There is. But it's Blatch's secret to tell."

Deanna frowned. "So, have you had any revelations about the case?"

"A couple."

Deanna sat up. "Let's hear them."

"Okay. But I think they'd go down better with a cappuccino." He gave her a soft smile. "At least, they would for me."

Deanna nodded. "Okay. I'm on it."

The bell hanging over the entry door chimed. Deanna walked down the hall to see who it was.

Deloris Blatch stepped in and closed the door behind her.

"Good morning, Deanna," she said quietly. "What can I do to help?"

"MARCUS IS INNOCENT," Deanna said as she showed Deloris how to use the cappuccino machine.

"I know," Deloris said in her soft-spoken way. "But even if he wasn't innocent, I'd love him just the same." She placed an empty cup on the machine and shook her head softly. "I don't know if it's wrong or right, but a mother's love doesn't vary with the facts. It's an unbreakable bond."

Deloris' words were meant to be tender and reassuring, but they cut Deanna's heart like a rusty switchblade. She lost her grip on the cup in her hand. It fell to the floor and shattered.

"Oh, geez," Deanna said. "Clumsy me!"

"Don't worry. I'll get it," Deloris offered.

"No. This is my mess to clean up." Deanna grabbed a broom and dustpan. "Why don't you take Smalls the one that's done. I'll bring out the others."

Deanna watched Deloris leave the breakroom, then bent down to sweep up the pieces of the broken cup.

I guess this is a reminder our bond wasn't that unbreakable, huh Melody?

SMALLS STOOD IN FRONT of the whiteboard looking like a substitute teacher who was out of his depth. His students, Deanna and Deloris, were doing their best to help him decipher Blatch's handwriting, and to make sense of the spaghetti-like flowchart scrawled on the board.

But no one's heart seemed in it.

"I'm sorry. I just can't think straight with Marcus in jail," Deanna said. "Maybe we should wait until he's released to sort all this out."

"That may be a while," Smalls said.

"Why?" Deanna asked. "What do they have on him?"

Smalls blew out a breath and studied the marker in his hand. "More than I'd like."

"Tell us everything you know," Deanna said. She glanced over at Deloris. The elderly woman nodded.

"Okay," Smalls conceded. "But I have to warn you, it doesn't look good."

"Why?" Deloris asked.

"You're aware of his," Smalls cleared his throat, "juvenile record, right?"

Deloris nodded. "Yes. My son has told me all about his past."

Smalls' face registered both pain and relief. "Okay. Good. So, the main evidence the cops have is eyewitness testimony putting your son at all four potential arson scenes, either on or near the date they happened. They've also got fingerprints—from Fenton Place. But hell, they probably could find mine there, too, if they looked hard enough."

"Why were *you* there?" Deloris asked.

Smalls gave Deloris a tight smile. "In case you don't know, Blatch and I are working a case for Mutual Peninsular. It involves Mercer Arms and Tandy Preston's place, two of the crime scenes in question."

Deloris nodded. "So why were you at Fenton Place?"

"Well, it looked like the same MO as Mercer Arms. Blatch thought it might be the same perpetrator. We went over to have a look."

"And the fourth crime scene?" Deloris asked.

"It was Deanna's place."

Deloris' eyes grew wide with alarm. She touched Deanna's arm. "Is everything all right?"

"Yes, I'm fine, Mrs. Blatch. So is my place. No harm done."

Smalls shot Deanna a look. "Unless you count the fact she managed to throw out the evidence before we had a chance to examine it."

Deanna smiled sheepishly. "Sorry. At the time, I—"

Deloris shook her head. "No. There's no need to apologize. She turned to Smalls. "That's water under the bridge we can never get back, Mr. Smalls. What have we got that we can work with *now?*"

Deanna smiled inside, happy for Deloris' support. "Yes, Mr. Smalls. What have we got *now?*"

Smalls frowned, but he was smart enough to know he was not only outnumbered, but was also being a bit of a shit.

"We've got *your* eyewitness testimony, Mrs. Blatch," he said. "You saw Gary Lee Preston yesterday. He's our prime suspect in the fires."

"Well then, how do we catch him?" she asked matter-of-factly.

"Very carefully, I suggest," Deanna said. "From what we know about this arsonist, he's deeply disturbed, and capable of almost anything."

"Disturbed how?" Deloris asked.

"I'd rather not say," Deanna said.

Smalls cleared his throat. "Okay, so here's the plan. I'll go visit Blatch in jail, find out what else they've got on him. Deanna, you do an internet search on lawn services. See if you can turn up anything."

"I can't. I have an appointment with a client in half an hour."

"I can do it," Deloris offered.

"Go down to the station?" Smalls said. "No offense, but—"

"No. The internet search. I can do it. I saw the van. With any luck, I might be able to find a picture of it, or a logo or something to jog my memory."

Smalls frowned. "Okay. But only if you promise me you won't take it any further. If you find the company, don't call the number. Don't go to the address. Don't do *anything* but let us know. Understood?"

Deloris smiled determinedly. "Understood."

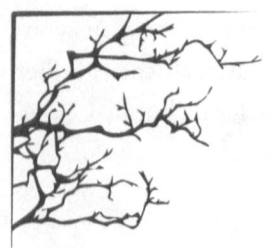

Chapter Fifty

HE'D BEEN QUICK.

And quiet.

No one had seen him.

Now he was back, safe in his nest.

He settled down to rest.

He was tired.

So tired ....

He closed his eyes.

The voices started.

Strange, unfamiliar voices.

His eyes shot open.

He grabbed his knife.

I'll be ready when they come.

He sat up and edged himself to the side of the door.

Then he waited quietly in the dark for the monsters to come.

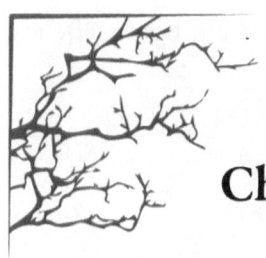

Chapter Fifty-One

DEANNA TOOK A DEEP breath, inhaling the sweet scent of fresh-cut grass. She rang the doorbell and braced herself. There was no telling what she might encounter during her next session with Conrad Count.

A short, plump, Hispanic woman answered the door.

Deanna smiled. "Consuela. You're back."

"Yes, ma'am. Come in. Mrs. Count waits for you."

She led Deanna into the kitchen, where Cecilia was fixing herself a highball. "Want one?" she asked.

"No thanks. I hope this doesn't mean you've found any more ... discoveries."

"No," she quipped. "Not unless you count finding Charles in the backyard again. Bastard. He says he's got plans to renovate the sprinkler system."

"And that's bad?" Deanna asked.

Cecilia frowned. "I don't need a man with his own plans," she hissed. "I need a man willing to follow *my* plans."

Deanna's eyebrow raised slightly. So much for the tearful woman she'd said goodbye to yesterday. Cecilia Count was apparently over her shock and making short work of rebuilding her walls. "I see Consuela is back."

"My powers of persuasion," Cecilia said sourly. "And a freaking holiday bonus."

"Where's Conrad?"

"In his room."

"Mind if I go on up?"

Cecilia opened the freezer and pulled out a gin bottle. "Be my guest."

CONRAD LOOKED UP AS Deanna opened his door.

"Hello, Dr. Young," he said woodenly, then looked down at the book in his hands.

"Hello, Conrad. What are you reading?"

"A stupid baby book." He held it up by one corner like it was covered with slime. "*Tommy's Big Red Engine*."

Deanna sat on the edge of his bed. "Why do you think it's a baby book?"

Conrad scowled and tossed the book on the floor. "The story is stupid."

"Stupid? How come?"

Conrad's blue eyes narrowed with frustration. He folded his arms across his chest. "Nobody dies. Or even gets burned up."

"Burned up?"

He shot her a look reserved for nincompoops. "Yeah. If you play with matches, you burn people up."

"Oh." Deanna nodded. "Do you play with matches?"

Conrad pouted. "Mother won't let me have any."

Deanna noted he hadn't really answered her question. Like his mother, Conrad's defenses were up. He was being especially evasive this morning, so she tried another tack.

"Does Freddie play with matches?"

"Sometimes."

"Does he burn people up?"

Conrad climbed off his bed. "I want to go out."

Deanna nodded. "Sure. It's nice and sunny. Why don't we go sit in the swing?"

"Okay."

Deanna stood, and was surprised when Conrad slipped his hand in hers and tugged her toward the door.

From the base of the stairs, Cecilia watched them descend, hand in hand. Her expression seemed to grow darker and darker with each step. When they reached the bottom, Cecilia stared at her son and said, "Conrad. Go ahead outside. I want to talk to your friend for a minute.

Conrad glared up at her. "She's *my* friend."

Cecilia blanched. "I ... I know. I want to ask her what kind of cookies she likes, so I can send some out for both of you."

"Ask Consuela. *She* knows," Conrad said. He stuck his tongue out at his mother, then stomped off toward the back door.

Cecilia watched him go, then turned sharply to face Deanna. "What do you think you're doing? Trying to be his mother?"

Deanna's mouth nearly fell open. "No. It was his idea to hold hands. He wants me to be his friend. Cecilia, that's a *good* sign."

Cecilia shook her head. "You two are ganging up against me, aren't you?"

Deanna stared at her, incredulous. "This isn't about *you*, Cecilia."

"Sure it is. Conrad thinks I'm his enemy, doesn't he?"

Deanna softened her tone and chose her words carefully. "I'm sure Conrad loves you. But he's also deeply disturbed by something. That's what I'm trying to get him to open up about. With your help, that is."

Cecilia's stony expression crumbled. She grabbed Deanna by the shoulders and sobbed into her blouse. "I'm sorry! I don't know what I'm doing. I don't know how to be a mother. *My* mother was ... was...."

Deanna patted her back. "I understand."

Cecilia pulled away sharply. "No, you don't! You don't have any idea what I've been through—the price I've paid to get where I am!"

Deanna nodded softly. "You're right. I don't. But I'm pretty sure we've both traveled down some similar roads."

Cecilia sniffed and studied Deanna's face. "What do you mean?"

"My mother wasn't the most loving person in the world either."

Cecilia stared at the floor. "My mother could cut me to pieces with a wave of her pinkie."

Deanna pursed her lips into a tight smile. "Mine, too."

Cecilia looked up, blurry-eyed. "Really?"

"Yes. I remember one time in particular," Deanna explained. "A party I'd arranged for her birthday. I'd just graduated second in my class with a doctorate in psychology. I'd also just landed a prestigious job in New York."

"What happened?" Cecilia asked, dabbing her eye with a tissue.

"We were having a celebratory toast. One of my friends asked my mother what she was most proud of about me."

Cecilia's face went blank. "What did she say?"

Deanna took a deep breath. "My mother told everyone that my greatest accomplishment was that I'd only had one cavity."

Cecilia winced. "Ouch."

"I know." Deanna laughed jadedly. "I'm sure my mother must've said something nice about me in her lifetime, but for the life of me, I can't remember what."

Cecilia chewed her lip. "I feel exactly the same. Why is that?"

Deanna shrugged. "As far as I can figure, pain sears in memories better than joy." She glanced in the direction of the back door. "That's why I'm concerned about Conrad. I think he's in pain. Divorce is especially hard on kids."

Cecilia nodded. "Well, please, go to him. Help him, Dr. Young." She grabbed Deanna's arm. "Then, maybe you can help me."

CONRAD WAS SITTING in the swing when Deanna walked into the backyard. She was a few steps away when she noticed the dingy, gray cat in the bushes nearby. It came running toward her.

"Come here, Smooches," Conrad said.

Deanna sat down on the swing beside him. "I thought the cat's name was Freddie."

Conrad looked at her sideways and giggled. "Freddie's not a cat."

"He's not?"

"No." Conrad giggled conspiratorially. "That's just what Mother thinks."

"Oh. Then who's Freddie?"

"He's—"

The back door opened. Consuela came out carrying a tray of milk and cookies. She took a step and nearly tripped. Then she looked down and screamed.

"Tata Duende!" she hollered and dropped the tray.

Milk splashed everywhere. Cookies skittered across the patio. Consuela threw her arms up and screeched, "Dios no nos falte!"

"What's goin on?" Deanna asked. "Are you okay?"

Hysterical, Consuela screamed again and ran into the house.

"Stay here," Deanna said to Conrad. She sprung from the swing and ran into the house. Consuela was yanking off her apron as if it were on fire.

Deanna grabbed her by the arms. "What is it? Tell me!"

"Tata Duende. Diablo! He come for us!" Consuela yelled. "Dios nos guarde!" She crossed herself, grabbed her purse, and ran for the front door.

"Wait!" Deanna yelled. But was met with only the slam of the door.

What the hell was all that about? Deanna wondered. She glanced around for Cecilia, then went back outside to check on Conrad.

He was next to the bushes, playing with the cat. As Deanna approached, he balled his fist and hid something behind his back.

Deanna eyed him curiously. "What've you got there?"

Conrad shrugged. "A present from Freddie."

Unnerved, Deanna grabbed Conrad by the shoulder. "No more games. I need to know right now. Who's Freddie?"

Conrad looked up at her with angelic blue eyes. "Freddie's a monster," he said. "He lives under the house."

Conrad smiled and took his hand from behind his back. "From Freddie," he said, and unfurled his fingers.

Lying in the center of his pink, little palm was a severed human thumb.

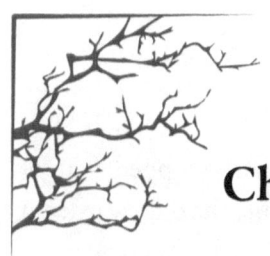

Chapter Fifty-Two

"THAT'S IT, MRS. BLATCH," the man sitting behind the desk at the bank said. "The valuation of your house is all in order. I just need your signature and we can fax the paperwork over to the clerk at the courthouse."

"Thank you, Don, for rushing this through at the holidays."

"You've been a good customer for twenty years." He leaned across the desk. "Deloris, are you absolutely sure you want to do this? I don't know your step-son—"

"Son."

"Yes, your son. But if he should skip a hearing or violate the terms of his release, you could lose your house."

"I appreciate your concern, Don. But I'm sure. After all, what good is a house if there's no one there to make it feel like home?"

Don nodded. "All right, then. Sign here."

Deloris picked up the pen and signed the document. "Now what?"

"That's it. I'll take it from here."

"Thank you so much, Don."

"You're welcome."

As Deloris stood up to leave, Don said, "You know, I still miss seeing Dave."

Deloris smiled. "Thank you. So do I. Marcus is all I have now. I'm sure you understand."

"I do. Children hold sway on us like nobody else."

Deloris nodded. "You really *do* understand."

ON HER WAY HOME FROM the bank, Deloris stopped at an office supply store to pick up printed copies of a file she'd forwarded to them—a list of lawn companies doing business in St. Petersburg.

After briefly scanning the list, she hurried home, anxious to grab a quick bite before heading back to the office to give Smalls and Deanna the list.

She pulled up in front of her house and parked, then thumbed through the list one more time to make sure she hadn't missed something.

Preoccupied, she failed to notice the white van drive by.

Fiddling with her keys as she walked up to her front door, she also failed to notice something sitting on the steps by the door.

She nearly tripped over it.

"Well, isn't that odd," she said, and picked up the empty soup can.

Chapter Fifty-Three

"THANKS FOR THE PEACHY-keen examination," Smalls said to the rubber-gloved cop who'd just frisked him in more places than he'd even thought possible. "Does this mean we're officially engaged, honeybun?"

The cop shot him a *fuck you* expression. "Second door on the left."

Smalls buttoned his pants and walked down the hall. He stopped at the second metal door he came to and turned the handle. Blatch was sitting inside at a wooden table, wearing what looked like army medical scrubs.

"Thanks for coming," Blatch said. "I'd offer you a cappuccino, but ...."

"This is bullshit," Smalls said. He drug a wooden chair up to the table across from Blatch and straddled it. "What're they holding you for this time?"

"More like *why* are they holding me."

Smalls flexed his jaw and grimaced. "This is all about Cathy, then?"

Blatch shrugged and shook his head. "It's gotta be. I'm no murderer."

Smalls' eyes narrowed. "They're charging you with *murder?*"

Blatch scowled. "Among other things."

Smalls blew out a breath. "Okay. Tell me everything you can remember about what Castleberry said to you."

"What else is there to tell? Castleberry's dug into my dirt as deep as he can go."

"How'd he know about your juvie records? You didn't even tell *me* about 'em."

"I didn't tell *anyone*, Smalls. I didn't *have* to. That's the point of being tried as a juvenile. The incident was supposed to stay sealed forever."

Smalls scowled. "Well, somebody squawked."

"Shit." Blatch hung his head. "I guess it's like they say, the past always catches up with you."

"They can't build a case on thirty-year-old ghosts. What else has Castleberry got? Any hard evidence?"

"Besides my prints all over the crime scenes?"

Smalls scowled. "Only at Fenton Place. And let me remind you, nobody got hurt there. It was Mercer Arms where Regina Krous got killed."

"But Davidson saw me at Mercer Arms. And the MO for both fires was pretty much identical. They could argue the only reason they couldn't find my prints at Mercer is because the place burned to the ground."

"Shit."

"There's more," Blatch said. "They've got the pen I used at Tandy Preston's place. Both her and my prints are on it, linking me with her."

"So?"

Blatch grimaced. "Castleberry thought it was 'pretty convenient' how I was the one who ID'd Gary Lee's body. He's holding me on murder and conspiracy to commit insurance fraud. He thinks Tandy and I cooked up some scheme to kill Gary Lee for the life insurance payout."

Smalls punched the table with his fist. "That's fucking bullshit! How'd Castleberry get the pen? Did Tandy give it to him?"

"I think so. From the sound of it, he interviewed her."

Blatch watched in silence as Smalls chewed his thoughts for a moment. Finally, his partner spoke.

"You're a skinflint, Blatch."

Blatch nearly fell over. "What?"

"No," Smalls said. "What I mean is, it's not like you to leave your pen behind."

Blatch shook his head. "How else could Castleberry have gotten it?"

"Davidson," Smalls spat. "When we did the stakeout at Tandy's. Remember? It was raining. He got in your car with us. He could've lifted the pen then."

"From the backseat?"

"Just an idea. I gotta say, I've got my doubts about that guy."

Blatch blew out a weary breath. "I hear you. But Davidson's in a tough spot, too. He's walking a tightrope trying to please a boss he hates. I know *exactly* how he feels."

"Still, I don't get it. That thing with Cathy. It happened six months ago. Why's Castleberry harassing you *now?*"

"I don't know. So he can make me spend Christmas in jail?"

"Huh," Smalls grunted. "I guess this means the party's off for to-morrow."

"No shit. Unless you feel like posting half a million bail for me."

Smalls whistled. "That's a lot of cash."

Smalls' phone pinged with a text. He glanced down at it. "Well, what do you know? Looks like there's a Santa Claus for bad boys after all."

"What are you talking about?"

Smalls looked up and grinned. "Your bail's been posted. What say we get the hell out of here?"

"But ... by who?" Blatch asked.

"By fucking Rudolph. For crying out loud, Blatch. What do you care? Let's go!"

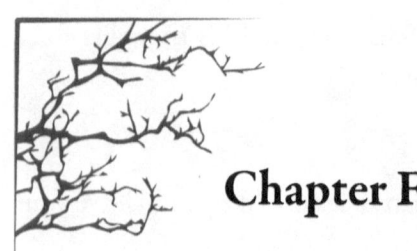

Chapter Fifty-Four

"NO, CONRAD! NO!" DEANNA screamed.

She grabbed the boy's arm and shook it until he unfurled his fist. The macabre, severed thumb fell from his small hand and landed in the grass.

Conrad stared up at her. His face a curious pout. "Why?"

Why? she thought, her mind half scrambled with fear.

Why?

Because there's a murderous psychopath under the house! He could be ... oh dear God!

He could be watching us now ....

Deanna's knees wobbled violently. She grabbed Conrad by the hand—*the same hand that had—No! Don't think about it. I need to get us both inside. Now!*

Her heart pounding in her ears, Deanna glanced around wildly, then yanked Conrad across the yard and up the back steps.

As she opened the back door, the hair on the back of her neck bristled.

Someone's watching us, she thought as she shoved Conrad inside. She ran in after him, then slammed the door and locked it.

"Stay right here," Deanna told the boy, then she ran to the front door and made sure it was locked.

"Cecilia?" she called up the stairs.

There was no reply.

Deanna hobbled on stiff legs back into the kitchen. Conrad was standing at the back door, looking out the window. She pulled him away.

"Stay beside me," she whispered.

Conrad nodded, his blue eyes reflecting her own fear.

She offered the child a weak smile, then pulled her cellphone from her purse. With Blatch in jail, she had no choice but to call Smalls. He picked up on the second ring.

"Smalls! It's Deanna!"

"Hey, Dee. Good timing. I'm just here springing Blatch from the hoosegow. Want to—"

Deanna could barely hear him over the thrumming of her pulse in her ears. "Smalls! Please, you've got to help me. I'm here at the Count place and ...."

Smalls' joking tone evaporated. "What? What's wrong?"

"Please, can you come over? We think ... that is, *I* think ...."

"Think what?" Smalls said.

"I think ... someone might be living under Cecilia Count's house."

Smalls voice faded to a dry whisper. "Where are you now?"

"Inside the house. Conrad, the child I'm counseling. He found a thumb in the backyard and said—"

"Dee, listen to me," Smalls said, his tone firm and reassuring. "Get everyone out of the house and to a safe place."

Deanna swallowed hard. "Where?"

"Somewhere out in the open."

Deanna tried to think. "I ... uh ...."

"The Publix parking lot on 38th. Can you do that?"

"Uh ... yes. I'll meet you there." Deanna hung up the phone and gasped. Cecilia was a few feet away, glaring at her from the bottom of the stairs.

"Meet who, where?" she asked angrily. "And what did you do to Consuela? I just convinced her to—"

"Be quiet," Deanna said. "Listen to me very carefully. We need to get out of this house. *Now!*"

Cecilia blanched. "What? Why?"

"I said, *now!*" Deanna reached into her purse and pulled out her Glock. She glanced around the room. "Where's Peter?"

Cecilia's eyes widened until her irises were completely rimmed in white. "Peter's at school. He has classes all day on Thursdays."

"Okay." Deanna shoved Conrad into Cecilia's arms. "Now, you both need to stay calm and quiet. We'll take your car." She pointed to the door with her gun. "Follow me."

"Oh my God!" Cecilia cried out. "Are you *kidnapping* us?"

Deanna's eyebrows shot up with surprise. "What? No! I think your life—Conrad's life—is in danger. I don't have time to explain. For once in your life, Cecilia, you need to trust someone. Trust me."

Cecilia studied her for a moment, then looked down at Conrad. He was on the verge of tears. He tugged her hand and said, "Let's go, Mommy."

Cecilia's hard expression melted. She looked up at Deanna and said, "Okay."

"KEEP AWAY FROM THE windows," Deanna warned as they inched through the living room. She edged up to the side of a front window and peeked through the blinds.

"I don't see anyone. Cecilia, do you have your car keys?"

Cecilia fished them from her purse with trembling hands. "Yes, right here."

"Good. Here's the plan. We're going to make a run for your Mercedes. Don't click the button to open the doors until we're at the car. Understood?"

Cecilia bit her lip and nodded.

"Everyone ready? Here we go."

Deanna flung open the front door and quickly surveyed the yard. She turned back to Cecilia and Conrad and whispered, "Let's go. Run!"

The three made a mad dash for the car, Cecilia pulling Conrad along by the arm. Halfway down the walkway, Conrad tripped and fell. Cecilia scooped him up, and, in a panic, clicked the key fob.

A sharp *beep* sounded. The doors to her Mercedes unlocked.

Shit, Deanna thought. She glanced back at the house. No one seemed to be chasing after them. "Take the backseat," she told Cecilia as they scrambled into the car.

"Give me the keys," Deanna said, slamming and locking her door. She turned toward the backseat and grabbed the key fob from Cecilia. "Lock your doors! Now!"

"Oh!" Cecilia gulped. As she scrambled left and right, clicking the locks in place, Conrad started to cry.

Deanna winced with worry. "Is he injured?"

Cecilia shook her head. "Just a scraped knee."

"Okay. Let's get out of here." Deanna turned to face the windshield and turned the key in the ignition.

Nothing happened.

She tried again.

The Mercedes wouldn't start.

"What's wrong with the car?" Cecilia asked. "You don't ... you don't think someone's tampered with it?"

"I don't know." Deanna pulled her cellphone from her purse. "I need to call my partners and let them know."

"Your *partners?*" Cecilia asked.

Crap, Deanna thought. "I'll explain everything right after I make my call."

A sudden, hard rapping on the car window startled Deanna so badly she nearly dropped her phone. Outside the driver's side window, a man was staring at her.

"What's Charles doing here?" Deanna asked, her voice barely audible.

"I texted him," Cecilia said.

Deanna stared at Cecilia in the rearview mirror. "I thought you hated him."

Cecilia pursed her lips. "So did I. But when I thought we might die ... I ...." She shook her head. "His face flashed before my eyes. I ...."

Charles knocked on the window again. His face was edged with impatience.

Deanna rolled the window down a crack.

"What's going on?" he demanded. He glanced back at Cecilia and Conrad. "Is everything okay?"

"Yes," Cecilia answered. "We're fine."

"Charles," Deanna interrupted, "I know this sounds strange, but I suspect a—" She glanced back at Cecilia and Conrad. "I think something may be amiss at your house."

Charles' impatient expression evaporated. "What?" He turned and took a step toward the house.

"Wait!" Deanna called out. "The situation could be dangerous!"

He turned back toward her. "Dangerous! How? Should we call the police?"

"Maybe," Deanna said. "But before we do that, I contacted two detectives I know. They'll be here any moment. I'll explain the whole situation when they get here. In the meantime, I think you should get in the car. For your own safety."

Charles stared sternly at Deanna for a moment. He pursed his lips and nodded. "I'll sit in the back with my family."

Deanna unlocked the car. Charles climbed into the backseat. Suddenly, Deanna felt her skin crawl.

Charles smelled faintly of gasoline.

Oh my God! Deanna thought. *Could he be involved in this some-how?* She kept her eyes glued on Charles as she lay down her Glock and texted Smalls.

Stuck at house. Car won't start. Hurry!

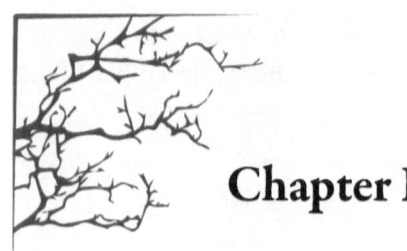

Chapter Fifty-Five

IT WAS TAKING AN ETERNITY.

While Deanna waited for Blatch and Smalls to arrive, her emotions flipped from sheer terror to abject embarrassment, then back again.

Have I overreacted? Is this all a stupid mistake? Deanna wondered as she watched the Count family in the backseat hugging each other and confessing their love for one another like passengers on a sinking ship.

There may be a psychotic killer under their house, or their child simply has an overactive imagination.

As she waffled between fear and humiliation, Deanna chewed her lip and took another glance in the rearview mirror.

Cecilia was wrapped in Charles' arms, her head on his chest.

The last words Cecilia said to Deanna echoed inside her brain.

"When I thought we might die ... his face flashed before my eyes."

Deanna cringed. She'd feared for her own life as well—and had experienced her own flashback.

The face that had appeared before Deanna's eyes had been Marcus Blatch.

Deanna shook her head softly and wondered, *Is it because I don't know many people here, or is it something more?*

A hand landed on Deanna's shoulder. She nearly jumped out of her seat.

"Sorry," Charles said. "I didn't meant to startle you."

"What is it?" Deanna asked, her voice a strange squeak.

"I was hoping you could fill me in," he said. "Cecilia said Consuela started this whole thing."

Deanna sucked in a lungful of air to calm herself, then turned to face him. "In a way, she did. She was upset by something she saw."

Deanna glanced over at Conrad. His blue eyes seemed lost in a storm of confusion. "But I think there's a lot more to the story than I can explain at the moment."

"What *can* you tell me, then?" Charles insisted, his tone growing impatient.

"Not a lot," Deanna confessed. "But I suspect someone Consuela knows may be involved in the arsons in the neighborhood."

"What?" Charles asked, his eyes wide.

"I don't want to say more—in front of Conrad," Deanna said, lowering her voice. "But he—we—found something in the backyard. Consuela saw it, too, and screamed out 'Tata Donde,' or something like that. I don't know if that's someone's name or what."

"I'll call her right now and find out," Cecilia said. She pulled out her phone, punched a number and listened for a moment. She clicked off and scowled. "No answer. Mexicans are so unreliable."

"Consuela's from Puerto Rico," Charles said. "Hold on. I'll google search Tata Donde." Charles took out his phone and scrolled through a few screens. "Here's a Tata Duende."

"Yes, I think that's it," Deanna said. "What does it say?"

Charles' brow furrowed. He shook his head. "It says here Tata Duende is the name of 'the little man of the forest.' He wears a funny hat and his feet are—" Charles looked up at Deanna. "This is nonsense!"

"Please, Mr. Count," Deanna said. "At this point, anything could be helpful."

Charles sighed and continued reading. "It says Tata Duende's feet are on backward. And he has no thumbs."

"No thumbs?" Deanna asked.

"Yes. It says he searches for bad people and takes their thumbs."

Deanna swallowed hard. "It's time I let you know then. The 'thing' we found in the backyard. It was a human thumb."

Cecilia's face collapsed. "You didn't tell me."

"I didn't want to frighten you any more than you already were," Deanna said. "But I found Conrad with the thumb ... in his hand."

Cecilia turned to her son, her face an awful blend of fear and disgust. "Conrad! Where did you find the ... the ... ?"

The boy looked up at his mother, his face stained with tears. "Freddie," he said, then flinched.

Cecilia scowled. "Don't lie to me! A cat couldn't—"

"Freddie's not a cat," Deanna said. "Isn't that right Conrad?"

The young boy bit his lip and nodded. "Freddie is Tata Duende."

Conrad's impossible confession sent fresh shivers down Deanna's spine. His desperate grasping for a fresh scapegoat made her wonder if Conrad was trying to aid the true perpetrator of these awful events.

Why? Because he was terrified.

Because the sick individual responsible for all this was close by. Dangerously close ....

Quite possibly even in the backseat.

Deanna ground her teeth and wished Smalls and Blatch would hurry up. She checked the time, then took a pensive glance in the rearview mirror at the dysfunctional family in the backseat.

Did one of you do this? she wondered.

Chapter Fifty-Six

THE CRAWLSPACE UNDER the Count house was dark and dank and smelled of death.

"Feels like I'm in a goddam coffin under here," Smalls growled as he inched his way along in the powdery sand beneath the wooden rafters.

Blatch squeezed his head and shoulders halfway into the opening of the crawlspace, then gave up. "I can't fit. You'll have to go it alone. But I'm right here." He shone his flashlight into Smalls' face.

"Great," Smalls grumbled. "Now I can't see a damned thing."

Blatch winced. "Take a minute and let your eyes adjust. And be careful!"

"Ugh! It stinks to high heaven under here," Smalls said. He moved forward another foot and gasped.

A dirty, severed eyeball stared back at him from the gloom.

"What the fuck!" he yelled, then jerked back and hit his head on a rafter. "Pull me out!"

"Shit!" Blatch yelled, and grabbed his partner by the ankles.

"Hold up!" Smalls called out. "It's a cat. A dead cat."

"Geez!" Blatch said. "You had me going!"

Suddenly, a hand landed on Blatch's shoulder. He dropped Smalls' ankles and spun around, reaching for his Glock. His hand froze.

"You scared the crap out of me!" he yelled at Deanna. "I told you to stay in the car."

Deanna winced. "I couldn't. It was just too .... I was worried about you two. Have you found anything?"

Blatch shook his head. "Just a dead cat."

"A cat? What's it look like?"

Blatch stared at her blankly. "I don't know. Why?"

Deanna shoved him on the shoulder. "Just ask Smalls."

Blatch bent over and called to Smalls through the crawlspace opening. "Smalls, what's the cat look like?"

"Dead, you ass-wipe," he hollered back. "And stinking to high heaven."

Blatch sighed and called back into the dark hole. "Can you be more specific?"

"Gray, I think. Hard to tell in this light."

"Smooches," Deanna said.

Blatch turned around and eyed her. "I don't think this is the time or the place."

"Wha?" Deanna blushed. "That's the name of the neighbor's cat. Ask Smalls to bring it out, if he can."

Blatch shook his head. "Okay. But he's not going to like it."

SMALLS DUSTED THE DIRT from his clothes and handed Blatch a bag containing the cat carcass.

"Did you find anything else under there?" Deanna asked. "Evidence someone's been under the house?"

Smalls shook his head. "Nothing."

Deanna stared at her shoes. "I'm sorry I put you up to this. I should've known better than to take the child's word so literally."

"Don't be," Smalls said. "The kid could be on to something. I think we should search the house."

Deanna looked up at Smalls, her eyes wide. "Really? I don't think the Counts will like that."

"Why not?"

Deanna chewed her lip. "To tell the truth, I think they—"

"Did you find anything?" Charles Count asked, walking swiftly up to them.

"No. Not under the house," Blatch said. "But to be sure, we'd like to search the premises. Or, if you prefer, we can have the police do it."

Charles stiffened. "No. I'd rather they stayed out of it unless absolutely necessary." He shot Deanna a hard glance. "You know, in case this turns out to be merely somebody's imagination run wild."

Chapter Fifty-Seven

LEAVING THE CONRAD house, Smalls insisted on going to one of his favorite haunts for lunch—the Dairy Inn on 9th Avenue North.

"I took one for the team crawling under that house," he said, brushing a cobweb from his shoulder. "And the place is open-air. The way I look and smell, that'll be a blessing for us all."

Deanna hadn't argued. Instead, she'd insisted on buying. They'd risked their lives to indulge her call.

A man living under the house. How stupid can I be to fall for that? she'd thought on the way to the restaurant. *I owe them a lot more than lunch.*

After ordering at the outdoor window, the three took their food to one of the handful of picnic tables scattered around the small, red-brick building.

Smalls wolfed down his chilidog in three bites. Deanna, on the other hand, was having trouble swallowing the nibble she'd taken of her plain hotdog.

"Not hungry?" Blatch asked, taking a second bite of his slaw-covered dog.

"No." Deanna winced. "I feel like a fool."

Blatch shrugged. "You made a bad call. In this business, not everything pans out."

Deanna sighed. "I guess you're right."

Smalls grunted and took a sip of coffee. "Are you absolutely sure you saw a thumb in Conrad's hand?"

"Yes. I mean, I'm pretty positive."

"Then why couldn't we find any trace of it?" Smalls asked.

Blatch leaned closer to Deanna. "You sure it wasn't maybe a shriveled-up hotdog or something?"

"A hotdog," Smalls said, shaking his head. "Classic." He got up from the table.

Deanna winced. "I ... I don't think so."

Deanna thought about Conrad's nasty habit of going through the garbage. Could the horrible thumb she saw really have been a piece of hotdog? But what about Consuela's reaction? Could Conrad have been pulling a joke on both of them?

"Sometimes our eyes can play tricks on us," Blatch said. "They make us see what we're expecting to see, instead of what's really there."

"I guess. But—"

"Hey guys! Look at this," Smalls called across the parking lot. He was standing by Blatch's sedan, the trunk open.

"What now?" Deanna asked.

"With Smalls, there's no telling." Blatch shot her a flirty smile. "Cheer up. We all make mistakes." He took the last bite of his slaw dog, dusted off his hands, and stood up.

Deanna picked up her nibbled hotdog and followed him across the lot to the sedan.

"What is it?" Deanna asked Smalls.

"Let me show you something." Smalls reached into a bag and pulled out the cat carcass. He held it up by its head.

Deanna dropped her hotdog onto the asphalt. "Geez, Smalls!"

"What?"

Blatch shot him a dirty look.

"I've got a point to this," Smalls said defensively. He pointed to a gaping hole at the base of the cat's neck. "See how evenly cut the flesh is here? Looks like a stab wound to me."

Deanna's nose crinkled. She gulped at the knot in her throat. "Why would someone do that?"

"To sever the spinal cord," Smalls said. "Paralyze the cat but keep it alive."

"For what?" Deanna asked, not really wanting to know the answer.

"What about the missing eye?" Blatch asked.

Smalls shrugged. "The creep who did this could've missed the spinal cord. The cat got away and ran under the house. Could've caught its eye on a nail or something. Like I did with my shirt." Smalls pulled at a tear in his sleeve.

"But what does all this mean?" Deanna asked.

Smalls studied her for a moment. "Looks like you weren't so wrong after all. Somebody in the near vicinity of that house is a pretty sick fucker."

"The Counts?" Deanna asked.

"Or some close neighbors," Smalls said.

Deanna shook her head. "But the search of the Counts' house didn't turn up anything."

"Sure it did," Smalls said. "I'm holding it right here."

Deanna cringed. "Please put that poor cat down."

Smalls smirked. "Yes, m'lady."

"So, where do we go from here?" Blatch asked.

Smalls lowered the cat carcass back into the bag. "Me? I'm gonna put this cat on ice and change my clothes. Meet you guys back at the office in half an hour."

"Why?" Deanna asked.

Smalls pursed his lips and looked her in the eye. "I think it's time we got serious about your psycho theory, Dee."

Chapter Fifty-Eight

THE VOICES FADED.

So did the light stabbing through the crack—a dusty, disintegrating sunbeam.

He was safe again.

Slowly, carefully, he reached for the door and pulled on the handle.

It didn't move.

Something's wrong.

He tried again. But the handle stuck tight, refusing to move.

A surge of hot panic shot through him.

They've locked me in!

His mind grew wild.

No! They can't do this to me!

Not again!

Chapter Fifty-Nine

SMALLS WAS CAPTAINING his chair at the head of the conference table. Blatch was presiding over his own, undecipherable scribbles on the whiteboard. Deanna was chewing her fingernails to the quick.

"All right, Dee," Smalls said. "It's time you told us exactly what's going on with your crazy client."

Deanna winced. "I can't. It's confidential."

Smalls scowled. "Sorry, but you've gotten us involved now. This has gone way past 'confidential.'"

Deanna shook her head. "I'm sorry, Smalls, but I can't tell you any specifics about my client. It's a breach of faith. And it's against the law."

Blatch put a hand on the conference table and leaned toward Deanna. "How about generalities, then?"

Her brow furrowed. "Like what?"

"Like what would a six-year-old boy be doing with a human thumb?" Smalls said.

Blatch shot her a pensive smile. "He's right, Deanna. You got us involved. We're part of this now."

Deanna chewed her lip. "But what if I was wrong about the thumb? What if everything was just a dumb misunderstanding?"

"What if you were *right?*" Blatch countered. "It would mean that it's very likely your client is part of the arson cases we're investigating."

"Arson and *murder*," Smalls corrected.

Blatch sighed and locked eyes with Deanna. "Those are serious criminal charges."

"Then shouldn't we be telling the police?" Deanna asked.

Blatch winced. For a myriad of reasons, he didn't want to involve the cops any more than they already were.

"Castleberry's already up Blatch's ass," Smalls said, mirroring Blatch's thoughts. "And if I heard him right, Charles Count told you *he* didn't want them involved either."

"But—" Deanna began.

"Look," Blatch said. "The police are already conducting their own investigation. And I doubt very seriously that they want to hear any clues from their primary suspect."

Deanna sighed. "You're right."

"Of course he is," Smalls said. He tapped his red pen on the conference table. "Now, I suggest we start looking at some suspects who *aren't* in this room."

ON THE LEFT SIDE OF the whiteboard, Blatch had written a list of names. They included Gary Lee Preston, Tandy Preston, Timmy Preston, Charles Count, and Cecilia Count.

"Okay, let's get Deanna up to speed on our main suspect, Gary Lee," Smalls said.

"Why is he the *main* suspect?" Deanna asked.

"He has the most to gain," Blatch said. "Two life insurance policies worth a total of two-hundred grand. One, he'd have to split with his wife. The second one, the one for Regina Krous, he could keep for himself."

"Huh," Smalls grunted. "Or, maybe the first policy is Tandy's payoff for keeping silent about the second one."

Blatch raised an eyebrow. "Good point."

Deanna shook her head. "The way I see it, Gary Lee has the most to *lose*, not gain."

"What do you mean?" Blatch asked.

"Well, he has to *die* to collect," she said. "Or fake his death and live the rest of his life on the run. To make a go of it, he'd have to leave behind everyone—including his girlfriend, Jenny. From what I know, most people can't do it. They miss their friends and family too much."

"But Gary Lee fits the profile to a tee," Blatch said. "And my own mother identified him as being alive yesterday. He works for a lawn service. That means he has easy access to the four-cycle fuel being used as incendiary devices in the arsons."

"And his thumbprint was on one of those cans," Smalls added.

"But what about the fact that his thumb was found *inside* one of the cans?" Deanna asked.

Blatch shook his head. "Maybe he cut it off himself. You know, to try and fool people into thinking he was dead."

Deanna shook her head. "I can't imagine doing such a thing." She sat back in her chair, then suddenly sat back up again. "Wait. Your mother! Did she notice whether the man she saw yesterday was missing a thumb?"

Blatch cringed. "No. I'll call her right now." He punched Deloris' number on his speed dial. She didn't answer. He clicked off and smiled sheepishly. "I forgot. I think she plays bridge today."

"Mommy leave you some supper in the oven before she left?" Smalls quipped.

"Maybe," Blatch said calmly. "You got something against love?"

Smalls' sarcastic face went scarlet. He cleared his throat. "Okay, folks. Moving on. What about Tandy and Timmy Preston? Are they mixed up in this?"

"I don't see how," Blatch said. "What good would it do either of them to start stirring up questions about whether Gary Lee was still alive or not? All it would do is slow down the death benefit payout she's been waiting on."

Smalls blew out a breath. "I agree. It doesn't make any sense for them to burn down Mercer Arms, either. Unless Tandy knew Gary Lee was the beneficiary of Regina Krous' policy."

"I doubt she did," Blatch said. "She didn't even seem aware of the policy on her own husband."

"What about Timmy, Gary's brother?" Deanna asked.

"Tandy's new boyfriend? That pothead couldn't organize a garage sale," Blatch said, "much less a conspiracy to commit murder."

"Okay. Let's put a pin in those two for now," Smalls said. "So, that leaves the Counts. Good old Charlie and CeeCee." He locked eyes with Deanna. "You think they could be up for it?"

"What would be the point?" she said. "They don't need the money. They already have everything."

"That's not what I heard," Blatch said. "Charles is tangled up in a real-estate development that's about to go bust. What if he conspired to burn down a couple of buildings so he could buy them on the cheap?"

"I don't know him that well," Deanna said. "But I just can't see him getting his hands that dirty."

"Of course not," Smalls said. "He'd hire some lowlife to do that part."

"But why involve his own family?" Deanna shook her head. "I don't buy it. Both Charles and Cecilia seemed genuinely upset today."

"Don't forget, Dee, they're both good actors," Smalls said. "Comes with the territory when you play politics."

"I agree with Deanna," Blatch said. "Charles doesn't seem like the type."

"Why not?" Smalls argued. "He fits the profile. He's white. And middle-aged."

"But he's got a family, and a damned responsible job," Blatch countered.

Smalls locked eyes with Deanna. "Being able to hold a job doesn't necessarily rule him out, does it, Dee?"

Deanna shook her head. "No, it doesn't. Still, both he and Cecilia seem too ... *fastidious* to be stabbing and torturing animals. Much less cutting off thumbs. Cecilia can't stand it if a single speck of dirt is on the floor."

Blatch sighed. "Good point. Okay, who else have we got?"

Deanna blew out a breath. "I hate to say it, but I don't think we can rule out Conrad Count."

"The kid?" Smalls asked.

"Yes."

Blatch shot her an incredulous look. "Why?"

"I'd rather not say at the moment. Can we just keep him on the B list?"

Smalls ground his teeth. "The B list? This isn't a celebrity party, Dee. Anybody else you can't tell us anything about?"

"Take it easy," Blatch said.

"Yes," Deanna said. "Conrad's au pair."

"Au pair?" Smalls said the word as if it tasted bad in his mouth. "What's her name?"

"Not her. Him. Peter Steiner."

"Peter?" Blatch said. "Hold on a second." His brow furrowed. "First Conrad. Now Peter." He looked over at Smalls. "The guy at the morgue said the assistant he fired was named Peter Conrad."

"Shit!" Smalls said.

Deanna gasped. "What?"

"The guy working at the morgue when Gary Preston died was named Peter Conrad," Blatch said. "This might sound crazy, but consider this: What if Gary Lee ran into somebody who looked like him. He gets this hair-brained idea to scam the insurance company. He gets a job at the morgue, then has his body double killed in an accident. Think about it. He'd be right there to handle the guy's dead body and fake his own death."

"But wouldn't Tandy know it wasn't him?" Deanna asked.

"Not if she was in on it," Smalls said.

"Or," Blatch said, "Gary Lee could've laid on the slab long enough for Tandy to identify him, then put his doppelganger in the body bag."

"That's cold-blooded," Smalls said. "But brilliant." He locked eyes with Deanna. "What's this au pair guy look like?"

Deanna winced. "White. European-looking, I guess. You know, slim, scraggly clothes. Long hair."

"Sounds a lot like my mother's description," Blatch said. "Which room was his?"

"None. He lives in the garage."

"Now I know why Cecilia Count didn't want us in there," Smalls said. "I figured she had a sex swing or something set up in there. Geez, Deanna. You should've told us about this guy."

"But he's too young to be Gary Lee," Deanna said. "Peter's just a college student. He can't be more than twenty-two."

"Are you saying you want us to believe this Peter Conrad name is some kind of coincidence?" Smalls said.

Deanna stood her ground. "I'm sorry, but it can't be Peter Steiner. Cecilia said he was away at school all day yesterday. He wasn't there when the thumb ... you know."

Smalls scowled. "If there really *was* a thumb."

"Hold on," Blatch said, raising his hand. "Mom—*Deloris* told me the lawn guy she saw yesterday had a nickname. Gone-bad."

"So?" Smalls said.

"Gone-bad rhymes with Conrad. She could've heard it wrong. She's getting up there in years."

Smalls frowned. "Are you saying there really *is* a guy out there named Peter Conrad?"

Blatch shook his head. "Right now, I don't know what I'm saying."

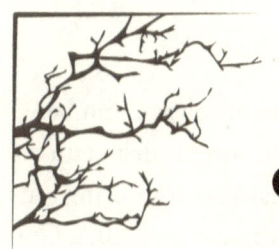

Chapter Sixty

DELORIS STOOD IN HER living room, admiring the star atop the Christmas tree. Then she closed her eyes and made a wish upon it—that everything would turn out all right for Marcus.

When she opened them, a glint of white caught her eye. She glanced out the front window just in time to see a white van with a yellow trailer go by.

"That's them!" she said aloud, and ran to the front door. She flung it open and scurried down the steps and out into the street.

The van stopped at the corner. A man started climbing out of the cab.

Deloris waved her arms at him. "Hello!" she called out.

The man turned around. Deloris recognized his face. He was the crew boss she'd seen yesterday.

"Excuse me," she said, huffing for breath as she ran up to him.

"What is it?" the man asked. "Are you all right?"

"I ... you were ... here ... yesterday," she said, gasping for air.

"Oh. Yeah. I remember. Mowed your front lawn. Did we do something wrong?"

"No!" Deloris said. "Just wanted to ... talk to Gone-bad."

"Who?"

"The young man who cut my lawn."

The man laughed. "Sorry. But 'Gone-bad,' as you call him, lived up to his name."

Deloris held her hand on a painful stitch in her side. "What do you mean?"

"He's gone."

"Gone?"

"Disappeared after lunch break yesterday."

"Oh." Deloris' face collapsed. "Do you have his phone number?"

"He didn't give me one. He was just a day laborer I picked up off the street." The man rolled his eyes. "That's what I get for paying him early. I don't think he would've had the money to eat if I hadn't. Guy looked like he was starving."

"Yes," Deloris nodded. "Right."

"What do you want with him?" the man asked. "He didn't say he'd work for you without me, did he?"

"No!" Deloris said. "Nothing like that."

"Good. These guys are always trying to undercut me." He handed her a business card. "And a lady like you. Well, you're better off not dealing with these kind of guys on your own. Who knows where they've come from."

"You're right," Deloris said, glancing at the card. "Still, if you see him, Mr. Green, could you let me know? I'll give you my phone number."

"Sure."

The man input Deloris' phone number into his phone. Deloris thanked him and limped back toward her house. As she passed Old Man Melman's place, she was surprised he wasn't out sitting on the front porch.

When she reached her front door, she was surprised again.

It was ajar.

I thought I closed it. I hope no mosquitos got in, she thought, and ambled inside.

Chapter Sixty-One

"LARRY? YOU GOT A MINUTE?" Deanna asked over the phone.

"Sure. What's up?"

Deanna padded to her couch in her bathrobe and took a sip of chardonnay. "I think this has been the longest day of my life."

"What are you talking about? Hanukkah started two days ago."

Deanna laughed. "Thanks. I needed that."

"You sound beat. What's going on? No more spider nightmares, I hope."

Deanna stopped short. "No. I hadn't even thought about them. I guess I've been so wrapped up in Conrad's case .... And now ... geez. Where do I start?"

"Don't tell me the cat dragged in more creepy gifts."

"No. I mean ... maybe. Larry, please don't think I'm crazy, but today I thought I saw Conrad playing with a human thumb."

"A real one?" Larry asked, his voice devoid of playfulness.

"Yes. A real, human thumb."

"Geez, Deanna!"

"I know. But then it disappeared."

"Disappeared?"

"Yes. Ugh. How do I explain this?" Deanna said. "You see, Conrad told me Freddie gave him the thumb."

"Freddie the cat?"

"Yes, that's what I'd thought all along. But then Conrad told me Freddie wasn't a cat, but a monster who lived under the house."

"Good grief. What did you do?"

"I had Blatch and Smalls search under the house."

Larry swallowed. "Did they find anything?"

"A dead cat."

"Hmm," Larry said. "That sounds ominous."

"No kidding. Larry, I'm afraid that Freddie might be Conrad himself—or rather, a side personality he's created to cope with his parent's divorce."

"Split personality? That's extremely rare, Dee. And even if it were the case, I doubt any child his age could cut off a grown person's thumb. That just doesn't make any sense."

Deanna sighed. "I know. But then, nothing in this whole case does."

"What do Smalls and Blatch have to say?"

"Blatch thinks there was no thumb. That it was a piece of hotdog the boy found in the garbage."

Larry sighed with relief. "I have to admit, that makes a lot more sense, given the soup can and bag of hair."

"I know."

"So, what do you want from me, Deanna?"

"Advice. Tell me Conrad isn't the next Jeffry Dahmer in training."

"Is that what you suspect?"

Deanna bit her lip. "I don't know. Sometimes I look at his angelic little face and think it's not possible. Then other times, the way he laughs when he describes 'squishing' people ...."

"But Conrad's always under supervision, isn't he?"

"He's always been in his room—or with his au pair Peter—every time I've come to see him."

"Do you suspect Peter of influencing him?"

"I don't know. Conrad spends a lot of time with him. And they play some semi-violent video games together. But it doesn't make any sense to me. Why would Peter want to get Conrad in trouble? He'd only get himself fired again."

"Again? Why was he fired before?"

Deanna hesitated. "Cecilia said the reason was unrelated to childcare. I think Peter performs other ... uh ... *household duties*, if you know what I mean."

"I see. Well, as you know, psychopaths don't typically function along normal social mores. They follow their own warped logic, which often comes across as illogical to us. Where is Peter from?"

"Somewhere in Eastern Europe, I think."

"Huh. That could make him a wild card."

Deanna frowned. "What do you mean?"

"Many of those places are desperately poor. People do whatever they must to survive. Who knows what kind of horrors Peter may have seen in his homeland. Either way, he won't have the same sensibilities as an American."

"I don't understand."

"Not everyone grows up with Mickey Mouse and apple pie."

"Oh," Deanna said. "What about Tata Duende?"

"Who?"

Deanna sighed. "Just a silly kid's story. Never mind."

Chapter Sixty-Two

DELORIS LOCKED THE door behind her and headed toward the kitchen. Halfway there, she heard something clatter to the floor somewhere in the back of the house.

"Marcus, is that you?" she called out.

No one answered.

She turned back and took a tentative step down the hall.

A dim light shone out the bottom of the bathroom door.

Deloris edged closer.

She heard the faint sound of water splashing.

She knocked on the door. "Marcus?"

"Yeah, Ma."

She felt herself relax with relief. "You okay in there?"

"Yeah. Just knocked over your hand lotion. Be out in a minute."

"Okay. I didn't see your car."

"I don't know why. It's right out front."

Silly me, Deloris thought. "Okay," she said, then padded back to the kitchen and set a kettle of water on the stove for tea.

THE WATER WAS HALFWAY to a boil when Marcus joined her in the kitchen. Concerned about her safety, he launched into a bit of a lecture. "Where were you when I came home, Mom? You know you left the door unlocked? It's not safe to do that anymore. The neighborhood's not like it used to be."

"I know," Deloris said. "I was in a hurry."

Marcus frowned. "That's no—"

"You see, I saw the van!" Deloris said, cutting him off.

"The van?"

"The lawn service van. I ran out to catch it!"

"Oh." Blatch's stern face melted. "That's great! What did you find out?"

Deloris beamed. "I got the owner's business card. It's right there." She nodded toward the counter.

Marcus picked up the card. "Greens for You," he read aloud. "Owned and operated by Kevin Green."

He smiled up at his mother. "Good work, Mom. I'm going to give him a call now."

She nodded. "I'll make some tea while you do."

Marcus dialed the number on the card. A man picked up.

"Kevin Green, speaking."

"Mr. Green? Hello. I'm Marcus Blatch. I wanted to speak to you a moment about Peter Conrad."

"Who?"

"One of your employees. My mother spoke to you a few minutes ago about him?"

"Oh. Listen. I'm afraid I don't know any more about him than what I told her. The guy only worked for me a few hours today. He took off after I paid him at lunchtime."

"Can you verify his name? Peter Conrad?"

"No. Not really. To be honest, the guy was in bad shape. I asked him his name, but his speech was pretty slurred. He muttered something that sounded like Gone-bad. That's all I got out of him. Listen, I don't normally hire guys like him. I only let him work because I felt sorry for him. He looked really down on his luck. And it's the holidays and all."

"I understand," Blatch said. "Thanks. If you see him again, would you call me directly?"

"Sure. But don't hold your breath. The way the economy is, I get so many faces through here I can't keep track."

"I understand," Blatch said. "And I don't mean to bother you, except that it's important. I'd appreciate anything you can do."

"Okay. Is he a relative of yours or something?"

"Or something," Blatch said. "Thanks again."

Blatch hung up. He set his phone down on the kitchen counter and picked up a crudely woven bracelet made of pine straw.

"What's with the bracelet?" he asked. "I found it by the front door when I came in."

"I don't know," Deloris said, looking up from pouring tea into cups. "I thought it was yours."

Chapter Sixty-Three

"SHUT THAT STUPID THING off," Blatch said as he walked into the conference room Friday morning.

Smalls smirked and flipped the off switch on the gyrating Santa. "Christmas kill-joy. So does this mean your party's off for tonight, too?"

Blatch flopped into a chair. "It's on—as long as I'm still out on bail, that is."

"Your mother is so sweet," Deanna said.

"And the lady puts her money where her mouth is," Smalls said. "Can't say I'd mortgage *my* house to bail you out."

Blatch sighed. "I'm lucky to have her. But she can't keep me out of prison if I'm convicted."

"You won't be," Deanna said, touching his arm. "Your mother was so worried about you yesterday. Did you know she came in to help us out?"

"Yes. She said you put her to work. Oh. By the way, she found the lawn service that hired Peter Conrad—or Gary Lee Preston—or whoever he is."

Deanna sat up in her chair. "She did? *And?*"

Blatch shrugged tiredly. "It was a dead end. The guy who hired him doesn't know the guy's real name, phone number, or where he lives. But I did find out one thing."

"What?"

"The guy wore gardening gloves, so neither my mother nor the man who owned the lawn service could vouch for whether he was missing a thumb."

"Shit," Smalls said.

"Exactly." Blatch drummed his nails on the table. "But it got me thinking about something last night. Deanna, what if there really was no missing thumb?"

Deanna winced. "I already admitted that I could've been mistaken."

"No," Blatch said. "I don't mean just the thumb you thought you saw. I mean all of it. Preston's thumb in the fuel can. Hell, even his *thumbprint* on the outside of the can."

"What are you saying?" Smalls asked. "That somebody's playing us?"

"*Me*," Blatch said. "They're playing *me*. Castleberry and Davidson."

"You think Davidson lied about the evidence?" Smalls asked.

"Maybe."

Smalls slapped the table with his palm. "I knew it!"

Blatch shook his head. "I've been so stupid. Remember that day Davidson was hanging around the hotdog stand on the corner by our office? He wasn't taking a break from traffic court. He was spying on me."

"How do you know that?" Deanna asked.

"Because it was Thursday."

"I'm not following you," Deanna said.

"Davidson told me he was in traffic court," Blatch said. "It's only held on Wednesdays. That's why, when I came back and talked to you guys, I thought it was Wednesday."

Smalls nodded. "I remember that."

"Davidson was lying to me," Blatch said.

"But why?" Deanna asked.

"I think he and Castleberry are trying to frame me somehow for this whole mess. Think about it. None of this thumb business was reported in the papers."

"It was for Mercer Arms," Smalls said.

"Yes. The first incident," Blatch admitted. "But it was quickly retracted."

"A mistake?" Deanna asked.

Blatch scowled. "Or a miscommunication between Castleberry and Davidson with their dirty little scheme."

Smalls whistled long and low. "Hold on, Blatch. You're talking pretty high-level conspiracy here."

"High-level, maybe. But not widespread." Blatch shook his head. "I'd lay money down it's just between those two. We need to check under every rock and figure out how they're connected."

Deanna shot Blatch a worried look. "Could Castleberry really hate you that badly for taking Cathy from him?"

"Yes, I think he could." Blatch looked down at the floor. "There's something I haven't told either one of you."

Deanna and Smalls exchanged glances. Blatch took a deep breath and continued.

"Cathy was killed in the same accident Gary Lee Preston was. I told you both it was a traffic accident. But it wasn't. It was a robbery. A liquor store."

Blatch winced as he recalled the event. "Cathy was working the beat. She answered the silent alarm. She got there just as Preston ran out of the store. She fired at him. Shot him in the spleen. He shot her back. Hit her in the neck."

Smalls and Deanna sat listening, silent and spellbound. Blatch sucked in a shaky breath.

"And me? I was off duty. In the wrong place at the wrong time. I just stood there, watching the whole thing. It was all over before I even thought to draw my weapon. They both bled out in the street."

He crumpled into a chair. "I failed Cathy. I got her killed."

Deanna reached toward Blatch. He pulled away. She glanced over at Smalls. He shook his head softly at her.

"I ... I'll make us some coffee," she said, and stood up to leave. Her cellphone rang. She grabbed it, smiled apologetically, and tip-toed out of the conference room.

"Hello? Dr. Young speaking."

"Dr. Young. It's Charles Count."

"Yes, Mr. Count. What can I do—"

"Please. Come over right away. We found something ...."

"What is it?"

"I can't explain on the phone. And please, bring your detective friends with you, if you can."

Chapter Sixty-Four

"I DON'T KNOW WHY I didn't think of it before," Charles said.

"Maybe because you would've had to confess to installing it," Cecilia said sharply. She glared at Charles. "What were you doing hiding a camera in the yard? Spying on me?"

Charles blew out a frustrated breath. "I was only thinking about your safety."

"Never mind all that right now," Deanna said. "What's on the surveillance tape?"

"It's kind of grainy, but I felt like it might be important," Charles said.

Smalls, Blatch, and Deanna squeezed onto a prim, white sofa and peered with anticipation at the huge TV monitor on the wall. A fuzzy, black-and-white video came on, showing the Counts' side yard at night.

The side door to the garage opened. Peter Steiner, the au pair, stumbled out. He was smoking a joint.

Smalls groaned. "Look, Mr. Count, we don't get—"

"Wait," Charles said. "That's not it."

Peter took a final hit off the joint and threw the stub in the grass. He went back inside and closed the door.

"I still don't—" Smalls began.

"Wait for it," Charles whispered. "Here it comes."

Suddenly, a boney hand jutted out from the bushes.

The hand grabbed the still-glowing marijuana stub and disappeared back into the bushes.

The hand was missing its thumb.

"Christ!" Smalls hissed. "When was this taken?"

"Night before last," Charles said.

"Shit. He could be anywhere by now," Blatch said.

"I've already checked the grounds and spoken with Peter about it," Charles said. "He doesn't know anything."

"What about Consuela?" Deanna asked, glancing over at Cecilia.

"She's still not answering her phone," Cecilia said. "I doubt we'll see her again."

"Do you use a lawn service?" Blatch asked.

"Well, yes," Cecilia said. "But only since Charles ...." She glanced at her husband, then looked down. "Only for a few months."

"What's the name of the company?" Blatch asked.

"Green man, or something like that," Cecilia said. "Why?"

"Just an idea I'm working on," Blatch said.

"Well, the lawn service won't be coming back, either, if that's what you're worried about," Charles said. "I'm moving back in. I'll be doing it myself from now on."

He gave Cecilia a tentative smile.

Cecilia smiled back at him, then glanced over at Deanna and shrugged. "The house was falling apart without him."

Deanna smiled and nodded.

Suddenly, the lights in the house blinked off, then came back on again. The TV monitor buzzed and faded to black.

Charles blew out a breath. "Speak of the devil."

Cecilia scowled. "It's that damned breaker box again."

"Where's Conrad?" Deanna asked.

Cecilia's face went blank. "Oh. I don't know. Upstairs, I think."

DEANNA WAS RELIEVED to find Conrad up in his bedroom, reading.

"Hi there," she said as she stuck her head into the room.

"Hello, Dr. Young," he said without looking up from his book.

"You really like to read, I see."

Conrad sighed. "Mother likes me to read."

"You know, I think I saw your friend today."

Conrad looked up, his face curious. "Peter?"

"No. Tata Duende."

Conrad stiffened for a moment, then went back to pretending to read. "Mother says Tata Duende's just a pretending."

"Maybe. But sometimes, people like to pretend—to be a pretending."

Conrad looked up at her with interest. "What do you mean?"

"Like at Halloween. People dress up and pretend to be someone else."

"Oh. Mother doesn't believe in Halloween."

"Well, I do." Deanna sat on the edge of the bed. "How about you?"

Conrad bit his lip, then nodded.

"Do you like to pretend to be someone else?" Deanna asked.

"Sometimes."

"Like who?"

Conrad smiled shyly. "Like Freddie."

"Is Freddie pretending to be Tata Duende?"

Conrad nodded.

"And you like to pretend to be Freddie?"

Conrad nodded again.

"Why?"

Conrad looked up at Deanna, his blue eyes a sea of unfulfilled wishes. "Because."

"Because why?" Deanna asked.

"Because Freddie can do whatever he wants. He's free."

AS DEANNA STARTED DOWN the stairs, she squinted against the white glare coming from the white lights on the white, perfectly conical, artificial Christmas tree in the corner of the white living room. As she reached the bottom of the stairs, she saw her partners talking with the Counts by the front door.

Blatch caught sight of Deanna. He looked up and smiled. "There she is," he said, then turned back to Cecilia and Charles. "I think it would be best if you all stayed in a hotel for the next few days."

"It's Christmas Eve," Cecilia argued. "We have dinner plans tonight, and ...." She looked at Charles.

He shook his head. "We couldn't find a hotel now if we wanted to, Mr. Blatch. Anyway, I'll stay here tonight—to make sure everything's all right."

Blatch nodded.

"Keep your doors and windows locked," Smalls cautioned, buttoning his jacket. "There's no telling if or when the ... uh ... *person* we saw on the video will come back."

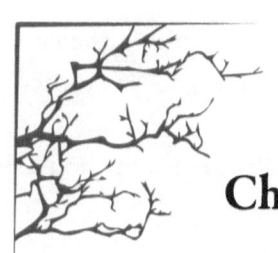

Chapter Sixty-Five

"GEEZ. THERE REALLY *is* someone out there without a thumb," Deanna said as the three climbed into Blatch's sedan. "I have to admit, part of me is relieved that I'm not losing my marbles."

"And the other part?" Smalls quipped.

Deanna winced. "Scared out of my mind, if you must know." She shut the car door and turned to Blatch. "Come on. Let's get out of here."

While Blatch cranked the engine, Deanna glanced over at the Count house. From the outside, it was a picture of gleaming, white perfection. But what lurked nearby—or within—was dark. And dirty.

And totally unclean.

"That place gives me the creeps," Smalls said from the backseat.

"Me, too," Deanna said. "It's so ... *cold.*"

Smalls grunted. "There's no room to breathe in there."

Deanna sighed and thought of Conrad's mournful expression. "I know someone else who feels the same way."

Smalls leaned toward the front seat and tapped Blatch on the shoulder. "I guess that video kills your 'no thumb' conspiracy with Castleberry and Davidson."

"Maybe," Blatch said. "Maybe not. I still feel like they're involved in this somehow."

Smalls groaned. "Geez, Blatch. You and Castleberry have been locked in a pissing match for ages. Can't you just let it go for one night? It's Christmas Eve, for crying out loud."

Blatch shot Smalls an angry look in the rearview mirror, then his face softened. "You're right. Let's have some fun tonight." He turned to Deanna. "Party at my place in an hour."

"I need to change clothes," Deanna said. "Drop me at my house? I walked to the office today."

"Sure." Blatch glanced back at Smalls. "You, too?"

"You kidding?" Smalls sneered. "I drove. Pardon me for getting all religious on you, but if God had intended us to walk, he wouldn't have invented tires."

Chapter Sixty-Six

"ARE YOU SURE YOU WANT to move back in?" Cecilia asked Charles. They were standing in the open doorway, watching Blatch's sedan pull away.

Charles turned to his wife. "Yes. If it's okay with you. I only have one condition."

Cecilia looked up at him. "Condition?"

"Yes. That you give us a fighting chance. I want Peter gone."

Cecilia pursed her red lips for a moment, then nodded. "Okay."

Charles offered her a tight smile. "Should *I* tell him, or should you?"

"I'll tell him," she said, then the white lights on the white Christmas tree blinked out.

Charles rolled his eyes and sighed. "I'll take care of it."

"Thanks."

Cecilia watched as he walked over and knelt down in front of the gifts under the tree. He rummaged around for a moment and called out, "Good grief! There must be ten strands of lights plugged into one socket!"

Cecilia winced. "Consuela."

"Figures." He got up off his knees. "I think there's some extension cords around here somewhere."

Cecilia winced again. "I think Peter's using them all in his ... in the garage."

Charles shook his head. "Geez! It's a wonder this place hasn't burned to the ground! I'll go check out in the toolshed. I think I left some in there before I ...." He looked up at Cecilia.

She smiled apologetically.

"Never mind," Charles said, and smiled back.

"HERE THEY ARE," CHARLES said as he came back in the front door, three green extension cords draped in his arms.

Cecilia bit her lip and shot him a dubious look.

"What?" Charles asked. "The color? Sorry they're not white."

"No," Cecilia said. "It's not that. It's Peter. He's gone."

"Gone?"

"Yes. He left a note on his bed saying he was spending the holidays with friends. He ... he asked me to give this present to Conrad." She held up a gift bag.

Charles frowned at it. "What is it?"

Cecilia shrugged. "I don't know."

Charles gave her a look. "Come on. You know."

Cecilia grinned guiltily. "It's a book. I'll give it to him now."

"No. Let's wait until morning," Charles said, dropping the cords by the tree. "We have the party to get to."

"Me, too?" Conrad called down from the top of the stairs.

Charles looked up and smiled at his son. "Yes, of course," he said. "You, too."

Chapter Sixty-Seven

DEANNA SLIPPED ON HER red leather pumps and opened the door. A gust of wind blew her blonde locks into her eyes.

"Darn. It looks like rain," she muttered. She'd planned to walk over to Blatch's party. *Just as well*, she thought. *I forgot to give the Counts their Christmas gift.*

She reshuffled the gift bag and bottle of wine in her hands, freeing up her right hand to grab an umbrella. She studied the odd assortment crammed in the umbrella stand by the door, a legacy from her hoarding mother.

Deanna picked one that matched her holiday dress, then scampered out the back door to the garage. She slipped into the Corvette, then lay the umbrella, gift bag, and bottle of wine on the passenger seat.

One quick stop, then off to the party, she thought as she cranked the ignition and pulled out into the alley.

She maneuvered the Corvette slowly down the brick streets, savoring the neighbors' sparkling holiday-light displays. When she got to the Count house, she was surprised to find the gate open and not a single light burning. Not even the Christmas tree.

Deanna shifted into first and started to drive away, then changed her mind.

Might as well get it over with.

She parked, grabbed her umbrella and the gift bag, and hurried through the gate. When she reached the front steps, she leaned over to set down the gift bag by the door.

That's when she felt it.

A sudden, odd jerk of her neck.
The ground came rushing up at her.
The world went dark.
And her red umbrella rolled slowly away on the wet lawn.

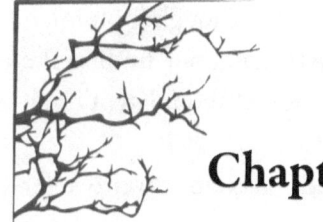

Chapter Sixty-Eight

"GOOD EVENING, MRS. Blatch," Smalls said as he folded his umbrella outside her front door. "Thank you for the invitation."

Deloris smiled at Smalls' formality as he tipped his hat to her. "You're welcome, Mr. Smalls. Please, come in!"

Smalls handed her a bottle of wine. "A little holiday spirit to share." He saw Blatch and handed him a brown paper bag.

"What's this?" Blatch asked.

"Your present. A bag of donuts. I was talking to a few cops today and asked around what you guys like."

Blatch laughed and picked up a gift from under the tree. "Here's yours."

Smalls shook the rectangular box. "What is it? Chocolates?"

"Nope. A carton of K-cups. Bailey's Irish Crème."

Smalls laughed and glanced around. "Nice. Just don't tell Deanna."

Blatch grinned. "Don't worry. She's not here yet."

"Let me get you a glass of punch," Deloris said.

"That'd be swell, Mrs. Blatch."

"Please, call me Deloris already!" she said, and headed off toward the kitchen.

"Were you really talking to some cops this afternoon?" Blatch asked Smalls.

"Yeah. Just asking around a bit. I was trying to find out how tight this Davidson kid is with Castleberry. Sanderson said if he was any deeper, his eyes would turn Castleberry brown."

"Huh," Blatch said. "That's too bad. I kind of liked the kid."

Smalls shrugged. "No accounting for taste. Thought you might like to know that nobody mentioned anything about finding Preston's prints or thumbs, either. Even when I asked about latent hitchhikers."

Blatch rolled his eyes. "Not everybody gets your weird references, Smalls."

"Maybe not. But I got a feeling your railroad theory may have a few tracks of truth to it."

"What do you—" Blatch said.

"Here's your punch," Deloris interrupted, handing Smalls a cup.

The doorbell rang. "Oh, that must be Deanna," Deloris said. She waltzed over and opened the door.

A scrawny, red-faced man in a bad suit shot her a crooked smile.

"Who's the boyfriend?" Smalls whispered to Blatch.

"Not boyfriend. Neighbor. That's Old Man Melman. The original Grinch."

Smalls snorted. "That explains why his suit is ten sizes too small."

Blatch shot the old man a look. "Yeah. Just like his heart."

"So where's Deanna, anyway?" Smalls asked.

"I don't know." Blatch frowned. "She should've been here by now. I'll give her a ring."

Smalls sipped his punch while Blatch made the call.

Blatch slipped his phone back into his pocket. "No answer."

Smalls grunted. "I don't blame her for being late."

Blatch eyed him. "What do you mean?"

Smalls shrugged. "What's the rush? She knows we'll just end up sitting around talking about psychos."

Blatch smirked. "Not while *you're* still around. We're not *that* rude."

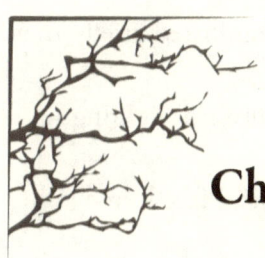

Chapter Sixty-Nine

DEANNA OPENED HER EYES.

For a second, she worried she'd been struck blind.

All around her was nothing but black.

She blinked again. She was lying on her stomach on the ground. She tried to turn her neck.

A stab of pain made her want to cry out. But something inside her warned her not to make a noise.

The smell of motor oil and gasoline was overwhelming. Even so, it wasn't enough to obliterate the sickening odor of filth—and rotting flesh.

Fear shot through Deanna's spine.

She tried to sit up, but something touched her cheek, pinning her down.

It felt like the cold, hard blade of a knife.

"No."

The word, a gruff growl of a sound, wafted at her in the dark.

Cold. Angry. Male.

"Who are you?" Deanna asked.

Her question was met by a sudden hiss of phosphorus.

Nearby, a blue spark came to life in the darkness.

Deanna watched, terrified, as the spark grew into a small, orange flame.

In the small circle of light emitted by the match, Deanna made out the filthy fingers of a bony hand.

It has a thumb, she thought numbly as the ball of light moved away from her.

The shadowy outline of a kerosene lamp illuminated briefly, then the lamp's innards caught fire.

Slowly, a yellow-orange glow bloomed outward, lighting up a tiny room stacked with gardening supplies.

Then, to Deanna's horror, a wretched, skeletal face leered at her from the gloom.

The face was both strange and vaguely familiar.

"You've been a bad girl," the man said.

His eyes, sunken and hollow, ignored her, fixating instead on the knife blade in his hand. He twisted the blade back and forth, mesmerized by the way it glimmered in the orange light.

"I'm sorry," Deanna said softly. "Please. Let's talk this out."

"No."

"Please," Deanna said.

Like a viper's strike, the knife shot toward her face.

Deanna turned just in time. The blade narrowly missed her eye as it drew a painful line across her cheek.

"I told you *no*," the voice said. "No means no."

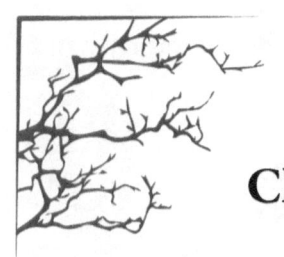

Chapter Seventy

BLATCH TOOK A SIP OF punch but couldn't swallow it. He was restless. Antsy. And it had nothing to do with Old Man Melman's dirty looks.

Deep in his gut, he knew something was wrong. But what?

Is this about Castleberry? he wondered. *Am I worried about getting arrested again?*

No. Blatch knew he could handle that, should it happen. Something else was bugging him.

He peeked out the front window. Deanna still hadn't arrived.

He called her number again.

Still no answer.

He glanced around at the others at the party. Everybody was laughing. Chatting it up.

Maybe this is all in my head.

He dialed Deanna again.

Nothing.

Screw this.

A strange impulse made Blatch suddenly sprint for the front door. Once outside, he hesitated for a second.

Right toward Deanna's place, or left to the Count house?

He took a step to the right.

It felt wrong.

Blatch turned left and bolted down the sidewalk, running for all he was worth toward the Count house.

As he rounded the corner of 11th Street, Blatch was relieved to see Deanna's Corvette parked outside.

But the relief didn't last.

There were no lights on at the Count house.

His gut had been right.

Something was terribly, terribly wrong.

Chapter Seventy-One

"DON'T MOVE," THE VOICE hissed between two crusty, sore-pocked lips.

In the lurid glow of the kerosene lamp, the man's gaunt cheekbones and tattered clothes gave him the appearance of a ghastly ghoul straight from a haunted house.

His hands, skeletal as claws, played with the knife, turning it over and over in his good hand.

The other hand, to Deanna's horror, bore a huge, black scab where the thumb should've been.

Deanna closed her eyes against the revolting image. Her mind raced desperately. How could she possibly reason with this psychopath?

His raspy breath grew nearer. Something warm and wet dribbled onto her cheek ....

Dear God, help me, Deanna thought.

Suddenly, a strange, crackling noise echoed in the small room.

Deanna opened her eyes. The madman's face was inches from hers. He raised the knife ....

No! Deanna screamed inside.

The crackling sound repeated.

Her attacker looked away.

A soft, buzzing sound began to hum in the room.

The man cocked his cadaverous head closer to the wall.

"God, is that you?" he whispered.

Deanna knew this may be her only chance. She inched her hand forward, toward a metal bucket near her head.

But her hand was shaking so badly it rammed into the bucket. The sound betrayed her.

"No!" her captor screamed as his head jerked around to face her. He raised his knife again ....

Deanna scrabbled frantically for the bucket ....

The knife came down ....

Chapter Seventy-Two

BLATCH RACED THROUGH the open gate toward the dark Count house. He turned on his cellphone flashlight and waved it around the walkway and front steps.

Sitting by the door was a gift bag.

Blatch angled the flashlight's beam toward the yard.

Up against the hedges, he spotted a crumpled red umbrella.

What he saw next made the hair on his arms stand on end.

Deanna's purse lay open in the yard.

He ran to it and picked it up. The strap was broken.

"Deanna!" he called out.

He shone the light around the yard wildly.

Nothing.

He stared out into the night and yelled.

"Deanna! Where are you?"

Chapter Seventy-Three

THE KNIFE MADE A BONE-chilling *screek* as it skittered across the surface of the metal bucket.

Deanna rolled sharply to her left and sat up, ignoring the sharp pain shooting through her neck.

She kept her eye on the knife.

The knife was everything ....

In the orange light, she caught the glint of the blade as it rose up to take another stab.

"No!" Deanna screamed, and leaned away. His arm grazed her shoulder as the knife whooshed by her.

Deanna scuttled backward until her back was against a wall. Bracing herself, she kicked out at her assailant.

Her heel met his chin with a sickening crack.

He fell backward, dropping the knife. "Ow! You hurt me!" he cried out like a sorrowful child.

Deanna braced for another kick, but his pitiful cry made her pause.

What's wrong with this man? she wondered.

Her hesitation was a mistake.

Her attacker lunged forward, grabbing at Deanna with both hands. One skeletal hand wrapped around her wrist and yanked hard.

Deanna spun around, knocking over the kerosene lamp.

"You'll pay for this!" her attacker hissed as he pushed her onto the dirt floor. His scabby thumb-less hand mashed down on her throat. His other hand grappled for the knife ....

Deanna knocked the blade away, then wrestled free from his chokehold.

She had to keep the maniac away from the knife ....

But it was like fighting a demon.

The creature before her was hollow-eyed. Skin and bones.

And he fought like a wild animal.

Before she could stand, he jumped on top of her, clawing at her arms with boney hands—snapping at her face with rotten teeth ....

Deanna fought back, elbowing him in the ribcage. He howled like a wounded animal.

She struggled to standing, just as a flame shot up where the kerosene lamp had fallen.

A cloth tarp had caught fire.

Deanna turned back to face her attacker. In the growing light of the fire, she saw his eyes for the first time.

They shone dark with rage and confusion.

Once again, he grabbed at her. He seemed oblivious to the danger of the spreading fire.

The flames grew higher. The room began to fill with acrid smoke ....

Please, Deanna pleaded as she wrestled with the madman.

Her arms began to shake from exhaustion.

Please! I don't want to die like this ....

Chapter Seventy-Four

FROM SOMEWHERE IN THE darkness, Blatch heard a muffled cry.

He cocked his head.

A banging sound echoed to his right.

He raced around to the side of the Count house. But as he rounded the corner, nothing looked a miss.

Straight ahead came the dull thump of something hitting metal.

Blatch sprinted forward a few steps.

He smelled smoke.

From the light of his cellphone, he noticed a white cloud unfurling from under the door of the toolshed.

He ran up to it. "Deanna?" he yelled.

"Marcus!" she screamed back.

"I'm here!" He focused his cellphone light on the shed's metal door. He hadn't searched it yesterday because it had been padlocked.

Today it was not.

"Are you okay?" he yelled, and grabbed the metal door. The heat seared his hand like a hot skillet.

"Help me!" Deanna cried back.

"Shit!" He pulled off his jacket, wound it around his hand, and yanked at the shed door.

It wouldn't budge.

"Deanna!" he called out. "The door is stuck!"

"Hurry!" she called back, then coughed.

"Stand back!" Blatch took out his Glock and hit the door handle with the butt of it.

He tried the door again. No movement.

An animal-like howl echoed from inside the toolshed.

Blatch felt the hair on the back of his neck stand on end.

"Dear God!" he yelled. "Hold on, Deanna! I'll be right back!"

Chapter Seventy-Five

WITH FLAMES LICKING at her feet, a sudden calmness came over Deanna. In the middle of chaos came clarity.

Deanna realized her attacker had a weakness.

When Blatch had banged on the shed door, the madman had let go of her.

He'd held his hands to his ears and howled.

The noise had hurt his ears.

"Don't stop!" Deanna had called out to Blatch. "Keep banging on the door!"

But Blatch hadn't. He'd stopped.

And now, the wild man before her was eyeing her once again. Only this time, he seemed desperate.

A wounded animal.

Deanna glanced around at the growing flames. Through the smoke, she spied a garden spade.

She lunged for it.

Her attacker lunged for her.

Deanna fell.

He fell on top of her, knocking the wind out of her.

Deanna gasped for air, her fingers just inches from the spade. As her attacker sat atop her, beating on her back, Deanna struggled forward until her fingers grasped the handle. With all she had left in her, she slammed the spade against the side of the metal shed.

A sharp clang reverberated through the shed.

Her assailant stopped his attack.

He fell onto his side and curled into a ball, covering his ears with his hands.

Deanna watched in stunned silence for a moment.

Then she coughed.

The reflex brought her back to reality.

If I don't get out of here soon, I'm going to roast alive.

Gagging for air, Deanna grabbed the knife lying on the ground. She squatted down by the shed door and tugged at the board wedged in place, barring the door from being opened.

It wouldn't budge.

"Come on. Help me!" she said to the man curled in a fetal position. "Help me, please! Or we'll both be dead!"

Chapter Seventy-Six

BLATCH SCOURED THE backyard for something he could use to pry open the shed door. He found a broom by the garage and ran back to the side yard.

Suddenly, the door to the toolshed squealed open.

Illuminated by the firelight within, a ragged creature from a nightmare stumbled out.

Blatch dropped the rake and pulled his gun.

"Stop right there," he said.

The creature turned and stared at him.

Deanna stumbled out beside him.

"Deanna!" Blatch yelled. "Get out of the way!"

"No!" Deanna screamed.

She ran between Blatch and her attacker and held out her arms.

"Don't shoot!" she yelled. "He's just a child!"

Chapter Seventy-Seven

"HE DIDN'T LOOK LIKE a child to me," Blatch said as he waited in the emergency room with Deanna.

"He's not," she said. "I meant he is *mentally*. He's suffering from either a lower mental capacity or a mental illness. I don't think he knew what he was doing."

"Miss, I need you to stop talking and let me finish this," the nurse said as she examined the cut on Deanna's cheek. "You got lucky. This isn't too deep. I think you can get by without stitches, but you need to watch out for infection."

"Thank you," Deanna said. "What about the man the ambulance brought in with us?"

"Doctor says he's severely dehydrated and malnourished. And he has second-degree burns on his hands and ears. Do you know him?"

Deanna shook her head. "No. But I think he may have wandered away from a mental facility or halfway house."

"He might be up for criminal charges, too," Blatch said.

"Not from me," Deanna said, shaking her head.

Blatch blew out a breath. He locked eyes with the nurse. "I suggest you keep him under careful watch."

The nurse nodded. "He's heavily sedated right now, and will be for a few days while we tend his burns and get him rehydrated."

"Good," Blatch said. "I'm a private investigator. In the meantime, I'll see what I can find out about him."

BLATCH HELPED DEANNA into his sedan and climbed into the driver's seat. He turned the ignition and shot her a sympathetic smile.

"How you feeling?"

Deanna shrugged. "Okay, I guess."

"Still up for a little Christmas Eve cheer?"

Deanna shot him a look, then smiled. "Sure. Why not. I hear the Blatch's throw one hell of a party."

Blatch grinned. "Word of warning. I've tried the punch. I wouldn't recommend it."

Deanna laughed. "Thanks for the warning." She glanced down at her torn, grease-stained dress. "I guess I'll need to go home and change first. This outfit doesn't match my bandages."

Blatch reached over and touched her arm. "You were brave tonight." He studied Deanna for a moment. "Are you really all right?"

Deanna smiled up at him and nodded. Suddenly, tears burst from her eyes and streamed down her cheeks.

"I will be," she said, her voice wavering. "If you'll just hold me and tell me everything's going to be okay."

Chapter Seventy- Eight

CHRISTMAS MORNING, Smalls turned his key in the office door and smirked sourly as the bell above clanged out its warning.

"Jingle bells my ass," he muttered, and pushed his way inside. He hung up his coat and hat, and made his way to the conference room.

"What the?" he said as he opened the door.

"Surprise," Blatch said.

Deanna laughed at Smalls' befuddled expression. "Merry Christmas, partner."

Smalls eyed Deanna's bandaged cheek. "Geez, Dee. Looks like Santa brought you more than you bargained for."

"SO *that's* why you two never made it back to the party," Smalls said, and slurped down the last sip of his cappuccino. "So, you capture the guy, and you *still* can't figure out who he is?"

"He wasn't exactly carrying a wallet," Blatch said. "And he's in such bad shape it's hard to make an ID on him based on looks alone."

Deanna sighed. "Given his mental capacity, I don't think he can be Gary Lee Preston. Not unless he's had some kind of traumatic brain injury."

"This thing keeps getting muddier and muddier," Smalls said. He eyed his two partners. "Kind of like you two."

Blatch's phone rang, saving him from coming up with a retaliatory insult for Smalls. "Blatch here."

"Detective Blatch? It's Nurse Jones, from the hospital."

Blatch's inner alarm sounded. "Is something wrong?"

"No. I just wanted you to know we found something in the man's clothes."

"Oh. What?"

"Initials. They were drawn on the inner waistband of his pants. The initials FK."

"FK. Thank you. That might prove helpful. Thanks for letting me know."

Blatch clicked off the phone. "Well, we have our first solid clue on our guy. His initials are FK."

Deanna's mouth dropped open.

"Freddie," she said. "His first name really *is* Freddie."

Chapter Seventy-Nine

"EXCUSE ME, I'M SORRY to bother you on Christmas Day, but do you have any idea what happened at my place last night?" Charles Count asked Deanna over the phone.

"We got home and the lights were out. The breaker box was tripped. And this morning I see the bloody toolshed had a fire in it! Cecilia found your gift at the door, and thought you might know something about it?"

Deanna winced. "Yes. I was going to let you know, but I thought I'd wait until nine o'clock, so as not to bother you."

"Oh. Well, yes. I appreciate that. Cecilia and Conrad and I ... we had a nice morning. I hope you did, too. It's a little late to ask, but I hope I'm not disturbing you."

"No. Not at all. Actually, I'm at the office, trying to identify the man who started the fire in your shed."

"The man?" Charles said, his voice wavering.

"Yes. Last night, I was—" Deanna stopped. This wasn't the time or place to explain the horrific details. "I ran into a man when I was delivering your gift."

Charles tone changed from aggravation to concern. "This man ... was he the one on the video? The one with the missing thumb?"

"Yes. We're pretty sure he is. We don't know his name yet. But we discovered his initials. FK. Does that ring any bells?"

"No. Not offhand."

"Okay." Deanna hesitated. "Mr. Count? I'd like to talk with Conrad about him."

"What? What would he know?"

"Maybe nothing. And, if you could, let's leave it for now. After all, it's Christmas."

"Right. I'll talk to Cecilia about it."

"Thanks."

As Deanna hung up the phone, she was haunted by the feeling that time was running out for FK. She needed to find out who this poor man was, before he was tossed back out on the street.

Before he had a chance to hurt anyone else ....

"WHO WAS ON THE PHONE?" Smalls asked as Deanna rejoined them in the conference room.

"Charles Count. I put him off about his toolshed. He has no idea who FK could be. Like I said before, I'm pretty sure the F stands for Freddie. Conrad must have spoken with him." Deanna shook her head. "I thought Freddie was his imaginary friend."

"Turns out, he's all too real," Blatch said, finishing her thought.

"I'd like to start making some calls," Deanna said. "See what we can find out about FK."

"But nobody's working today," Smalls countered. "It's Christmas."

Deanna shot him a look. "Only if you're a Christian."

"YOU WERE RIGHT, AANYA Gill's working today," Blatch said. "She's running a search for next of kin for both Regina Krous and Gary Lee Preston."

"Fat lot of good it'll do," Smalls said. "Deanna and I already tried searching for them on the internet."

"Maybe she knows some tricks we don't," Blatch said.

Smalls sniffed and shrugged his shoulders.

"I spoke with Larry," Deanna said, coming back into the conference room. "I wanted to get a second opinion on FK's behavior. Larry agreed with me. He acted more like a delusional schizophrenic than someone with a brain injury."

"What's it matter?" Smalls asked.

"Well, if FK's schizophrenic, he's probably been sick for a long time," Deanna said. "That would rule him out as being Gary Lee Preston. But if he's suffering a brain injury, he still could be Preston."

"What about his age?" Blatch asked. "Is that a fit with Gary?"

Deanna thought of her ordeal in the toolshed and shivered. "He was so horribly skinny—and filthy." She shook her head. "I got a good look at him and I still can't tell you for sure how old he is."

"Okay," Blatch said. "Enough about this guy. We've done all we can for the moment. We'll start making inquiries at foster homes and halfway houses tomorrow. But for now, let's let them have their holiday in peace."

"What about Davidson and Castleberry?" Smalls said. "I don't think those fuckers deserve any holiday peace."

Blatch glanced over at Deanna.

She nodded.

Blatch turned back to Smalls.

"Okay. So, what've you got in mind?"

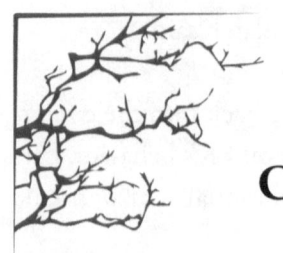

Chapter Eighty

SMALLS WALKED INTO the conference room and set two brown bags on the table. Both bore the lopsided ice-cream cone logo of the Dairy Inn.

"*This* is your idea of sticking it to Davidson and Castleberry?" Blatch asked.

Smalls stared at him. "Yeah. It's time to put this 'thumbs or no thumbs' theory to rest."

Blatch shook his head. "And you thought eating hotdogs would do it?"

"We need fuel to think. And I couldn't resist their greasy deliciousness," Smalls deadpanned. "Besides, the Dairy Inn was the only place delivering on Christmas Day."

"Ugh," Blatch groaned, then reached for a bag.

"SO, THE QUESTION IS, who's the conspiracy nut? You or Davidson?" Smalls asked, then bit into his chilidog.

Blatch glanced over at Deanna. She shrugged as if to say *he's right*, and took a healthy bite of a hotdog garnished with mustard and relish.

"Want to hear my theory?" Smalls mumbled through his mouthful.

"Do we have to?" Blatch asked.

Smalls swallowed. "Cathy was in on it."

Blatch choked on a sip of soda. "What?"

"Yeah," Smalls said. "She and Castleberry set up the robbery six months ago, along with Gary Lee Preston."

"What are you talking about?" Blatch growled. He shot to his feet.

"Hear me out," Smalls said. "I'm not your enemy."

Blatch shut his mouth and sat back down.

"Why do you think you just happened to be in the wrong place at the wrong time, Blatch?" Smalls asked. "I think Cathy, Castleberry, and Preston were setting you up. They staged the liquor store robbery in order to fake Gary Lee's death and split the insurance payout. After all, they had the perfect witness. *You*."

Blatch sat there in stunned silence. Smalls studied his partner for a moment, then continued.

"But things didn't go to plan. Cathy misfired and shot Gary Lee fatally. But he had just enough juice left in him to fire back, killing Cathy instantly. That left Castleberry holding an empty bag."

Smalls leaned over and touched his partner's arm. "Cathy wasn't your fault, Blatch. And Castleberry might be mad about losing her, but he's even madder about losing out on his share of a hundred grand."

"But ... there's no proof," Blatch said.

"Maybe not," Smalls said. "But it sure makes the pieces fit. The only winners in the whole mess were Tandy Preston and Regina."

"How do you figure that?" Deanna asked.

"Well, Tandy Preston was too close to Gary Lee for them to go near. But Regina Krous was another story."

Blatch looked up. "You're not saying *Castleberry* started the fire at Mercer Arms."

Smalls blew out a breath. "I'm only saying it would be his only way to salvage the deal."

"How?" Deanna asked. "Regina Krous' policy was payable to Gary Lee Preston. According to your theory, he's dead."

"Thus the need to resurrect him," Smalls said.

Blatch shook his head. "That explains his fingerprints. His thumb."

"Bingo," Smalls said softly. "Castleberry had to resurrect Gary Lee long enough to stall the benefit payout until he could find the next in line to collect."

"Who is?" Blatch asked.

"I don't know," Smalls said. "I haven't gotten that far."

Deanna looked at both men. "I think I know."

Chapter Eighty-One

DEANNA TOUCHED THE bandage on her cheek and turned to Blatch. "You said Gary Lee Preston had a girlfriend. Jenny, right?"

"Yes."

"And Regina Krous had a life insurance policy payable to Gary Lee Preston."

"Yes."

"Please tell me you're going to get to some kind of point soon?" Smalls said.

Deanna shot him a look. "I will if you quit interrupting me."

Smalls rolled his eyes. "Okay. Okay. Continue. Please."

"Jenny's a common nickname for Regina. What if Gary and Regina had a child together, back when they were high-school sweethearts?"

Blatch stared at her. "Go on."

Deanna bit her lip. "What if that child had mental health issues ... of a serious enough nature that he was institutionalized as a possible threat to his mother, or society in general?"

"Wait a second," Blatch said. "Are you saying the guy who attacked you—the one we left in the hospital last night—is Gary Preston and Regina Krous' *son?*"

"Yes."

Smalls hooted. "Hot damned! I think she's right. It makes the insurance piece fit like a glove!"

Deanna smiled sadly. "I believe they both took out policies that would pay for their son's care if either one of them should die. The policies were made payable to either parent, because their son himself didn't have the mental capacity to be legal guardian for himself."

"Hold on," Blatch said. "Gary Lee didn't have a policy payable to Regina."

"I think maybe he did," Deanna countered, "and Tandy made him change the beneficiary. How could he refuse her without spilling the beans about his son?"

"She said she didn't know anything about it," Blatch said.

"She could be lying," Smalls said.

"Or Gary could've missed a few payments, so the policy lapsed," Deanna said.

Blatch shook his head. "And now, Castleberry needs this disabled boy to collect the insurance benefit."

"I think so," Deanna said.

Blatch's phone rang. He glanced at the screen. "It's Aanya Gill from Mutual Peninsular." He picked up the phone.

"I have news," she said.

"Mind if I put you on speaker? I'm here with my partners."

"No, that's fine," she said.

"Go ahead."

"It took a little digging because records of this type are sensitive," she began. "But Gary Lee Preston and Regina Krous had a son. Frederick Lee Krous. He'd be almost twenty now. He was born with what was called "a severe dissociative disorder." He was living in an institution in Georgia until ten days ago, when he was transferred to a new facility in Tampa. But ... well, the records indicate he never arrived."

"Never arrived?" Blatch asked. "Who was doing the transport?"

"I don't know. I'd have to look into that more."

"Thank you, Ms. Gill. You've been a big help."

Blatch clicked off the phone. "If Frederick Krous was a risk to society, the transport company could've requested police support."

Smalls blew out a breath. "Or maybe a nice policeman volunteered to do it alone."

"Castleberry?" Blatch asked.

"More likely Davidson, his lackey," Smalls said. "And they haven't claimed the life insurance benefit yet because somehow, Frederick Krous gave them the slip."

Blatch's phone rang again. "It's the hospital." He picked up.

"Mr. Blatch?"

"Yes."

"It's Nurse Jones again."

"Yes. How can I help?"

"I just thought you'd like to know, your mystery patient has a visitor."

Blatch frowned. "A visitor?"

"Yes. A police officer. He says he knows him. That's good news, right?"

Chapter Eighty-Two

"IT'S OVER, CASTLEBERRY," Blatch said as he burst into Frederick Krous' hospital room.

"What are you talking about?" Castleberry hissed.

"Really?" Blatch said. He eyed his former boss with disgust. "Okay, then. Explain why you're here, visiting this man."

Blatch glanced at the emaciated, comatose young man lying in the hospital bed.

"I always make the rounds on Christmas," Castleberry said, and held up a red sack.

Fuck, Blatch thought.

"Seems like quite the coincidence," Smalls said, entering the room with his weapon drawn.

"You put that gun away before I arrest you right here!" Castleberry hissed. "This is a *hospital!*"

"Yeah," Smalls said. "But you're no Santa."

"I beg your pardon?" Castleberry said.

"Check his sack," Smalls said.

Blatch snatched the bag away before Castleberry could react. He dumped its contents on the floor.

Smalls snorted. "Well, who knew garbage was the in thing this season?"

"I'm just here to spread Christmas joy, nothing more," Castleberry countered.

"Oh really?" Deanna said, marching into the room. "Tell it to Santa." She held up Smalls' gyrating Santa doll and flipped on the switch. Santa's pants dropped to his knees.

"What the hell is this all about?" Castleberry yelled.

"We wondered how you found out about our friend Freddie here," Blatch said. "God knows, it wasn't due to your amazing detective work."

"Figured you had to be listening in," Smalls said. "Then, lo and behold, but what to our wandering eyes should appear, but a little black bug up our dear Santa's rear."

Deanna showed him the listening device between Santa's legs.

"You can't pin that on me!" Castleberry said.

"We can if your prints are on it," Blatch said. "Yours or Davidson's."

"Davidson's?" Castleberry asked.

Blatch grabbed Castleberry by the arm. "Save it, Bad Santa. You're not getting a dime off Freddie Krous."

Chapter Eighty-Three

THE OLD-FASHIONED, colored lights strung across the dark little bar lent a sad, *Charlie Brown Christmas* effect to the place. *Jingle Bell Rock* played on the radio, but even its spunk and cheer wasn't strong enough to chase the gloom from the corners of the room.

Deanna sat on her stool and sipped her chardonnay, happy not to be spending Christmas night in her crumbling mansion with her mother's ghost. Sharing the time with Blatch and Smalls was infinitely better, even if the two men were at each other's throats.

"I don't know who's more pathetic," Smalls said. "Castleberry, or *you* for striking that stupid-ass deal with him."

"What else could I do?" Blatch said. "You think I could just march the bastard into the police station and say, 'Book your captain'? The evidence we've got on Castleberry is flimsier than what he has on me."

Smalls blew out a breath. "I know. But if Castleberry burned down Mercer Arms, he murdered Regina Krous."

"That's still a big *if*," Deanna said. "While you two were arguing, I think I figured out one way to explain Gary Lee's thumbprint at the scene of that fire. But I warn you, it's not pretty."

"What? Spill it," Smalls said.

"First, someone would need to procure Gary's thumb."

Blatch winced.

"I told you it wasn't pretty," Deanna said. "That means they had to have access to his dead body. And *that* means it was either someone at the morgue—"

"We know that," Smalls interrupted. "One of Castleberry's cronies."

"Or at the funeral," Deanna said.

"Tandy didn't have a funeral for Gary Lee," Blatch said.

"Oh."

"But there *was*, a viewing ...."

"That could work," Deanna said.

Smalls scowled. "What do you mean, *work?*"

Deanna set down her glass of wine. "Bear with me. What if Regina Krous got her son Freddie out of the facility in Georgia to attend his father's service? Freddie could've cut off his father's thumb at the wake, as some kind of macabre memento."

Blatch cringed. "You think Freddie's capable of that?"

Deanna bit her lip. "Yes. From what I've experienced of him, he lives in his own, strange reality. Truth be told, I think he's responsible for cutting off his own thumb."

"But why?" Blatch asked. "I mean, where would he come up with a sick idea like that?"

"Who can say for sure?" Deanna shook her head. "Maybe Freddie cut his father's thumb off to keep as a souvenir. Or a good luck charm—so he never had to be alone."

Smalls grunted. "I think Castleberry made up the thumb story and torched Mercer Arms himself." He shot Deanna a sour smirk. "That makes more sense than your convoluted story."

"Look," Blatch said. "Castleberry refused to tell me whether or not he actually has Preston's thumb in evidence. But even if he does, wherever it came from, we've got to let the cops take it from here. We did our job. We know Gary Lee's dead, and we found his true beneficiary."

"So, that's it?" Smalls grumbled. "We're gonna make fifty bucks off this whole deal?"

"Yeah," Blatch sighed. "I guess so. It stinks, but that's the story of my life."

"Shit," Smalls spat. "Even Scrooge had a better ending than this crappy Christmas Story."

"Story," Deanna mumbled absently.

"What?" Blatch asked.

"Story," she repeated. "I think ... I wonder."

"Wonder what?" Smalls asked.

Deanna shook her head. "Nothing. I need to talk to Cecilia Count."

Chapter Eighty-Four

"THANKS FOR COMING WITH me, Marcus," Deanna said as they stepped up to the front door of the Count house.

He took her hand. "Of course. I didn't want you coming back here alone. Not after last night ...."

Deanna squeezed his hand and rang the bell. Cecilia Count answered the door.

"Deanna. Mr. Blatch. Come in. What's this all about?"

Conrad came running up, holding a red firetruck. "Look what I got from Santa!"

Deanna winked at him, then locked eyes with Cecilia. "I hope you don't mind?"

"No. He loves it," Cecilia said.

Charles came up and shook Blatch's hand. "Thanks for coming. Can I get you two anything? Glass of wine, perhaps?"

"No thanks," Deanna said. "But *you* might need one after you hear what we have to tell you."

Charles' face grew serious. "What?"

"The young man who started the fire. We know who he is. And we think he'd been living in your garden shed for the past week or so."

Cecilia's face collapsed. "What?"

"The man is mentally ill," Deanna explained. "I think Conrad was feeding him."

Charles looked over at his son, who was happily playing with his firetruck. He turned to face them, his face aghast. "My God! Did he hurt Conrad?"

"No," Deanna said. "I don't believe so. But he's the one who was giving Conrad his 'gifts.'"

Cecilia's face registered her meaning. "So Conrad didn't ... Conrad isn't—"

"No," Deanna said, and took her hand. "I think he's a healthy little boy."

Cecilia burst into tears. Charles wrapped his arms around her.

"Thank you, Dr. Young," he said. "You've made this a very happy Christmas for my family."

"You're welcome," Deanna said. "But I've also come to beg a favor. I need to talk to Conrad for a minute. Alone."

Cecilia and Charles exchanged a glance, then nodded.

"Of course," Cecilia said.

"MOMMY SAYS SANTA IS just a pretending," Conrad said as he zoomed his firetruck across his bedroom floor.

"Not everything is a pretending," Deanna said.

He looked up at her with angelic blue eyes. "No, ma'am."

"Freddie wasn't a pretending. I met him."

Conrad's eyes grew wide. "You did?"

"Yes. Freddie is sick, so he went to a place where he can get well. I don't think you'll see him again."

Conrad looked down. "Oh."

"You did a very good thing, giving him the soup."

Conrad looked up and nodded. "He had to eat it, or he'd die."

"Why?"

"The story said so."

Deanna's brow furrowed. "What story, Conrad?"

"The one in the book Peter reads to me."

"Oh. Can you show me the book?"

"Sure." Conrad went to his bookshelf and picked out a slim, paperback book. He handed it to Deanna.

On the cover was an illustration of a boy with wild hair and long fingernails.

"Do you mind if I borrow your book?" she asked.

Conrad nodded.

"Okay," he said, and went back to scooting his firetruck across the floor.

"WHAT WAS ALL THAT ABOUT?" Blatch asked as they climbed into her Corvette.

"It's a story," she said.

"You mean, 'It's a long story,' don't you?"

"No. It's a story." Deanna fished around in her purse and pulled out the book. "Here. Read it."

Chapter Eighty-Five

AFTER DROPPING BLATCH off at the office, Deanna had headed home. As she walked from her garage to her backdoor, she heard a sharp cry. She looked up and saw a black bird circling overhead.

She watched the raven for a moment, then her cellphone rang. She fished through her purse and snatched up the phone.

"Did you read it?" she asked Larry. She'd found Conrad's little storybook online, and sent her old colleague a link to download a copy.

"Yes, I read it," Larry said.

"Can you believe it?" Deanna asked. "It's all about wicked children and the horrific things that happen to them!"

"I'm at a loss for words," he said.

"All of Conrad's imaginary friends are in there," Deanna said. "'Gustus' is *Augustus*—the boy who wouldn't eat his soup, so he died. And Peter, the boy who wouldn't cut his hair or fingernails. And Frederick, the boy who killed birds and tore the wings off flies—"

"And Conrad," Larry interrupted. "The boy who sucked his thumbs—"

"So *they were cut off!*" Deanna said, nearly breathless from the horror of it.

Larry exhaled loudly. "All described as 'Merry Stories and Funny Pictures.' Dee, this book. It's ... well, I don't know what to say."

"Conrad's au pair was reading these stories to him!" Deanna said. "Who could write such a thing?"

"Apparently, a German psychiatrist," Larry replied dryly. "But you have to understand, Dee. This book was written back in the 1800s—when people still thought *shock therapy* was a good idea."

Deanna's eyes grew wide. "Shock therapy! Oh my lord! That's it!"

"What's it?"

"I couldn't figure out how Freddie Krous found out about these stories. But I just remembered something. When he was holding me captive in the toolshed, an electrical socket buzzed. Freddie leaned toward it and said, 'Is that you, God?'"

"I'm not following you," Larry said.

"That wall socket goes directly into the garage, where Peter Steiner read Conrad those stories. Freddie must've been able to hear him through the opening."

Deanna chewed her lip. "Oh, geez! Freddie must've thought God was speaking to him through the electrical outlet! That's why he leaned over to hear ... that's how he got those burns on his ears."

"Dear God," Larry said. "Could that really be true?"

Deanna grimaced. "How else could he have known about them? Given his mental state, I doubt Freddie can read. He had to be *told* the stories somehow."

Deanna gasped. Her mouth fell open.

"What?" Larry asked. "What is it, Dee?"

"I know why Freddie attacked me Christmas Eve. To him, I was like the boy named Robert in the book. The foolish one who played in the rain and was swept away in the clouds."

"What do you mean?"

"I was carrying a red umbrella, just like Robert. Just like Regina Krous ...."

"Who's she?"

Deanna pursed her lips. "The woman who died in the fire at Mercer Arms. A witness said she was carrying a red umbrella that day. She was also ...." Deanna's voice trailed off.

"Also what?" Larry asked.

"Freddie's mother."

"Oh."

The two sat in silence for a moment, listening to each other breathe over the phone. Finally, Larry spoke.

"Dee, I'm sorry, but I have to ask. Did Regina smoke?"

Deanna's brow furrowed. "I don't know. Why?"

"In the book, Harriet, the girl who plays with matches, burns down her house. She burns to death along with it."

Deanna's jaw went slack. "Oh, Larry. You don't think Freddie set the fire at Mercer Arms—and killed his own mother?"

"I don't know," Larry said. "It's too terrible to think about. It's like a Greek tragedy."

"Or a horror story." Deanna shook her head. "A faulty electric socket that brought a Frankenstein child to life."

Larry sighed. "At least Conrad doesn't seem to have any ill effects from it."

"No," Deanna said. "He seemed perfectly all right to me."

"Good," Larry said. "Let's hope so. After all, when you think about it, each of us is just a conglomeration of the stories we tell ourselves."

Chapter Eighty-Six

"WELL, IT'S OFFICIAL," Blatch said, hanging up the phone. He glanced around the conference table at his partners, Deanna and Smalls. "Freddie Krous will be investigated for the arsons and the murder of his mother."

"He can't possibly be found culpable," Deanna said. "Freddie's mentally disturbed. *Severely.* He should never be let out of that care facility in Georgia again."

"But someone *did* let him out," Blatch said. "And if there's any justice in this world, the trail of who did will lead to their conviction, for Regina Krous' sake."

"Right," Smalls grunted, and glanced at his watch. "Well, good day's work for a Monday, people." He smirked and added, "And we all survived the holidays."

"Is that another sick joke?" Blatch asked. "It's getting harder and harder to tell with you."

Smalls shot Blatch a quizzical look. "I don't know what you're talking about."

He turned to Deanna. "And I gotta admit, I kind of like the new name we came up with for the agency. *Mind's Eye Investigations.* It's got that certain ring to it, don't you think?"

Deanna grinned. "Yes, it does."

"Good. It's all settled then," Smalls said. "I'm calling it a day." He swiveled his chair at the head of the conference table, stood up, and shot his partners a look.

"See ya, wouldn't want to be ya," he quipped, and headed out the door.

"Finally, something we both agree on," Blatch said, elbowing Deanna.

She laughed. "Aw, come on. He's not so bad."

Blatch grinned. "I guess I'll get used to him. You know, I never gave you your present."

"You didn't have to—"

Blatch handed Deanna a small box wrapped in plain, brown paper.

"Sorry about how it looks," he said. "My mother's into this recycling kick. We're reusing paper grocery sacks instead of buying wrapping paper this year."

"I like it," Deanna said, admiring the gift. "Especially this little pine-straw wreath thingy." She looked up at him. "Did you make it?"

"No. I found it on my doorstep." Blatch smiled modestly and shrugged. "I thought it added a festive flair."

Deanna laughed. "I haven't seen anything like this since college, when I sat in on an art therapy class at a mental health facility."

Blatch's smile faded. "You're kidding."

Deanna looked into his eyes. "No. Why?"

Blatch bit his lip. "My mother .... You see, the day I found that thing, Freddie had mowed her lawn. Deloris gave him a glass of water. You don't think Freddie left it there ... as some kind of warning?"

Deanna shook her head softly, then looked down at the crudely fashioned ring of pine straw.

"No. I think Freddie meant it as a thank-you gift."

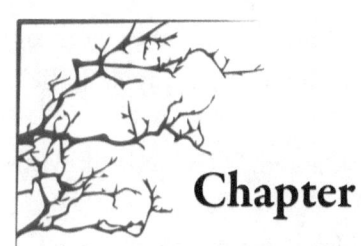

Chapter Eighty-Seven

"SO, DO YOU HAVE PLANS for New Year's Eve?" Blatch asked Deanna as they grabbed their coats and locked up the office for the day.

She wagged her eyebrows at him coyly. "I don't know. Let me check my calendar."

"Well?" Blatch asked as he followed her into the elevator.

Deanna grinned and made a pretense of flipping through her appointment book. "Don't rush me."

"What's the hesitation? Is it because I'm a jailbird?"

Deanna shot him a smirk. "I thought you said all charges against you were dropped."

"All except *one*," Blatch said.

Deanna's eyes widened. "Which one?"

"I still have a criminal desire for you."

Deanna's cheeks blushed.

"Aw. Don't tell me you're shy," Blatch said, flashing her a charming, boyish smile.

"No," she said. "Embarrassed. That line's so bad it could give Smalls a run for his money."

Blatch winced, then snuck a peek at Deanna's notebook. "Hey. You really *do* have some appointments in there."

"Yes," she said, and snapped it shut. "If you must know, the Counts have retained me for family counseling."

"That's great! But what about your office situation?"

The elevator pinged. The pair stepped out into the lobby.

"I'll be meeting with them at their house for another week or two," Deanna said. "By then, my office should be ready at Jodie's place."

"Where are you off to now?" Blatch asked. "Have a drink with me?"

"I can't. I'm going to visit Freddie. He's being transferred to a facility in Tampa in the morning."

Blatch opened the lobby door for Deanna. "I feel sorry for him."

"Yes," Deanna said as she brushed by Blatch. "Me, too. I wonder what it's like to be caught up in a dream world that's mostly nightmares."

"I don't know," Blatch said. "And I don't *want* to know."

As they walked to the parking garage, Deanna sighed. "You're right. In a way, I guess, we all live in our own little worlds."

"And I'm glad you're in mine," Blatch said.

Deanna smiled up at him, then reached inside her purse for her car keys.

An envelope fell out.

Blatch leaned down and picked it up.

"What's that?" he asked.

"A Christmas card from Larry. With everything going on, I forgot about it. Do you mind if I open it now?"

"No. Go ahead."

Blatch watched as Deanna tore into the envelope. She pulled out a greeting card featuring a lavish, old-fashioned Christmas scene on its cover.

Not your typical Larry, Deanna thought as she opened the card. Silently, she read the quote inside:

> *"Someday you will be old enough to start reading fairy tales again."* C.S. Lewis

Below the quote, her friend had written the words,

Remember, most of them have happy endings.
Love, Larry

"What's it say?" Blatch asked.

Deanna closed the card and smiled up at him.

Then she gently touched his arm and said, "Why don't you pick me up at eight."

READY FOR MORE FROM Deanna, Blatch and Smalls?

Follow me on Amazon and Bookbub and you'll be notified when this next mystery in the Mind's Eye Investigations series is ready for release!

Follow me on Amazon:

https://www.amazon.com/-/e/B06XKJ3YD8

Follow me on BookBub:

https://www.bookbub.com/search/authors?search=Margaret%20Lashley

Really love Mind's Eye Investigators?

Join my psychological suspense newsletter and get all the latest on new releases, flash sales, contests and more! As a welcome gift, I'll send you a free copy of Golden Years, a short story you can't get anyplace else! Click here to join:

https://dl.bookfunnel.com/7fb48pi0up

More Mysteries by
Margaret Lashley

The Val Fremden Mystery Series
https://www.amazon.com/gp/product/B07FK88WQ3
Freaky Florida Mystery Adventures
https://www.amazon.com/gp/product/B07RL4G8GZ

Want to Contact Me? Here's How:
Website: https://www.margaretlashley.com
Email: contact@margaretlashley.com
Facebook: https://www.facebook.com/valandpalspage/
Or click the link below and ask to join the Lunacy Lounge, my private Facebook group!
https://www.facebook.com/groups/ValTalk/

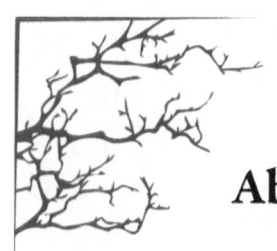

About the Author

MARGARET LASHLEY IS the author of the best-selling Val Fremden Mystery Series featuring an extremely reluctant amateur sleuth in her mid-forties. Now she's turned to the dark side with the Investigative Insights Series!

A true fan of the underdog, Ms. Lashley specializes in flawed, yet approachable characters readers can see themselves in. She's also a master of plot twists you'll never see coming. And in each of her books, there's a deeper subtext, exploring the ups and downs of being a woman in this day and age.

Margaret is a native of Florida, and lives in sunny St. Petersburg.

Personal Note from Margaret:

Why do I love underdogs? Well, it takes one to know one. And, for most of my life, I've been one, big time.

During my illustrious career, I've been a roller-skating waitress, an actuarial assistant, an advertising copywriter, a real estate agent, a house flipper, an organic farmer, and a traveling vagabond/truth seeker. But no matter where I've gone or what I've done, I've always felt like a weirdo.

I've learned a heck of a lot in my life. But getting to know myself has been my greatest journey. Today, I know I'm smart. I'm direct. I'm jaded. I'm hopeful. I'm funny. I'm fierce. I'm a pushover. And I have a laugh that lures strangers over, wanting to join in the fun.

In other words, I'm a jumble of opposing talents and flaws and emotions. And it's all good.

I enjoy underdogs because we've got spunk. And hope. And secrets that drive us to be different from the rest.

So dare to be different. Dare to be yourself.

www.ingramcontent.com/pod-product-compliance
Lightning Source LLC
Chambersburg PA
CBHW030418180626
46812CB00005B/2066